Pr

"A cl[...] [...]f both [...]t Carolyn Blue is a confident and witty detective with a taste for good food and an eye for murderous detail. A literate, deliciously well-written mystery."   —Earlene Fowler

"Not your average who-done-it . . . Extremely funny . . . A rollicking good time."   —*Romance Reviews Today*

"An entertaining amateur-sleuth tale . . . Fun."
                                                —*Painted Rock Reviews*

"Fairbanks has a real gift for creating characters based in reality but just the slightest bit wacky in a slyly humorous way . . . It will tickle your funny bone as well as stimulate your appetite for good food."   —*El Paso Times*

"A fast and funny whodunit."   —*The Best Reviews*

"Nancy Fairbanks scores again . . . A page-turner."
                                             —*Las Cruces (NM) Sun-News*

"Nancy Fairbanks writes a delicious . . . amusing amateur-sleuth story."   —*Midwest Book Review*

"Humor, entertaining characters, and a puzzling mystery round out the mix . . . A not-to-be-missed read."
                                                —*Roundtable Reviews*

Berkley Prime Crime titles by Nancy Fairbanks

Turkey Flambé

Nancy Fairbanks

BERKLEY PRIME CRIME, NEW YORK

THE BERKLEY PUBLISHING GROUP
Published by the Penguin Group
Penguin Group (USA) Inc.
375 Hudson Street, New York, New York 10014, USA
Penguin Group (Canada), 90 Eglinton Avenue East, Suite 700, Toronto, Ontario M4P 2Y3, Canada
(a division of Pearson Penguin Canada Inc.)
Penguin Books Ltd., 80 Strand, London WC2R 0RL, England
Penguin Group Ireland, 25 St. Stephen's Green, Dublin 2, Ireland (a division of Penguin Books Ltd.)
Penguin Group (Australia), 250 Camberwell Road, Camberwell, Victoria 3124, Australia
(a division of Pearson Australia Group Pty. Ltd.)
Penguin Books India Pvt. Ltd., 11 Community Centre, Panchsheel Park, New Delhi—110 017, India
Penguin Group (NZ), 67 Apollo Drive, Rosedale, North Shore 0632, New Zealand
(a division of Pearson New Zealand Ltd.)
Penguin Books (South Africa) (Pty.) Ltd., 24 Sturdee Avenue, Rosebank, Johannesburg 2196, South Africa

Penguin Books Ltd., Registered Offices: 80 Strand, London WC2R 0RL, England

This is a work of fiction. Names, characters, places, and incidents either are the product of the author's imagination or are used fictitiously, and any resemblance to actual persons, living or dead, business establishments, events, or locales is entirely coincidental. The publisher does not have any control over and does not assume any responsibility for author or third-party websites or their content.

PUBLISHER'S NOTE: The recipes contained in this book are to be followed exactly as written. The publisher is not responsible for your specific health or allergy needs that may require medical supervision. The publisher is not responsible for any adverse reactions to the recipes in this book.

TURKEY FLAMBÉ

A Berkley Prime Crime Book / published by arrangement with the author

PRINTING HISTORY
Berkley Prime Crime mass-market edition / November 2007

ISBN: 978-0-425-21904-1

BERKLEY® PRIME CRIME
Berkley Prime Crime Books are published by The Berkley Publishing Group,
a division of Penguin Group (USA) Inc.,
375 Hudson Street, New York, New York 10014.
The name BERKLEY PRIME CRIME and the BERKLEY PRIME CRIME design are
trademarks of Penguin Group (USA) Inc.

PRINTED IN THE UNITED STATES OF AMERICA

10 9 8 7 6 5 4 3 2 1

For the Bookies:

Becky
Nan
Sue
Sandra
Gloria
Carol
Holli
Linda

So many wonderful books read,
so many lively discussions.
Thanks for inviting me to join.

Author's Note

The seed idea for this book occurred to me when I read about people setting kitchen fires trying to deep-fry their Thanksgiving turkeys—how crazy and dangerous is that? The idea morphed into flambéed turkeys—another dangerous idea, as it turns out—when I realized that, one, the book would be published close to Thanksgiving and, two, Carolyn's book, *Eating Out in the Big Easy*, had been in process so long that New Orleans, the setting, had virtually washed away in Hurricane Katrina. A truly heartbreaking event for one of America's most delightful cities; for its citizens, many displaced and trying to get home; and for all of us who love New Orleans and want to keep visiting—and eating inordinate amounts of wonderful food there.

Then I made a trip to New York City to celebrate a new contract with my longtime agent and friend, Richard Curtis, and my kind-hearted, market-savvy editor, Cindy Hwang, who, when I returned from Italy with nasty cases of bronchitis and identity theft, said, "Don't worry about the deadline." Of course, I did and was determined to get this book in on time.

Richard, Cindy, my husband, and I had a great lunch together at Balthazar, to which Bill and I arrived half frozen (desert dwellers that we are) and late, having lost ourselves on the subways and streets of Manhattan. The trip also included a superb performance at the Metropolitan Opera and trips to places I'd never visited, such as Brooklyn and Queens, to sample ethnic foods in ethnic neighborhoods, an experience I highly recommend. All that was research for this book, plus some interesting things my husband found in a book I gave him for Christmas, about immigration from Sicily to New York City, and frequent visits on my part to the Internet.

My thanks to reader Freda Branch of Michigan, who wrote to tell me about the cilantro allergy, to which she is subject, and the delightful website ihatecilantro.com; I've included the site in the book. Check it out. Mrs. Terri Christopher in the book is named in memory of Lillian Susan Terriah Christopher, called "Terri" in college, at the request of her daughter Alexis. Alexis was the successful bidder at the 2006 Malice Domestic live auction, the prize being to name a character in my next book. Alexis, I hope you enjoy Mrs. Christopher. As always, thanks to my readers, who buy and read the books and email me. I've made wonderful long-distance friends through my website, such as Barbara Gausman of Liverpool, New York, with whom I correspond regularly.

This year I joined the Cozy Armchair Group on the Internet, a collection of cozy mystery writers and readers. We discuss one cozy mystery a month and all sorts of other things, not to mention getting seriously silly on occasion. The site is run by Pamela James and moderated by Terri Parsons and Glenda Stice. If you love cozies and haven't yet joined, give it a try. It's a hoot.

Last, I'd like to thank my friends Mary Sarber, retired librarian and book reviewer, and Betty Parker, antiquarian bookseller in Albuquerque, New Mexico. We went to Left Coast Crime in Bristol, England, then traipsed around rural England in March 2006 and had a wonderful time, even if it was *cold and windy*. They're wonderful friends and travel companions, and my next book will be set in England and dedicated to them.

Happy reading,
NFH

1

Lighting a Culinary Fire

Carolyn

Well, this is it, I thought as I picked up the silver pitcher with its slender spout and flammable cognac contents. I glanced around the large penthouse room that housed my publisher's facility for dining and receptions, a lovely room with white half-circle columns against the walls; ornate white woodwork surrounding light-green, moiré silk–covered walls; and French doors, which led to a two-sided balcony overlooking the streets of Lower Manhattan.

The crowd was starting to quiet down for the big event—all the cookbook authors, culinary writers for newspapers and gourmet magazines, food critics, reporters, photographers, Pettigrew and Sons, Inc., editors and authors (Allison Peabody, Janet Fong, and Annunziata Randatto, to name a few), and representatives from book wholesalers and sellers, all of whom had passed through the receiving line and been introduced to me by Gaius Petronius (Petey) Haverford, managing editor and nephew of the publisher—what a name for a flirtatious young man with spiky yellow hair!

My editor, Roland DuPlessis, fatter than ever and decked out in an evening jacket with green velvet lapels and matching jeweled waistcoat, was beaming at me and letting the moment lengthen to increase the suspense. Flambéing my popular turkey recipe had been his foolish idea. Paul Fallon, the vice president of the newspaper syndicate that published my columns, was in attendance with his live-in lover, Francis Striff, an industrial chemist and colleague of my husband, Jason. My agent, Loretta Blum, face surrounded by a big corona of frizzy black hair, squat figure bedecked in a flashy and probably expensive gown, had stood beside me in the receiving line, loudly whispering information about everyone who was about to shake my hand, while scarfing down canapés and champagne and trying to steal some of the Pettigrew authors away from their own agents. Even my friend Luz Vallejo, a retired vice lieutenant, who had helped me solve the murder of the musical director of Opera at the Pass, and later accompanied me on a memorable/disastrous cruise, was in attendance. However, she was deep in conversation with Roberto Santibanez, a handsome Mexican from Guanajuarto who owned restaurants and specialty food shops in the United States and wrote Mexican cookbooks for Pettigrew.

The only people who weren't here were Jason, who had had a terrible chemistry emergency back home—Luz had been surprisingly nice about taking his place at the last moment—and the publisher and owner of Pettigrew and Sons, Inc., Claudius Pettigrew. He was expected to attend, but he had yet to arrive. Petey had assured me that his uncle had probably forgotten because he was likely reading some wonderful book he'd already read several thousand times. It was just one of those things that happened.

I, however, thought that Mr. Pettigrew, whom I had yet to meet, didn't like my book, or believed it was going to be a failure because Roland had nitpicked so long over the recipes that *Eating Out in the Big Easy* was now about a city that had been all but destroyed by a hurricane. That likelihood was certainly making *me* nervous, that and having to flambé my lovely, golden turkeys, three of which were gleaming sumptuously on china platters along the buffet table. Roland nodded pompously, as if he were the queen at some steeplechase in which one of her horses was running. At the signal, the tinkling of a handheld silver bell (Who did he think I was? The maid?) my fingers tightened on the handle of the pitcher as I stepped closer to the largest turkey.

It had a wide, shallow cup stuck into the top on a long spike that probably reached all the way into the dressing, that delicious mixture of spices, herbs, fruit, ground meat, and bread crumbs that was as tasty, in its own way, as any dessert. After filling the cup to the brim with cognac, I flipped a small lever, which opened little holes, lit the cognac with the fancy lighter Roland had provided, and stepped back. I have to admit that I had produced a lovely sight. The cognac flamed, rivulets of fire ran down the sides of my turkey, and the crowd let out an admiring "Ahhhh!" I had created a turkey volcano. Applause broke out, cameras flashed, and I bowed—as Roland had instructed me to, after he won yet another argument.

Then I stepped to the smaller turkey on the left, taking the lighter with me and picking up a pitcher that held a thickened cognac, which would cling to the turkey skin rather than drip. I was to make criss-cross patterns on this one and then set them aflame on top, a much harder task. I painstakingly drizzled the first line from the left center, over the top and onto the right center, unhappy because the liquid didn't seem to be sticky enough. Before I began the first crosshatch from right to left, there was a *whoosh*ing sound, and someone in the crowd said, "Look at that!" Cameras flashed. I glanced to the side to find that the center turkey was flaming a bit higher than it should and little fires were alight where the cognac had dripped into the wide platter.

Frowning, I did the crosshatch and started left to right two inches from the first line. *Pop! Whoosh!* My hand shook, and my third line wavered a bit. How embarrassing! I finished and swiveled my eyes. Turkey number one was burning halfway to the ceiling. I know that happens sometimes, because of too high an alcohol content in the brandy, but it shouldn't be happening now: I'd tested this bottle. As I started line number four with a firm grip on the pitcher, I could hear whispering, then a little shriek coming from behind me.

"Spectacular, isn't it?" said Roland.

Then, "Looks to me like someone needs to get a fire extinguisher." That was Luz, and everyone heard her. I could tell because her comment set off an argument while cameras flashed and Roland bellowed, "Nonsense. This is high cuisine at its most memorable."

"Right." My friend agreed. "It's almost as high as the ceiling. Carolyn, you better back away!"

I had managed to finish two more lines by *not* looking to my right. Someone grabbed my drizzling arm as a little fireball flew sideways and landed on my second turkey, which, of course, went up in crisscrossing lines of flame. I was so close to the new conflagration and so frightened that I dropped the pitcher and allowed myself to be dragged to safety while ladies screamed, reporters scribbled, and the tablecloth caught fire. Roland attempted, unsuccessfully, to put out various parts of the fire with a candlesnuffer, and finally Petey Haverford raced forward waving a long pronged fork, which he plunged into the side of the middle turkey. He then held it aloft like a rotund torch. "Someone get a fire extinguisher," he shouted, and headed for the French doors.

"Why hasn't the sprinkler system gone off?" asked Roland, finally sounding worried. He looked up at the coffered ceiling as if he could command a shower to fall and douse the second turkey, which was sending off small fireballs of its own while the spilled cognac from the pitcher I'd dropped burned merrily up and down the buffet table.

"Way to go, Carolyn," Luz whispered into my ear. "How did you manage that?"

Of course, I had no idea. I'd flambéed things before, though not willingly because I don't like fire; I don't even have a gas range, which is unheard-of for a woman who writes about gourmet cooking. But nothing untoward had happened during my previous ventures into setting fire to food.

"Petronius Haverford, what do you think you're doing?" called the commanding voice of Mrs. Christopher, the white-haired, stately lady who had been the executive assistant to the publisher for forty years and pretty much ran everything and everybody at Pettigrew's, according to Loretta, my agent. She had warned me not to get on the wrong side of Mrs. Christopher, who was called Terri by Mr. Pettigrew and, presumably, her late husband, but absolutely no one else.

However, Mrs. Christopher didn't manage to stop Petey, who had thrown open the French doors and rushed out with his flaming turkey held high. I could see the burn marks along the ceiling that marked his passage, and Roland followed him with the second turkey. "Roland, come back here," Mrs. Christopher ordered.

"Well, those two are in deep shit," said Luz.

"Maybe the turkeys will burn out quickly," I replied, wishing Jason were here. He'd know whether that was likely.

Roland's turkey evidently triggered the sprinkler system, but not before he got out the open door.

Luz had been edging me toward the doors on the wall perpendicular to the one that had provided escape to Petey, Roland, and the two turkeys. My lovely silver velvet dress, which Loretta had personally picked out for me at her uncle Bernie's wholesale establishment, now hung off me, damp, unsightly, and uncomfortable.

Everyone else was trying to get away from the fires and the water, pushing and shoving, reporters calling in stories on cell phones, photographers snapping last pictures of the growing conflagration, ladies weeping, men cursing. It was a disaster. No one would ever buy my book after this debacle, and there was the publisher's chef trying to carry away the third turkey, which was not on fire. I yanked my arm away from Luz's grip and headed back. "Stop that, Franz," I ordered and wrested the turkey away from him.

He wouldn't let go. "Vill burst into flames," he predicted. "Must be get rid of it."

"Absolutely not," I said, and stamped on his toe, which made him relinquish the last bird. "Someone has tampered with my turkeys, and this one is evidence."

"For God's sake, Carolyn," hissed Luz, "let's get out of here before the damn draperies catch fire and trap us, and the worthless sprinkler system ruins my dress."

The sprinkler heads certainly weren't covering the room. Everything to which the turkeys had set fire was still burning, but Luz's dress, lucky her, hadn't been caught by the water like mine, so I allowed myself to be tugged out to the balcony that fronted the side street. But I didn't give up the third turkey, and it weighed twenty pounds. At Thanksgiving Jason always carries the turkeys for me. So where was he when I really needed him?

2
Chaos in the Streets

Luz

A balcony on the twelfth floor of a New York building in November is frigging cold, I can tell you. I was about to freeze my ass off, and Carolyn was wet and shivering, but it wasn't like we could go back inside when the place was in flames. Where was the damn fire department? Most of the people must have been on the flaming-turkey balcony, because I could hear the racket. Maybe they'd found a fire escape and were fighting to get on. Well, I could elbow my way through any crowd of foodies and writers, but I wasn't real sure my knees would carry me down twelve flights of fire escape or that Carolyn would be willing to give up the turkey, which she still clutched to her chest with both arms.

Greasy turkey after falling water was going to do in that dress. I'm happy to say mine, which a cruise line had provided me after losing my suitcase, had survived the turkey roast and sprinklers. Not likely I'd ever be able to afford another dress even close to it; I'll still be wearing it when I'm eighty, if I live that long. My arthritis meds are bad for the health, even if they do keep me moving.

But I was going to have to kick off my fancy shoes and leave them behind; no big loss. The sandals with their frigging high heels hurt like hell. So why had I worn them?

Pride! One of the seven deadly sins. I hadn't wanted to seem like some wetback country bumpkin in the big city. I'd have to go to confession when we got home, and Father Gabriel would say, "About time, Luz. So get on with it. I always look forward to hearing about your sins." He'd love this confession—I'd shacked up with the ship's doctor on that cruise. Well, nobody can say traveling with Carolyn Blue isn't interesting. Better than sitting home with a narc dog, who's in worse health than me.

"Get a grip on your turkey, Carolyn. Let's go see what all the noise is about on the front balcony."

She hefted the bird, arms circling it, fingers laced, like it was a big brown sack of cement, and followed while I cut a path through the people standing on our side of the building. I could hear sirens now. About time! Some of the shivering guests tried to stop her. The dumb shits wanted to know why she'd "attempted to burn down the publishing house with flaming turkeys." At least she didn't answer: Either she was furious or in shock.

We rounded the corner and got caught in a bigger crowd, lots of them hanging over the edge of the balcony, looking down. I spotted the owner's assistant and figured her for the most sensible person there. She was standing in front of the French doors, arms crossed, face set in stone, keeping one eye on the gawkers and the other on the smaller amount of fire still flickering inside. Evidently their useless sprinklers had done some good. "Excuse me, ma'am," I said politely. "What's happening?"

She turned to us. "Petronius and Roland threw the turkeys off the balcony. I believe it has caused problems down below, but I didn't care to view the damage, whatever it may be. Mr. Pettigrew is *not* going to be pleased." Then she studied Carolyn. "Why are you carrying that turkey, Mrs. Blue?"

"It's evidence," said Carolyn through chattering teeth.

"She's in shock," I added hastily.

"I'm not surprised," said Mrs. Christopher, who was always polite to the authors and addressed them formally, unlike her treatment of the Pettigrew employees. Carolyn's weird agent had told us this on our first day in New York, when we visited her office.

"There's a bench over here, Mrs. Blue," she said. "Why don't you sit down? Your turkey must be heavy."

"The chef tried to make off with it," said Carolyn indignantly. "I'm not letting it go until the authorities arrive."

"Ah." Mrs. Christopher nodded. "Come along. There's room for you and the turkey on the bench."

For a wonder, Carolyn went off with her. Courtesy works pretty well with Carolyn, which is why we sometimes get into it. She thinks I'm rude. Go figure. I went off to find Petey and the fat editor. Also, I wanted to see what was happening in the street, and it wasn't pretty. Fire engines, two of them, with crews of guys in hats and raincoats dragging out hoses. One police car and more coming. I could see their flashing lights both up and down the street.

There was a car on fire in front of the building and a wrecked limo that had squashed a lavender metallic VW bug. I wouldn't have expected a lavender car in NYC. El Paso, yeah. The Hispanic population is into color, but I'd figure New Yorkers would think lavender was tacky. They'd probably faint if they saw some of the bright blue-green or red low-riders at home. The owners like to drag race in the streets and get themselves busted by the cops.

Firemen were trying to cut into the VW while medics waited to get in and pull out victims. Guys wearing Yassar Arafat headdresses and fancy New York suits surrounded the limo, shaking their fists and yelling at the cops. Other cars had smashed into one another or run up on sidewalks behind the first wreck. And all these people spilling out of an Irish pub—that's what dumbhead Petey called it. They were carrying beer mugs, singing, laughing, and generally getting in the way. "So, Petey, did you see the whole thing?" I asked. "How did it go down after you pitched the turkey? Think they'll arrest you?" I asked.

Petey looked like I'd just told him his fly was unzipped.

What the hell did he figure was going to happen when the cops found out he'd dropped a flaming turkey into the street?

"Why would they arrest me?" he asked. "Roland and I just tried to save the building. Wow! Did you see those turkeys go up? And the tablecloth? This is the most exciting party Pettigrew has ever thrown."

"Don't be an idiot, Petey. This may have ruined the book launch," said Roland, "and I talked your uncle into paying for it. People will be laughing at Carolyn rather than buying her book."

I hadn't thought of that, but maybe Carolyn had, and that explained why she was so glum.

"Well, how were we to know that the turkeys wouldn't go out on the way down?" said Petey. "You'd think the wind or something would put the fire out." He looked back at the room from which he'd run with the turkey held over his head. "Roland and I saved people's lives. And now the fire's stopped burning inside . . . well, almost." Then he looked over the balustrade. Several people had managed to get out of the VW with help, but a crumpled figure in the driver's seat had to be removed.

"I don't think anyone was hurt in the car that caught fire," he said kind of hopefully. "One of the turkeys went straight down, hit someone on the sidewalk, and bounced under the car. It was parked illegally. You should have seen the people inside scrambling out." He started to laugh and then noticed a reporter listening and scribbling notes. "Very frightening," Petey added, looking at me. "You can imagine."

"Damn right," I agreed. "Not every day a flaming turkey rolls under your car. Frigging hilarious. What happened with the limo and the VW?"

"Well, that was my turkey," said Petey. "I didn't realize I had such a good throwing arm. Adrenaline, I guess, although I did play cricket at Cambridge. My turkey hit the windshield of the limo, and the driver tried to swerve out of the way and smashed into the VW in the opposite lane, ramming it into another car. If he'd just kept going straight, the turkey would have rolled off the hood, and there wouldn't have been an accident. Limousines always have unbreakable glass."

"Maybe the guy panicked when he saw a flaming turkey heading for his windshield. He might have thought it was a firebomb."

"Or a meteor," suggested Petey enthusiastically. "Something to tell his grandchildren."

"Are you out of your mind, Petronius?" demanded Mrs. Christopher, emerging from the crowd and tapping him smartly on the shoulder.

"Come on, Mrs. Christopher," he said plaintively. "You've known me since I was a little kid. Couldn't you call me Petey?"

"I could not. You have a perfectly respectable name. You were named after the famous Roman satirist and arbiter of taste, Gaius Petronius, the Emperor Nero's *arbiter elegantiae*."

"And look what happened to him," Petey whined. "Nero made him commit suicide."

"But he did maintain his dignity by satirizing the emperor in his will. No one ever accused Gaius Petronius of creating an embarrassing situation by throwing burning turkeys onto a busy street."

"All those people and cars shouldn't be down there," said Petey defensively. "It's a weeknight."

"Corrigan's is celebrating a saint's day. St. Laurence O'Toole, a twelfth-century Bishop of Dublin," said Roland. "Imagine leaving one's home to drink Irish beer and eat Irish food. One wonders about the deteriorating taste in this city."

I figured Roland was making that up. I'd never heard of any saint named Laurence O'Toole, and my mom used to read us the life of a different saint every night. Not that I listened: After a hard day of punching out little boys who got smart with me or hassled my sisters, I usually fell asleep before Mom finished the latest grisly tale of saint-hood.

"If you knew the street would be crowded, Roland, why did *you* throw that turkey?" asked Mrs. Christopher, her mouth grim. "Both of you, and the publishing house, may be sued for property damage and personal injury."

You had to like the woman even if she was prissier than Carolyn. She wasn't letting the two idiots talk their way out of this mess. But then she turned to me, and I figured I might be in for a tongue-lashing, too, although I'd had nothing to do with any of this. I was just here letting my curiosity get the best of me, like any former cop would.

"Ms. Vallejo, I suggest that you rejoin your friend and take her back into the room. The fires have subsided, and she'll be more comfortable out of the cold."

I did that while Mrs. Christopher herded the other guests inside. I could hear Petey, that bastard, saying, "It was Carolyn's fault. They were her turkeys."

3

Pestered by Pettigrews

Carolyn

I don't know why Luz and Mrs. Christopher thought I was in shock. I wasn't! Well, maybe a little. It had, after all, been a terrifying experience, seeing my beautiful turkeys turn into firebombs while those rivulets of fire ran across the tablecloth where I'd spilled the cognac. And then shivering in a heavy, wet dress on a cold balcony while my publisher's party room, not to mention my career, went up in flames. Under the circumstances, I could hardly be blamed for feeling shaken. I shivered and hugged the last turkey close lest someone else try to take it away from me. I'd been sabotaged. I had no doubt of it, and I was furious, not to mention determined to find the villain.

Luz and I would investigate. When I looked up, she was standing in front of me like the good friend she was, ready to help me prove my innocence. "Let's get in out of this frigging cold," she said, as foulmouthed as ever, and I didn't even mind, for once. "Between the sprinklers and the guy in the tall white hat with the fire extinguisher, the fire's out." She helped me up and didn't even try to take away my turkey, although I might have let *her* carry it for a while if she'd asked. It was awfully heavy.

"So he was willing to help with the fire once he realized

he couldn't get the evidence away from me," I muttered. I had settled on the chef as the most likely culprit. His attempt to make off with the third turkey was an excellent clue. I wasn't sure just how he'd managed to ruin the flambéing ritual. Maybe he had tampered with the cognac, but if so, why did he want to take the last turkey? I hadn't poured anything on that one.

Maybe he'd slipped something inside the turkeys that would explode once I set them on fire. If so, he couldn't afford to let anyone find the bomb or whatever it was. I'd made the stuffing and basting sauce myself and stuffed the birds early that morning, then painted a mustard paste on the hot turkeys before turning down the temperature. I was then assured that I could leave the roasting and basting to the staff in the kitchen.

That's when Luz and I met Loretta at her uncle Bernie's to shop for my gown. Luz and Loretta's uncle talked arthritis while I tried on everything my agent chose, most of which I wouldn't have worn to a dinner party at a house of ill repute—not that I'd ever willingly enter a house of ill repute. The silver dress, with its gold embroidery, had been the only acceptable choice, but now it clung damply to my forty-something figure and made me look like a bedraggled sheep.

"Don't admit to anything," Luz whispered into my ear as we edged into the dripping room where all the food, including my lovely dressing, had been removed or destroyed. However, the liquor flowed freely under Petey's enthusiastic direction.

I wanted to ask what she meant by that. Admit to what? I hadn't done anything wrong. I— "Carolyn," Petey cried and threw his arms around me. "Jolly good party. Best we've ever had up here. Uncle Claudius usually opts for more sedate affairs. Let me take that turkey. Your arms must be—"

"No," I snarled and pulled away from him. Had he been the one? Playing some kind of stupid joke, on which he was now congratulating himself?

"Well, okay, dear heart. How about some champagne? Or a cocktail? You must be parched after all your good work."

"I'll have a bourbon and Coke," I said, remembering how good that had tasted when I was hiding out in a thriller writer's cabin on a cruise ship and just horribly traumatized.

Petey gave me a surprised look and sent a waiter away to fill my order. Roland had rushed up, overheard, and admonished me: "You'll never build a following of real gourmets if you drink things like that, Carolyn. Bourbon and Coke is so tacky. Take my advice and have something fashionable."

"I took your advice about flambéing the turkeys, and look what happened," I retorted. "I could order bourbon and . . . and sewer water, and no one would buy my book now."

"Nonsense," my agent intervened, having joined our circle. "Any publicity is good publicity. Everyone in the business knows that. Well, plagiarism doesn't go over well, but—"

"Isn't Carolyn a delightful dark horse?" exclaimed Petey. "I'd never have expected her to be so much fun. Tell me, Caro— May I call you that? I heard your Chicano friend—"

"No," I snapped. "And you're an idiot!" I didn't care if he was the publisher's nephew and probable heir to the kingdom, not after he'd thrown the turkey over the balcony and my editor had followed right after him.

Petey Haverford laughed and said I wasn't the first woman to call him an idiot, but that everyone agreed he had the best eye in town for a bestseller. "Do you know any fun writers of bestsellers?" he asked. "If you do—"

"I only know the thriller writer Owen Griffith," I replied stiffly, "and he has a publisher, not to mention having been accused by my mother-in-law of having an affair with me." I'd snatched my bourbon and Coke from the waiter and took two big swallows while clinging to the turkey with my other arm. "I doubt that he'd take any advice from me, even if I wanted to give him any. Which I don't."

"Owen Griffith? He's fabulous! I'll talk you into bringing him to us. Won't I, Rollie?"

My editor remarked that he thought I was angry with them both.

"Very perceptive of you, Roland," I remarked, and had another gulp of bourbon and Coke. I was feeling somewhat better, except for my arms. "Why did you throw the turkeys over the balcony? They were evidence."

"Of what?" asked Petey, looking puzzled.

"Of whatever was done to my turkeys. I ought to sic my mother-in-law on you. She's the meanest feminist in the country."

"Really?" Petey looked interested, and I had to wonder what silly scheme was running around under his ridiculous, spiked blond hair. I'd heard his uncle was very conservative. How did he put up with such a nephew, and in a position of responsibility, no less? But maybe the answer to that was obvious: Mr. Pettigrew hadn't come to the party. Maybe it wasn't me he disliked—yet. It was his nephew.

Suddenly I was being introduced to Petey's tall, silver-haired mother, Lavinia Haverford.

"*Mater*," he said. "I call her *Mater* because we all have these Roman-Empire names. *Mater*, our incendiary gourmet here, Carolyn Blue, has a feminist mother-in-law. Caro, my mother, who's a feminist herself. She holds séances at our brownstone to connect with dead feminists. Can you believe it? Think your mother-in-law might be interested? She doesn't write books by any chance, does she?"

Vera did write books, but she was the last person I wanted to summon to New York. My visit was already a disaster.

"Not *Gwenivere* Blue!" cried Mrs. Haverford. "I've read her wonderful *Women of the World, Unite!* You *must* invite her to come and visit me. All my friends would be so delighted to meet her. She can stay at the house and talk to our group, the Carolyn Heilbrun Memorial Book Club. Perhaps we could even arrange for her to attend a séance. We've been talking about trying to connect with Emma Goldman. You *have* heard of the wonderful feminist labor leader? I'm sure she and your mother-in-law would be soul mates." Mrs. Haverford's laughter was as silvery as her hair, as silvery as my soggy gray gown had once been. "Well, soul mates on either side of the grave. Emma Goldman is dead, of course, and your mother-in-law isn't, or so I assume."

Before I could admit that I *had* heard of the famous anarchist, commotion heralded the arrival of a tall bearded man, rumpled, rather scruffy, and definitely unsteady on his feet. Everyone stopped chattering and drinking and simply stared. Except me. I finished off my bourbon and Coke and signaled a waiter for another. How had the poor fellow managed to get upstairs? The elevator had been guarded for the invitation-only event. Several people had tried to get in and been turned away. I took this interloper to be drunk as well as homeless. But for the condition of his clothes and hair, he might have been a handsome man.

"Uncle Claudius, what happened to you? I was afraid you'd forgotten entirely," Petey cried. "Come and meet our author."

A path opened immediately for Uncle Claudius, who walked uncertainly in our direction, leaning on Petey when he arrived and saying, "My apologies to all. I became so enchanted by the new edition of Spencer's *Faerie Queen* that I lost track of the time. Fellow from Columbia did it. Why couldn't your father have sent him to us, Petronius? You should keep your eye out for opportunities like that."

"*Pater* probably doesn't know anyone in the English department, Uncle Claudius. He's a biologist. And as delicious as the *Faerie Queen* is, it's not going to be a bestseller, now is it?" Petey looked cheerfully smug.

"Don't be a philistine, my boy," Claudius said and turned to me. "You must be Mrs. Blue. Do excuse me for arriving late for your fete, my dear, but the most extraordinary thing happened to me. I was walking toward the entrance when a large, flaming object dropped onto my shoulder, knocking me to the sidewalk, and setting fire to my beard. Fortunately, some quick-witted fellow put the fire out but almost smothered me in the process. Then other people wanted to send for an ambulance, but I said I thought that I'd just sit for a minute or two until I regained my wits. After all, one can never count on an ambulance to take one to a suitable hospital. Then to my amazement, a car burst into flames quite close to me, and all sorts of hubbub ensued. I made my way into the lobby to sit down, but I suspect it may have been a terrorist attack of some sort. In what an uncertain world we live!

"Carlos, I'll have a flute of champagne, if you'd be so kind," added Uncle Claudius. "Nothing to eat, I think. I'm still a bit disconcerted." Uncle Claudius then gazed around the room, obviously bewildered at its condition. I swallowed down a groan. My turkey had knocked over my publisher and set his beard on fire? How much worse could things get?

That's when both the police and fire departments arrived, hoses and guns at the ready.

4

The Embattled Author-Arsonist

Luz

Uh-huh! The shit's about to hit the fan, I thought, as the firemen clumped into the room, all suited up in rubber coats, boots, and helmets, followed by both uniformed and plainclothes cops, if I was any judge, and I was, having been a vice lieutenant before rheumatoid arthritis screwed up my career and my life. I had been circulating, drinking martinis, which tasted like horse piss—give me a good margarita any day—and collaring reporters to let them know that it was Petey and Roland, not Carolyn, who were responsible for what had happened on the street. I doubted that she even knew what was going on down there. She hadn't looked over the balcony—too busy clutching her turkey.

How could such a well-meaning, good-citizen type like Carolyn get into so much trouble? Well, she was about to find out what a couple of flaming turkeys could do to a busy city street. If it had happened in El Paso on a weeknight, only a couple of drunks would have been around, and they'd have figured they were seeing things and sworn off the bottle for about ten minutes, or they'd have thought aliens were coming over from Roswell to get them so they'd better hide out behind a Dumpster in

some alley. Anyway, I figured I'd better get over there before Carolyn opened her mouth and gave the cops the
wrong impression.

Serve and protect had been our motto in the El Paso Police Department, especially when it came to the clueless,
like Carolyn, so I grabbed a drink off a tray and handed it
to the latest reporter I'd nabbed. Why couldn't they have
gone home after they got their stories? Free alcohol was
the answer. The nosy bastards phoned in to their editors
and then kept drinking. Maybe if they got drunk enough,
they'd pass out. I handed a drink to every news shark I
spotted on my way to get Carolyn's back.

The firemen were looking around for more fires to put
out and assuring people that their arson expert knew where
the missiles had come from and would be right up to investigate. Since they mostly threatened food writers with the
arson inspector, they got replies like, "What missiles?" and
glared under their helmets at the simpletons who didn't
know they were in big trouble.

A cop arrived wearing the rattiest green wool overcoat
I've ever seen, probably something he got from the Good-
will, which made you wonder whether New York detectives were as badly paid as El Paso detectives, but with a
higher cost of living to deal with. Anyway, the cop kept
asking who was in charge until he found his way over to
the homeless guy who'd stumbled in and joined Carolyn's
group. She was probably asking about the diet of the
homeless. I remember her asking about what drug dealers
ate over in Juarez.

"Okay, who shot the firebombs into the street?" snarled
the cop.

"What firebombs?" asked the homeless guy, who didn't
sound like a homeless guy and didn't even smell bad. Go
figure. If he was the person in charge, he sure had eccentric taste in clothes—him and the cop.

"Detective Worski!" Carolyn exclaimed. "Don't you remember me? I helped you with the investigation of Max
Heydemann's death. In the deli. It was . . . let me see . . ."

"I remember you," said the detective, looking glum under his stubbly double chin and above his thrift-store coat. "You were always calling me with more information, most of it useless."

"It was not," Carolyn retorted. "I was your best source of inside leads. I even pointed you toward the assassin."

"But you said he was a woman," Worski countered.

She shrugged. "But then I recognized him when he was dressed as a man and called you from the theater. And I did stop him from killing Jason. Furthermore, I intend to help you with this case. First, you need to know that there were no firebombs, just the turkeys Roland and Petey threw over the balcony."

"You were the one who set them on fire, Carolyn," said Petey.

"Turkeys?" Detective Worski glared at her.

In his place I would have glared at her myself. "I'm Retired Lieutenant Luz Vallejo of the El Paso, Texas, Police Department," I intervened. "Don't worry, Detective. I'll try to keep Carolyn off your back. I know what a pain in the ass she can be. No offense intended, Carolyn."

Worski grinned. "Detective Ivan Worski, NYPD," he responded, and shook my hand while Carolyn sent me a hurt look. "This is my partner." He gestured toward a dark-haired woman who had just arrived at his side. "Detective Juana Benitez. So, witnesses say a lump of flaming stuff fell from the balcony up here, hit some old guy who was gone by the time I got to the scene—"

"That would be me, Claudius Pettigrew," said the homeless guy. "I own the building and the publishing house, although I can't tell you what happened here. Obviously something unusual, given the events on the street and the state of this room."

I was torn between wondering if Benitez was Mexican or some other Hispanic type and being amazed that the homeless guy was the head honcho.

"They were flambéed turkeys, which had been sabotaged," said Carolyn irritably. "I've never flambéed anything before that kept on burning and set fire to other things. Both Mrs. Christopher and I tried to stop Petey and Roland from throwing the turkeys over the balcony. I do hope no more damage was done, and I apologize to you, Mr. Pettigrew—about your beard and your shoulder. It must have been a very terrifying experience to be hit by a burning turkey."

"Not at all, my dear," said the old guy so courteously I was surprised he didn't bow and kiss her hand. "Given the speed with which everything happened, I hardly had time to be more than astonished."

"So you set the turkeys on fire, Mrs. Blue, but someone else tossed them over the balcony," growled Detective Worski. "That's your story?"

I couldn't blame the poor guy for looking as if he thought she'd made it up. "It's that high cuisine," I remarked. "She writes about and even cooks all sorts of fancy stuff."

"It's not a *story*!" Carolyn protested. "That's what happened, and—"

"Carolyn makes a great gazpacho and terrific sangria," I interrupted, more to shut her up than anything and maybe score a few points for Carolyn with the Hispanic partner, "and if you know her, you know she wouldn't do anything to hurt anyone, especially since the whole thing screwed up the launch party for her book. So no motive. Right?"

Worski frowned at me and said, "What are you? Her lawyer?"

"And *here*, Inspector Worski, is the first piece of evidence." Carolyn tried to hand him the turkey.

"What the hell?" He backed away.

"I managed to keep the chef from running off with it when the other two began to burn in a very frightening manner. I do think he's the most likely suspect. Why would he want make off with the turkey unless he's the person who tampered with it?"

"O-kay," said Worski slowly. "Benitez. Take the turkey."

His partner looked at it with distaste, but put out her hands to follow orders. No luck there. A fire department guy who had been listening, said, "I'll take that turkey," and snatched it away from Benitez, looking sort of surprised at how much it weighed. "This is an arson, obviously, and I'm on the arson squad. We'll need this . . . ah . . . bird as evidence."

Well, that explained why the turkey staggered him. He didn't build up muscles hauling around heavy hoses; he just sniffed for accelerants when the fire was out, which he was doing right then: sniffing the turkey.

"No gasoline," he muttered to himself and upended the bird to sniff the butt.

"Do be careful," Carolyn gasped. "It occurred to me that someone might have tucked a bomb of some kind inside each of the three turkeys after I finished making the dressing and stuffing them. I went back to my hotel then, so there would have been a whole day for someone to insert an explosive device. Of course, it may have been the cognac. I don't know what a criminal would do to cognac to make it burn like that. I'd tested the bottle I planned to use, and it was fine. It produced a nice, moderate blue flame at that time, but I suppose someone could have mixed in or substituted something later."

"Look," said Worski to the arson inspector, "there're at least three people injured down there, one of them unconscious, not to mention a burned-out car and a lot of damage to other cars. One of those is the limousine of an ambassador to the UN. We'll probably have the damned State Department breathing down our necks before this is over. I don't give a shit if you guys take the turkey, but I want to hear what you find out ASAP. Got that?"

"Oh, my goodness," said Carolyn weakly. "People were injured? I can't believe this!"

"It wasn't your fault, Caro," I said quickly. "You didn't throw the turkeys overboard. Roland and Petey did that."

"I know, but—"

"And we'll find out who's been screwing with your turkeys. Okay?"

"Okay." She nodded. "Thank you, Luz."

"Sounds to me like at least three of you are up for first-degree assault at the least," said Worski, while his partner tried to wipe grease off where her fingers had touched the turkey before the arson guy grabbed it. He didn't look too happy to be stuck holding the turkey either, so he bellowed for someone lower on the food chain to take the evidence.

That guy arrived, pissed off, and muttered, "So what do *I* do with it? Serve it back at the fire house?"

Everyone in the room crowded around trying to eavesdrop, the reporters first in line with drinks in hand, talking into their cell phones.

"I assure you, Detective Worski," Carolyn was saying earnestly, "I intend to help you solve this horrible crime, whether or not you want my help, and Luz, who knows all about crime, will be at my side."

"So you've worked on flaming turkey cases, have you, Lieutenant?" asked Worski sarcastically.

I grinned. "There's always a first time. Right? Something to tell the grandkids."

"Would you like a Bio-Wipe, Miss—ah—Detective?" Carolyn asked Benitez, pulling one of those little tinfoil packs out of her handbag.

Leave it to Carolyn to come equipped with whatever anyone was going to need. She probably had a fire extinguisher in that purse but had been too shocked to remember it when the tablecloth went up in flames.

"I believe, given the seriousness of the charge mentioned by the detective, that Pettigrew's must consider bringing in our private detective to investigate this matter. You ladies needn't trouble yourselves." Claudius Pettigrew smiled at Carolyn and me and wandered off to find Mrs. Christopher.

Worski groaned. Can't blame him for that. No cop wants a P.I. messing around in his case.

5

Reliving a Ghastly Evening

Carolyn

I sat on the bed in my beige New York hotel room, my back against the suede headboard, wondering what in the world I was going to tell Jason. He'd call again, having already left two messages, which I'd missed because of all the ghastly things that had happened that evening—the injuries my turkeys had caused in the street, the fact that I myself was a suspect and had been told, after questioning—everyone there had been questioned at least briefly—that I couldn't leave the city, nor could Petey Haverford or Roland, my editor, not to mention the chef, who would be warned, if and when they found him.

I'd pointed out to Detective Worski that the chef's disappearance was suspicious when, at the least, he should have stayed to prepare more food to replace what had been burned up or ruined by the sprinklers and fire extinguishers. Instead Franz had tried to snatch away my turkey, the only evidence I had, and then disappeared after wielding the fire extinguisher for a short time. Very suspicious indeed. They were looking for him, but goodness, he could have escaped on a plane to Brazil by now.

"So what do you think?" asked Luz. Being unable to twirl because of the rheumatoid arthritis in her knees, she revolved slowly to model the blue evening dress that had been saved from the explosion on the *Bountiful Feast* cruise ship. Given what had happened on our last trip together, most people would have refused to travel with me again. Luz, however, hadn't even hesitated when I called at the last minute and asked if she'd like to fill in for Jason and accompany me to the New York launch of my first book. "Damn right," she'd agreed. "Doing stuff with you is always a hoot."

She looked at herself in the long mirror on the bathroom door. "So is this something I can wear to an opera?"

"It's perfect," I replied morosely, and it was. She, who had once been more comfortable wearing jeans and a gun, now had a whole closet full of designer clothes as a result of our cruise ship losing her minimalist wardrobe the first day aboard. I'd felt underdressed the whole time because she looked so stylish.

"Good." Luz pulled the dress over her head, hung it up in the very crowded closet area the two of us were sharing, and headed into the bathroom with a T-shirt over her arm. At least she was going to wear *something* to bed. Sharing a room with a naked woman made me uncomfortable, but not as uncomfortable as the ringing of the telephone beside my bed. That would be Jason, and I still didn't know what, if anything, to tell him about my evening at Pettigrew and Sons. If I told him the truth, he probably wouldn't believe me. If he did believe me, I'd be adding another ton of bad news to the terrible weight he already carried.

Jason wasn't with me because there'd been an accident in his lab, two students poisoned by heavy metals in an, as yet, unexplained mishap. Poor Jason. He couldn't leave, no matter how much he'd wanted to be with me for my big night. There was an investigation going on. The students were in the hospital. Not that there wasn't an investigation going on here—with people in the hospital. I picked up the phone and greeted my husband.

"So how did it go?" he asked, trying to sound enthusiastic.

"It was—spectacular," I replied. It certainly had been that.

"Did everyone like the turkey?"

"They'd never seen anything like it," I replied truthfully. I'd never seen anything like it myself. I could have cheerfully strangled Roland, had I been able to get my fingers around his pudgy neck, for insisting that I fix a Thanksgiving turkey recipe that had been very popular in my column. But people do not flambé their Thanksgiving turkeys, which also had been his ludicrous idea. For the book launch, the turkeys needed extra flair, he'd said. What an irony. The *flare* had turned out to be more than he, or I, bargained for. What a stupid, disastrous idea, and after he'd delayed the publication of my book about New Orleans restaurants and cuisine so long that the New Orleans I wrote about had been washed away before *Eating Out in the Big Easy* could even make its way into the bookstores. Two reasons that no one would ever buy it.

"So how are things there, Jason?" I asked, anxious to say no more about the party. "Are the students going to be all right?"

"I don't know," he replied, voice dull with apprehension. "Both are on ventilators, and one's still unconscious. The doctors are trying to precipitate the metals out of Jose's blood. He's the worst off because he got most of it. Nate's levels are much lower. As soon as he saw Jose go down, Nate dragged the poor fellow as far as he could and then used a cell phone to call for help. I'm beginning to think my objection to cell phones is ill judged. There are times when . . . well the thing is, *how* could it have happened? Jose knew how dangerous the fumes were, but he wasn't even wearing a mask. And he couldn't have been paying attention, or his experiment wouldn't have boiled over. We've had to clear the whole building."

"I'm just so glad you weren't there." A shiver passed up my arms at the thought that Jason might have ended up in that hospital, too. But then again, if he'd been in the lab, the accident wouldn't have happened.

"Federal agents are all over the place," my husband muttered.

They'll probably be out in force here, too, I thought gloomily. If the authorities still thought it had been a fire-bomb, they'd have to call in the—what?—DEA? "Well, let's hope the students recover. Surely it can't be that bad."

"It can be lethal," said Jason, sounding a bit snappish. But of course he was upset. So was I. "Anyway, I'm happy that things went well for you. Did you meet lots of review-ers and food people?"

"Lots of reviewers and food people," I agreed. "And other cookbook authors and people from the publishing house and culinary magazines. It was very . . . exciting."

Luz had just come out of the bathroom, her long T-shirt barely covering her hips, leaving in view long brown legs marred with a bullet scar on one thigh and puffiness in both knees.

"Well, we'd both better get some sleep, Jason," I said. "I love you."

He said he loved me, too, and started to ask why he hadn't been able to get hold of me earlier. "Goodnight, sweetheart," I interrupted and hung up.

"You didn't tell him, did you?" asked Luz accusingly.

"I couldn't. The students are still unconscious, and—"

"And you think he'll take the news better if he hears it *after* they've died?" Luz asked.

"Maybe he won't hear about it at all."

"Like that's going to happen! He's not going to notice if they throw you in jail?"

"*I* didn't do anything wrong," I protested. "Someone tampered with my turkeys. We just have to find out who did it."

"All those years investigating crime, and now I have to find out what happened to three turkeys," muttered Luz. "Shit." She eyed her bed with a puzzled look and asked, "What the hell is this thing anyway? How come they don't have regular blankets?"

"It's a duvet. They pride themselves on their European-style bedding and their top-of-the-line mattresses and pillows. Didn't you read the brochure?"

"Oh, right. Like I'm going to read about the beds. Hell, I can't even watch TV without getting the creeps. Half the time the people look like dwarfs." She glared at the TV, with its wide, shallow screen, hanging across from our beds. Then she climbed into bed and turned out the light under its beige rectangular shade.

I had to floss my teeth in the dark while dreading what morning would bring. And worse, remembering what had happened during the well-attended, much-anticipated, thoroughly appalling party to launch my bad-luck book.

6

The Morning After

Carolyn

I woke up feeling no better than I'd felt when I went to bed after the turkey debacle at my book launch. Because I was so stressed, I insisted that Luz and I eat in the hotel coffee shop, where we could get more than the continental breakfast. Of course she didn't want to. The donuts, rolls, croissants, and coffee were free. The eggs Benedict I craved weren't, but I prevailed by offering to pay for her breakfast, too. Still, Luz sulked over her eggs, bacon, and pancakes, so I devoted myself to the courtesy newspaper that had been left at our door.

Not my best decision. The front-page story contained gory details about the "terrorist attack" on Lower Manhattan in front of the Pettigrew Building, from which the attack had been launched, "according to government sources." The victim in the lavender Volkswagen was a nineteen-year-old girl named Li Yu Yan (also known as Birdie Li), granddaughter of Mr. Li Cheng Bao, president of the Wise Dragon Benevolent Society.

"This is so sad," I murmured and read the article to Luz. "She's only nineteen and her doctors don't expect her to regain consciousness. I think I'd better pay a condolence call on her grandfather. He deserves to know what really happened and that we plan to find the culprit who tinkered with my turkeys."

Luz frowned and replied, "You should stay away from those people. They might sue you. And you don't know what a benevolent society is. It could be some bunch of gangsters."

I had to laugh. Why would gangsters call themselves a benevolent society? "They probably help the poor and the new immigrants in Chinatown, Luz, and if you think it's dangerous, you can come with me."

"I'm going over to see what Worski and Benitez are doing. You should come with me. And if you're not going to follow my advice, you should at least have a cell phone so you can call me if you get lost or in trouble."

I replied that Jason didn't like cell phones and that I wasn't a child who needed someone to keep track of her. Visiting Mr. Li was the proper thing to do, and I was going to do it.

Luz snorted and wolfed down the last bite of her syrup-soaked pancakes. Back in the room I got a telephone number for the Wise Dragon Benevolent Society and made an eleven o'clock appointment with Mr. Li to discuss his granddaughter's accident, about which I had information he'd want to hear. I'd no sooner accomplished that task than I had a call from Jack Armstrong—what a silly name; I remember my mother laughing about "Jack Armstrong, the all-American boy," or was it my grandmother? This Jack wrote vegetarian cookbooks for Pettigrew and wanted to take me out to lunch since he'd been unable to attend my book launch. I told him that he hadn't missed much and that I'd be in Chinatown around noon, so we arranged to meet at the Lotus Blossom Dining Room. *Excellent* I thought. *I'll use the luncheon for an ethnic Chinese section in my book.*

"You don't have to worry about me, Luz," I informed my roommate. "I'm going to leave as soon as I've brushed my teeth in order to find Chinatown in time to sightsee or at least keep my appointment with the Chinese grand-father."

Luz

With Carolyn gone, I got out Detective Worski's card and called his station house for instructions on how to get from the hotel to the precinct by subway. Then I went out, walked down into the bowels of the damn city, and boarded a train. Wouldn't you know? The frigging subway was mobbed, and some smug, middle-aged guy plopped down in the last free seat and opened his newspaper. It was a disabled-section seat at that. I glared at him for a few minutes while being bumped around, and when he didn't get off at the next stop, I gave him a hard nudge with my foot and said, "Hey, *pendejo*, you don't look disabled to me. I've got bad knees, so why don't you be a gentleman and give me that seat?"

The bastard lowered his paper, looked me up and down, and said, "You don't look disabled either. If you can't stand up in a rush-hour subway, you should have taken a cab."

He was right, but damned if I was going to pay for a cab when I'd bought a week's subway pass. "I'm a tourist with one of those tourist passes," I snapped.

"I hate tourists. Always thinking they can take seats away from hard-working New Yorkers." He snapped his paper and went back to reading. If they'd had a conductor or driver or anything in the car, I'd have reported Mr. Hard-Working New Yorker for being able-bodied and hogging a seat that I was entitled to. One look at my knees and a sub-way employee would probably have put him off at the next stop.

"Yo, lady, you can have my seat."

I looked two seats down the aisle, and this big black kid in a leather jacket grinned at me—eighteen, nineteen, something like that. He had a bunch of studs in one ear. Looked like a gangbanger to me, or maybe a gay guy with the earrings and all—Carolyn won't let me say *queer* any-more—but I wasn't about to be picky. A seat was a seat, and my knees were already aching. I took it. "Thanks," I said. "You're a credit to your city. I'm Luz Vallejo."

"I'm DeShawn." He didn't even need to hang on the pole. He was so tall he just grabbed the overhead bar.

"Nice to meet you, DeShawn. So, I used to be a cop. What do you do for a living?" If he said he was a criminal, I'd be sorry I asked, but I figured to be polite and show an interest in the kid, kind of a reward for good behavior.

"Got a part-time gig deliverin' stuff on a bicycle. That's hot. Scootin' in between the cabs. But I aim to be a rapper pretty soon."

That had to be the dumbest ambition I'd ever heard of. Here the kid was raised to give up his seat on the subway to someone my age, and his idea of a career was being a rapper. Black people had been coming up with great music before I was born, and now all they liked were songs about rape and murder, songs with no melody. I wondered what Carolyn thought about rap and had to laugh. Rap lyrics made my occasional swearing sound like Christian rock.

"Why you laughin'?" DeShawn demanded. "That a ole lady thing or a Latina thing?"

"It's a cop thing," I improvised hastily. "Those rappers are a bunch of criminals, always shooting someone or get-ting shot."

"Like cops ain't doin' the same thing but don' make no money at it," said DeShawn scornfully. "If you're a cop, I want my seat back."

"I'm retired."

"You get shot?"

"Yeah, but I got bad knees from arthritis. Listen, kid, you can take my word for it. Being a cop is more fun and less dangerous than being a rapper. Besides that, everyone hates rappers and loves cops."

"Other way around in my hood, lady." He looked good-humored again, as if I was some poor, dumb hick who didn't know the score.

"Well, speaking of ladies, what does your mother think of you being a rapper?"

I had him there. He just shrugged, mumbled something I didn't catch, and shifted his weight from one unlaced high top to another. "Ain't no cop shop gonna want me to join up."

"Unless you've got a record, I don't see why not. We have African-American officers on the force in El Paso even though we don't have hardly any black citizens. If you've got a high school diploma and you're willing to take a few college courses while you're on the job, some police force would probably snap you right up." Why was I telling him this stuff? I didn't know if any PD would take him on. For all I knew, he couldn't read and write. God knows we graduated enough kids back home who couldn't.

"So how many blacks you got in uniform in this El Paso? One? Two?" He was laughing at me. "I come down there, you gonna give me a recommendation?" The woman sitting next to me got off the train, and DeShawn sat down beside me. "You sayin' I'm gonna like this place?"

"Probably not," I admitted. "Like I said, we're short on blacks and long on Mexican-Americans like me, and it's hot as hell most of the time, but—"

"Hot sounds good. Where you think my ancestors come from? The North Pole? You just don' wan' me showin' up at your house."

I didn't want the kid to think that. "How old are you?" He said twenty-one, which I doubted. I fished in my pocket for my billfold and got a business card out. I still carry them. Sometimes it helps to ID yourself as a cop, even if you're retired. On the back I wrote my name and the phone number of the hotel. "I know a couple of people in the NYPD." I didn't mention that they were investigating my roommate. "Give me a call. Maybe I can get you an interview." Mr. Rap Star's mouth dropped open when I handed him the card. "I'll be here at least till the weekend." Maybe longer if they wouldn't let Carolyn go. "And what's your last name?"

"Brown, but I ain't got no card."

"That's okay. DeShawn Brown."

"You for real?" he asked.

"Sure," I said, getting up because I had to change trains, which meant more damn stairs. *Hijo*, but this city was hard on the disabled. Maybe I should start looking for elevators in the subways. Surely by law they had to furnish them. I grinned at DeShawn and said, "Anything to keep a good kid from getting himself shot singing dirty songs that would embarrass his mother."

7

The Chinese Cell-Phone Lady

Carolyn

I didn't have too much trouble finding Chinatown, just a few wrong trains, but what a delight the neighborhood was! One of my favorite buildings stood five stories high with the upper floors sporting those tipped, tiled pagoda roofs, large windows set off by red columns and horizontal, colorful rows of designs, with shops on the lower floor. Young Asians crammed a Starbucks located on the ground floor, and on the sidewalk older Asians patronized street vendors selling their wares under umbrellas.

With ample time before my eleven o'clock appointment at the Wise Dragon Benevolent Society, I wandered and looked in windows full of hanging ducks, and at the windows of beauty shops, acupuncture establishments, trading companies, sellers of cosmetics, giant lobsters, unidentifiable vegetables, unusual pharmaceuticals, and herbs, all housed in old New York buildings adorned with Chinese symbols and English translations for us tourists.

Evidently the place had once been Little Italy, for several Italian restaurants remained. Had I not splurged on such a big breakfast, I'd have been tempted to drop into Vincent's Original for a pastry I'd enjoyed on the Amalfi Coast, not something I'd seen since in El Paso.

And everywhere people shouted in machine-gun Chinese on their cell phones, many ladies much older than I, which made me feel so old-fashioned and technology challenged. Luz's advice that I should have my own cell phone echoed in my head, so I stopped by an tiny, middle-aged lady and waited politely for her to finish her call. In return, she eyed me narrowly and ended her conversation on the spot. Surely she didn't think I'd been eavesdropping. I can't understand a word of Chinese.

"Excuse me for bothering you, ma'am," I said humbly, "but I couldn't help noticing that you have a cell phone. I don't, and—"

"No have cell phone?" she broke in. "Why not? Everyone have cell phone."

Well, at least she spoke English. "My husband is very thrifty," I explained.

She nodded approvingly. "Thrifty husband is good thing. When husband die, you not be poor widow abandoned by children."

I was surprised to hear that she thought my children would abandon me, but I persevered, saying, "I was hoping you could direct me to a shop that sells cell phones. Obviously I need one here in New York City."

"So you are tourist. Even people not live in New York need cell phone, and my son sell cell phone. Very prosperous. Make you good deal so thrifty husband not beat you. Come." She took my arm and hustled me down the street. "Come, come. Not walk so slow. Walk fast and be healthy like me. You need good herbs from herb doctor for energy. I can recommend wise ancient cousin who sell many fine ones. What your name?"

"Carolyn Blue," I gasped.

"I Madam Ming."

By the time we reached the cell-phone shop, I was panting and could hardly acknowledge the introduction to her son, a nice young man who spoke perfect English. She instructed him to find me a cell phone that would work both here and in whatever backward place I lived. "You make this lady good price because she married to thrifty husband who will ask cost when he see phone. She lucky white woman have thrifty husband because everyone know white children not take care of aging mother, like good Chinese children. Drop off in old-lady home full of crazy people. Very too bad."

I wanted to protest that I had lovely children, who would no doubt take care of me should I need their support in my old age, but the son was already arranging phones on his counter and explaining their functions, their minute plans, their roaming charges, and all sorts of things I didn't really understand. He evidently understood from my expression that I had no idea what he was talking about, not to mention what I wanted.

"Madam Blue," he said politely, "where do you live? Do you travel in foreign countries where you would want to use a cell phone?"

"Yes indeed," I said enthusiastically, thinking how wonderful it would be to avoid hotel phone systems that were expensive and confusing, not to mention having the ability to call the United States and talk to my children, publisher, agent, or, best of all, Paul Fallon, who handled my columns. "And I live in El Paso, Texas."

He nodded sympathetically. "Gunfighters and saloons. I have heard the song. Do you have a good camera, or would you wish to take pictures with your phone? I can sell you either."

I thought of how I'd looked in Lyon, France, with my hair all messy from riding in a convertible Austin Healey and knew I didn't want to take pictures with my cell phone, so I told him I already had a delightfully lightweight digital camera, with which I took thousands of pictures during my travels, and that I even knew how to get the pictures from the camera's memory card to my computer, a feat I felt quite proud of mastering. I showed him the camera, and his mother doubted that it was a good one for a tourist.

Lucky for me her son approved of my camera. "Japanese, but very good," he said. Then he produced the phone he thought would meet all my requirements at a reasonable price, a phone for which I could get a service that was not only reasonable but was running an excellent special. The phone even came in pretty colors and was very light-weight, which I liked a lot, but the instruction booklet was big enough to make my heart sink.

"I can show you how to do most things you need to do with the phone," he assured me. The man must be a mind reader, or maybe he was simply used to dealing with technophobes.

His mother was nodding and saying, "Good teacher. Teach me in ten minute use my phone. Very easy. No problem."

I asked timidly what this marvelous phone and service were going to cost me and almost fainted when I heard the price. Jason would not be happy.

"Can sell extra phone for thrifty husband only thirty dollar extra," said the mother. "Is so. Son will tell you." He nodded and went her one better by offering the second phone for twenty dollars.

How could I pass that up, even if Jason did suspect cell phones of causing brain damage or tumors or some such? I agreed to the purchase and got my first lesson: how to put in a list of numbers I'd want to call. I'm embarrassed to say that I did poorly, so the son had me write down the numbers—Luz's cell phone, the hotel, Mrs. Christopher at Pettigrew's, my home, my husband's office, my children, my father, and last, at Madam Ming's insistence, the number of her nephew who drove a cab, should I need one. "Nephew not successful like son but safe driver and has own cab. You like him. He give discount. Tell him Auntie Ming send you."

I was delighted to have the number of a safe driver who provided a discount. I could take more cabs. The son showed me how to get to the list, choose, and dial a number, and how to hang up. Then he demonstrated how to find messages left for me and return the calls. What more did I need? I'd read the instruction booklet when I got home and had more time. For now I only needed to remember his instructions.

I proved to myself that I could make a call by calling Luz and giving her my number. However, we had to plug the phone into the charger in order to do that. The son then replaced the uncharged battery with a charged one, which I considered very thoughtful of him, and knocked some off my bill because the battery was not new. However, he insisted on selling me a backup battery. Oh well, Jason wouldn't see the bill for a while, and meanwhile I was in touch with the world should I need help. I handed over my credit card.

The son ran the card to see if I was good for the price of my purchase. In the meantime I asked his mother, after glancing at my watch, if she could direct me to the Wise Dragon Benevolent Society.

"Why you go there? Is handsome building. You take picture?"

"I'm going to see Mr. Li Cheng Bao."

She frowned. "You know Mr. Li? He maybe not see you."

Goodness, she was nosy. Was that a characteristic of older Chinese ladies? "I've never met the gentleman, but I do have an appointment." She and her son muttered to each other in Chinese, which I didn't think was very polite since they both spoke English. "Is there a problem?" I asked. "I'm going to pay a condolence call. His granddaughter was seriously injured in an auto accident, so I—"

"I think because my mother has brought you here, I will give you a twenty percent discount," said the son. He then tore up the credit card ticket and started another one. "Li Cheng Bao would wish it."

"As I said, I don't know the gentleman," I reminded him, not wanting them to think they had to give me special attention because I'd mentioned the name of someone they obviously respected, which is not to say that I wouldn't welcome the discount.

"Is okay," said the mother. "You tell Mr. Li you buy phone from us and get very good deal."

I couldn't imagine how I'd manage to bring that up in the course of conversation but promised to do so if I could. Then I took down directions and went off the find the Wise Dragon Benevolent Society, where I arrived with ten minutes to spare. I sat in a plain room presided over by a very pretty young Asian woman, awaiting my appointment and reading the instructions for my new phone. I found the phone booklet very daunting. Maybe I'd have to read it in the hotel room at night in case I needed to return for more personal help. Mr. Ming was a better teacher than whoever wrote the booklet.

8

A Subway Perv
and a Chinese Grandfather

Luz

I'll bet I walked four miles counting stairs to get between subway trains that would take me to Worski and Benitez. Just because my knees hurt and DeShawn gave me his seat, was I being a sucker to befriend a kid I didn't know? Well, hell, it couldn't hurt to put him in touch with the detectives. Of course maybe Benitez didn't like blacks; some Hispanics don't, but I'd had a great black woman on my vice squad during the good old days. She busted more johns than anyone I ever worked with, and you never had to worry about her getting raped. That woman had muscles *and* good looks. She was a natural. She's a sergeant now in internal affairs. Hates it, but she's looking to transfer to drive-by shooting, which has been getting lots of business lately.

Benitez and Worski better have something to tell me. Like they'd found the chef, and he'd confessed to basting the turkeys with kerosene. Some jackass in my subway car—we were all holding the poles because the seats were full—pinched my ass. That was his mistake. I turned around and kneed him. Bastard went down screaming like a baby. What the hell did he expect? That I'd say "Thanks, buddy," and blow him a kiss? Since I had to let go of the pole to turn, I fell on top of him. People were jumping out of the way and into one another and cursing in forty different languages.

By the time we got to the next stop, a cop was waiting for us. Maybe they have cameras in the cars so they can respond to trouble. I scrambled off the pervert, while he screamed at the cop that I'd attacked him. "Yeah, right," I agreed. "After he pinched my ass." I took out my ID card, which said I was a retired police lieutenant, and passed it to the subway guard. "No reason a visitor should have to put up with perverts on the subways. I'm on my way to see Detectives Worski and Benitez at the station in Lower Manhattan," I told him. "If you want to cuff him, I can just take him with me." The subway cop laughed, cuffed my *pinche* friend—little multilingual pun there; Carolyn would be proud of me—left him huddled on the floor, and took my name.

He said to the guy groaning and bitching about his injury, "Looks like you pinched the wrong bottom, buddy." Then to me, "We've had trouble with this one before. I'll just go on downtown with you and turn him over to your friends. Maybe they'll want to question him in a soundproof room." The pervert started to cry while we stood over him for the rest of the ride and then hauled him to his feet for the walk to the Lower Manhattan station. He did a lot of sniveling about being in too much pain to stand up, but, hell, my knee was killing me because he had a bony crotch.

Once we got him to the detectives' grimy office—made EPPD accommodations for detectives look downright fashionable—Benitez, who's never going to win the Miss Congeniality Puerto Rico contest, listened to my story and said, "Well, get used to it, Vallejo. The subways are full of pervs, besides which, we don't do perverts up here unless they rape someone." The subway cop had to walk my prisoner back downstairs to the desk sergeant, while Benitez went off to look for Worski but not before saying that they weren't really interested in seeing me. They wanted to get hold of Carolyn, and she wasn't answering at the hotel.

"She's gone to see the grandfather of the girl who was hurt in the VW. And she doesn't have a cell phone."

"You're shitting me. Everyone has a cell phone."

While Benitez was gone, damned if Carolyn didn't call to tell me she'd taken my advice and bought a cell phone from the son of a lady she met on the street in Chinatown. Trust Carolyn. The instructions were probably in Chinese, and it only worked in Hong Kong and New York City. I took down her number, but I didn't pass it on to Worski and Benitez. They could just find her on their own if they hadn't cleared her yet. And they hadn't. They told me they couldn't do anything about the drunken limo driver who'd plowed head-on into the VW after the flaming turkey hit his windshield, because he and everyone in the limo had diplomatic immunity. Benitez told Worski that Carolyn was paying a condolence call on a victim's grandfather, who ran the Wise Dragon Benevolent Society.

"Li Cheng Bao? The kid in a coma's his granddaughter?" Worski groaned. "And Mrs. Blue is going over there? Well, hell, she's a woman who courts trouble."

"Tell me about it," I muttered. "I ended up in Juarez with a gun in my ear when she decided to question a guy from one of the drug cartels at a mariachi club. So you think she's in danger at the Chinese place?"

"For all I know the old guy might like her, but he doesn't have a rep for liking whites. We try to send the Chinese cops over when we have to talk to him."

"What about the chef?"

"Can't find him. He's not at home. None of the neighbors know where he went. Tell Mrs. Blue she's still our prime suspect, her and her turkey-tossing buddies at the publishing house." He shook his head in disbelief. "Would you believe that we had another turkey-tossing case in New York? Woman on Long Island, driving along, minding her own business, and this frozen turkey crashes

through her windshield, smashes her face, and puts her in
a coma. The kid who tossed it bought it with a stolen credit
card. He and his buddies found themselves in serious shit."

"There's no comparison between the two cases," I
snapped. "Carolyn didn't—"

"Well, you'd say that, not being a disinterested party.
Tell her she'd better get her ass in here before I have to put
a warrant out for her arrest. We need to talk to her."

"I'll tell her," I said, but I wouldn't; I'd forget. Then I
mentioned DeShawn, who'd been well brought up enough
to give me his seat on the subway and who might be a
good prospect if they needed to fill some black-cop quota.

"You think a would-be rapper is what the NYPD is
looking for?" asked Benitez. "They're all carrying illegal
weapons and shooting one another."

"Right," said Worski. "And if he's serious about being a
cop, he needs to apply to the academy. We're not re-
cruiters."

So I found myself out on the street again with the idea
that they weren't doing much except figuring to hang the
turkey caper on Carolyn and friends.

Carolyn

Mrs. Ming had been right about the exterior of the Wise
Dragon Benevolent Society. It, too, had red pagoda roofs,
as well as stone dragons guarding the door and red ones
decorating rows of tile on the exterior floor demarcations,
but the secretary's office and the office of the president
were plain to the point of looking monastic. Mr. Li Cheng
Bao rose courteously from behind his desk. The man was
as short as Mrs. Ming, but wearing a beautifully tailored,
conservative suit and a stern expression. Mrs. Ming had
looked a bit frumpy, but she'd certainly been animated,
even opinionated.

"You have something to tell me about my granddaughter?"
Mr. Li asked. "I don't believe we have met. I assume you
somehow became acquainted with my granddaughter, be-

cause she was accustomed to making friends with Occidentals." He didn't look as if he approved of that. "Please be seated, madam."

"I didn't know your granddaughter," I said as I took a straight-backed, unpadded chair in front of his desk, "but it was one of my turkeys that hit the window of the limousine that ran into her car, for which I am so sorry and offer my condolences. I imagine it must be very painful to have a young granddaughter hospitalized in such serious condition. I do hope she's come out of her coma."

"She has not, but fortunately it was not one of my grandsons. They are all hard-working, intelligent, dutiful young men. Li Yu Yan, my granddaughter, was given to driving about the city in an unsuitable German car with white friends, of whom I did not approve."

Somewhat confused by this response, I said, "I realize that you are trying to make me feel better about the whole disastrous event, which is very kind of you under the circumstances, but I must tell you that I am not responsible for the fact that the turkeys more or less burst into uncontrollable flame when I set them afire. This was not supposed to happen, and I can only surmise that—"

"The police led me to believe that the offending limousine was firebombed, not that they provided much insight on the accident. I do not understand your reference to turkeys. Is this Occidental slang?"

"Oh, goodness, you must have thought it was a terrorist event. I hope that idea doesn't become a popular misapprehension. I was simply flambéing three turkeys for a publisher's party, and the two I lighted set the tablecloth afire. It was quite unexpected and frightening, and after that people panicked, thinking the building would burn down, so they plunged forks into the two turkeys, which were charring the ceiling, and ran out to a balcony to throw them away. A foolish thing to do, in my opinion, but I assure you—"

"Do you usually set fire to food, madam? It seems a strange custom. I can understand fireworks on holidays,

which is an Asian custom of long standing, but not exploding food."

I sighed. This was not going well. "Flambéing the
turkey was my editor's idea. A sort of show-offy thing. The
turkey is a perfectly delicious Thanksgiving dish without
having any cognac poured on it and lighted. I think that
someone who wished me ill tampered with the turkeys
after I prepared them. The culprit must have wanted to ruin
the party held in honor of my book's publication."

"You are a writer then? A time-honored profession."

I thanked him and added, "What I came to say, Mr. Li,
as well as offering my condolences, is that I intend to find
out who is responsible for your granddaughter's injury,
even though I have to assume that they did not mean to
cause that in particular, just to make trouble, which they
did. A great deal of personal and property damage resulted
from those two flaming turkeys. Once I have discovered
the culprits, I shall inform the police so that the criminals
can be brought to justice, and, of course, I shall call to inform you when my investigation provides results. The publishing house has even hired a private investigator to work
with me."

Mr. Li, still frowning, remarked that I was an unusual
woman, who not only cooked turkeys, which might be expected of an Occidental woman, but also wrote books and
investigated crimes. "Have you experience in criminal investigation, madam?" he asked as an afterthought.

"Unfortunately, I do. I travel a good deal with my husband and often find that crimes have been committed on
which I can tender some observations."

"How unfortunate your husband must feel to accompany you on such travels. Perhaps he was badly named. I
myself am a mostly fortunate man, having been given a
propitious name by my parents."

"Really. What does your name mean?" I asked, thinking
that Jason's name might well be unfortunate. After all, the
Jason who went looking for the Golden Fleece and who
married Medea was certainly beset by troubles.

"Cheng Bao means Successful Leopard," said Mr. Li, "and I consider it improper for a woman to spend time pursuing criminals, no matter what her interest in the crime."

How very chauvinistic of Mr. Li to say such a thing. My mother-in-law would have been furious had she heard him.

"And now I see that I have another appointment. I appreciate your . . . honesty in coming here to explain the circumstances surrounding the injury to my granddaughter. I will have to consider your culpability when further information can be gathered on the event."

Obviously I was being sent away. Really, he was a scary sort of man. Maybe Leopard was a good name for him. Trying to end our meeting on a friendlier note, I mentioned that I had a luncheon date myself at the Lotus Blossom.

"You will like it," said Mr. Li. "Tourists always do, especially those who know little about Chinese food."

Well, that wasn't very nice, I thought as I left the office while Mr. Li picked up his telephone.

9

Eating Kosher at the Cratchetts'

Luz

Since the police didn't seem to be getting anywhere, I decided I'd better try to get in touch with the private detective Mr. Pettigrew had mentioned hiring. I called Mrs. Christopher, who provided the name, Abraham Cratchett, and two phone numbers. Then I called this Cratchett and identified myself as a friend of Carolyn Blue, a person who had been there for her flaming-turkey party and wanted to help with the investigation, having been a police lieutenant.

Cratchett said he was looking at security tapes from Pettigrew's front door and tradesman's entrance, and he had copies of the security sign-in sheets. He figured it might take him a couple of days, since he didn't know all the Pettigrew people coming and going on the tapes, so if I knew who had been at the party, he could use my help.

"Terrific. I'll come right over, Cratchett, and I know this kid named DeShawn Brown you could hire part-time. He's interested in being a cop and—"

"Bring him, too. You're free help, right? Ten dollars an hour is what I pay for part-time. My office is in Bensonhurst."

Since I didn't know Bensonhurst from bratwurst, which

is some kind of sausage I've heard of but never eaten, I told
him where I was, and he gave me his address and directions. Then I called DeShawn's cell and shouted at him
over the traffic noises. Obviously he was out on some
street jammed with drivers honking their horns. He
thought being a private detective sounded cool and offered
to ride his bike to Bensonhurst between twelve and one.
Well, that was easy, I thought, and took the subway to my
destination, which is in Brooklyn.

Bensonhurst was not much like the New York I'd seen
so far. Cratchett's address turned out to be this old three-
story wooden house, painted white ten or twenty years ago
with a curved window on the second floor and faded red
roofs made of curled-up shingles—a little porch with a
pointed roof on the first floor, and three pointed roofs on
the third floor: two in front, one lower than the other, and
one on the side, with only one little window up there. I
wondered who got to sleep in the attic. Tiny Tim? I'd read
the book about the Cratchetts by some old, white-guy author. Or maybe I saw the TV show.

A woman with thick glasses and curly gray-black hair
answered the door. She was his mother, Rachel Cratchett.
Jesus, a private eye who lived with his *mother*?

"Come in out of the cold and sit down, dear," she said,
giving me a big, welcoming smile. "Abraham will be up in
a minute. It's been a while since he's invited a girl home to
meet me."

What the hell does that mean? I wondered as I took a
seat in an old-fashioned room with crocheted stuff stuck to
the chairs and a television that my grandmother would
have been embarrassed to own. Ten inches? Probably
black-and-white.

"You're Hispanic? Your last name sounds Hispanic. I
don't suppose you're Jewish."

"No, ma'am, Catholic."

"Well, that's all right. I married a Catholic, and it's
turned out well. Of course, our Abraham was raised Jewish. He said you were a policewoman. My husband's a de-

tective with the police here in Brooklyn. I hope you want children. I'd certainly like to have grandchildren."

Did she think I was her son's *novia*? "I'm on the old side for having children, ma'am, late forties going on fifty. Anyway, I've never met your son."

"Well, he's a fine boy. His father would rather he'd joined the police, but I wouldn't have that. It's bad enough worrying about my husband, as you can imagine, your being a policewoman."

"Retired," I said hastily.

"Did you and Abraham meet through an Internet dating service?" Mrs. Cratchett chuckled. "My mother met my father through a matchmaker. Grandfather insisted. I suppose it's not that different. You and Abraham could adopt children if you hit it off."

"Mrs. Cratchett, I'm here to look at tapes for a case your son's working on, not to . . . ah . . . meet him for a blind date."

"Well, I might have known," she said sadly. "No matter how many young ladies I invite to dinner, Abraham's always too busy with his work to ask them out. Oh, here's someone else." She rose to answer the doorbell.

"That'll be DeShawn. He's going to help, too."

She let my subway pal in, somewhat surprised at his size, or maybe it was his color, and her son came up from the basement, after which we had to have lunch because Mrs. Cratchett insisted—matzoh ball soup, which was okay, but no big deal. I'll take *menudo* or *tlapeno* any day over chicken soup with a giant bread ball bobbing around in it. Then we had cream cheese and smoked salmon sandwiches on black bread. They weren't tacos, but they weren't bad either. During the soup and sandwiches, Mrs. Cratchett told us how her grandfather bought this house years after emigrating from Russia and kept it in the family even after the Italians moved into Bensonhurst and took over.

Finally she brought in what she called a blintz casserole, apologizing for the fact that she hadn't made the blintzes herself since she was editing some Jewish manuscript for a publisher and didn't have the time. The casserole turned out to be dessert, and it was really tasty. When I said so, she insisted on giving me her recipe. Like I was going to make a Jewish dessert—or any dessert, for that matter. I'd give it to Carolyn. Jewish was ethnic, I figured, and should fit right into her new book.

While I was poking at my food, DeShawn was shoveling it in and saying Mrs. C. was "some great cook." Abraham was describing his computer system, which DeShawn got real excited about, so maybe DeShawn was going to give up his rapper ambitions and take to being a private eye. He said, "You pro'bly thinkin' I'm just the muscle, but I know computers, too, man. I'm just what you need in the private-eye business—an' faster on a bike than any mothafu—"

"DeShawn, I can see that I'm going to have to reform your vocabulary if you're going to work with Abraham," interrupted Mrs. Cratchett. "Won't you have seconds on dessert? I do like to see a growing boy eat heartily."

"Don't mind if I do," said DeShawn, helping himself to another large serving.

While I was visiting a Chinese gentleman in New York and eating a Chinese lunch, a friend was served lunch by a third-generation Jewish lady in Bensonhurst, who gave her this tasty recipe. For those of us who don't want to spend forever making time-consuming sections of a recipe, much less the whole thing, this dish is both tasty and quicker to prepare than the original must have been.

Blintz Casserole

- Melt ½ *cup butter* and pour into two medium-size oblong Pyrex casserole dishes.

- Open *3 boxes of frozen cheese blintzes (18 blintzes)* and place the blintzes on top of the butter.

- Mix *6 eggs, 16 ounces sour cream, 5 tablespoons orange juice,* and *1 tablespoon vanilla,* and pour over blintzes.

- Cover with plastic wrap and refrigerate overnight.

- Preheat oven to 350 degrees.

- Bake about 1 hour and 10 minutes uncovered.

- Serve with *sour cream, a mixture of cinnamon and sugar, favorite jam,* or *fresh raspberries.*

Carolyn Blue,
"Have Fork, Will Travel,"
Brooklyn Intelligencer

10

Lunch with Jack Armstrong

Carolyn

My appointment with Mr. Li hadn't taken that long, so I strolled along, looking into shop windows as I followed the secretary's directions to the Lotus Blossom. On such bustling sidewalks my slow pace caused some dismay. I found myself having to stop to apologize when people ran into me, and with each stop I noticed three young men walking not too far behind me. *Probably a coincidence*, I thought, but to test them, I ducked in a jade shop that caught my eye and looked at various earrings and pendants taken from under the counter by the shopkeeper.

Sure enough, one of the young men sauntered inside and leaned on the counter near the door, while the other two lounged outside. Why in the world would they be following me? Were they purse snatchers? Then I remembered Mr. Li making a phone call as I left, instead of keeping the appointment he'd mentioned. Maybe he had sent them after me because he thought I needed protection, pursuing criminals being, in his opinion, too dangerous a job for a woman. Really, that was rather touching. Of course, he might just want to know immediately, from his own sources, what had happened to his granddaughter and thought having me followed would lead him to the information.

Highly amused that I was being tailed through Chinatown, and perhaps beyond, I continued to look at jade and even asked the cost of a particularly pretty pendant. "Seventy-five dollar," said the shopkeeper.

"Excuse me, young man," I called out, repressing a grin, "but I know little about the quality of jade and the price. Do you think seventy-five dollars is a fair price for this pendant?" That took him by surprise. Obviously, the tailee isn't supposed to chat with the tailer. The young man shrugged, and the shopkeeper, casting a nervous glance his way, immediately offered me the pendant for forty dollars. Goodness, the Lis and their associates did wonders for the price of merchandise in this part of the city. I bought the pendant, and the shopkeeper, still peeking at the young man, threw in a little chain.

"Wasn't that nice of him?" I said to my shadow, who muttered that he should get a cut of the discount. Then I smiled at the other two young men and headed for the Lotus Blossom with my trio of bodyguards behind me. *What fun! Wait till I tell Luz about this*, I thought. The Lotus Blossom looked pretty much like Chinese restaurants I'd patronized in the Midwest and the Southwest. I'd expected something more exotic. It didn't even have ducks hanging in the window.

I told the waitress that I was meeting Mr. Armstrong and was ushered to the table of a very large man who took both of my hands in his and studied my face, as a doctor might if he were looking for signs of illness before the purpose of the visit had been mentioned. Even his nose had the same blobbish shape as the rest of him. *He was the diet cookbook writer?* I hoped they didn't put his picture on the inside covers of his books. The camera makes one look fatter than one is, not that he was exactly fat. It's just that every part of him looked outsized and soft.

Then we sat down, and he recommended seven vegetarian dishes, after announcing that he was a vegan and never ate anything that came from an animal. If that was true, how had he managed to acquire his present girth? I ordered the orange beef, which was marked spicy, and he ordered the seven vegetarian plates for himself, which explained the inexplicable. Many had nuts in them. I supposed that enough fruits, vegetables, and nuts could make one huge, and obviously he had the appetite to achieve that goal.

"A vegan diet is an excellent road to long life and good health," he said once our waitress had left with our orders. "For instance, I am at my perfect weight: not thin enough to endanger my endocrinal and metabolic systems, not heavy enough to damage my joints. And as a vegan, I will never suffer from diabetes and am unlikely to develop cardiac or circulatory problems."

"I don't have any of those problems," I replied and took a sip of my tea. *His perfect weight? Not likely.*

"Ah, but you will develop problems, Mrs. Blue. Sooner or later. It's a given considering your present diet."

"You don't know how I eat," I retorted, becoming irritated.

"Of course I do. You fixed turkey for your book launch. I heard that it had pork and beef in the dressing. Look how that turned out!"

"Are you saying that the unfortunate turkey problem was caused by——"

"It wouldn't have happened if you'd served a nice salad, or even a sweet potato casserole, since you wanted to celebrate Thanksgiving. Sweet potatoes are very healthful. Your book is about New Orleans; you could have served beans and rice. That would have been appropriate. By the way, do you know those three Chinese fellows drinking tea over there? They're staring at you."

"Not personally, no, but they are associates of a Mr. Li, who is the head of the Wise Dragon Benevolent Society. At least, I think they are." Mr. Armstrong did not look happy to hear that. "Furthermore, I didn't want to serve sweet potato casserole or rice and beans. I write about gourmet food."

"Well, you're setting a poor example for your readers," he lectured as our food was served and he began shoveling drippy vegetables into his mouth with chopsticks.

I asked for a fork, afraid I might drizzle the orange sauce into my lap if I used chopsticks, which wouldn't have worried me so much if my escorts hadn't been keeping such a close eye on me over their teacups and cigarettes. I could have sworn there was a NO SMOKING sign on the restaurant's door, but their waitress didn't reprimand them. Maybe because they were the magical Mr. Li's associates. My orange beef was delicious, both sweet and spicy. I'd have offered Mr. Armstrong a taste, but he'd probably have refused and given me another lecture.

Instead I told him that I thought my turkeys had been sabotaged, watching him closely for signs of guilt, and that I intended to find out who had done it. "Can you recall anyone who might have wanted to spoil the launch party?" I asked, thinking all the time that it might have been him because he didn't approve of meat.

"Possibly Allison Peabody," he replied. "She writes about gourmet food, too, and might not like it that you were given a launch party, which she's never had. And of course, she's a carnivore. Eating meat makes one aggressive. Those men are still staring at us."

"Oh, don't mind them," I said airily, not at all upset that they were upsetting him. "Were you at Pettigrew's the day the turkeys were cooking in the publisher's kitchen? Maybe you saw someone suspicious."

"I believe I told you, when I called to arrange our lunch, that I was busy throughout the day and evening."

"So you did. Are we going to have dessert?"

"We're going to leave," he said, shoveling into his mouth the last of some broccoli drenched in what looked to me like oyster sauce, and waving the waitress over. Weren't oysters meat?

"I think those young men are dangerous. You obviously know nothing about Li Cheng Bao. Nobody does. I'll give you a ride as far as my place, and you can get a cab from there." He paid in cash and hustled me out of the restaurant where, to my dismay, he pointed out a large adult tricycle built for two and said, "Given your unhealthful diet, I hope you get daily exercise, Mrs. Blue."

"Not if I can help it," I snapped. "I don't have a weight problem, as you can see."

"No exercise! Well, then you can peddle, and I'll take the rear seat." Having made that astounding suggestion, he settled me on the front seat and got on behind. "Just push the pedals. I'm sure you remember how from childhood. Children are very healthy." He clasped my waist in his pudgy hands as if we were on a motorcycle. "Do get going. It's quite easy to propel this machine because of its leading-edge design, and it won't tip over, not to mention the fact that it doesn't cause pollution or use gas."

Hearing the laughter of the three men behind us, I now wanted to get away, so I tried to pedal, and it was awful. I only made it to the end of the block before I gave out, probably due partially to Mr. Armstrong's weight on the backseat. Who ever heard of a tricycle built for two? Quite disgusted with me, he changed places and whisked us through the unhappy sidewalk crowds, who had to jump out of our way, and across streets, where we were honked and laughed at. It was truly embarrassing, and the three Wise Dragon associates kept right behind us without undue exertion.

Mr. Armstrong lived upstairs in a building that housed a fragrant herb shop, a photography establishment, a noodle cafe, and a bicycle shop, where he probably had his tricycle serviced. He offered to take me upstairs, where I'd be safe, but I declined, thoroughly humiliated and angry, not to mention giving serious thought to his culpability in the destruction of my turkeys, my party, and the cars and people on the streets below.

The three followers walked up, laughing, and leaned against the door of the noodle cafe. Ignoring them and feeling thoroughly exhausted, I sat down on the doorstep in front of the apartment entrance and called Luz on my new cell phone to tell her that I considered Jack Armstrong a good suspect because he detested the eating of meat, even turkeys. I didn't mention the tricycle.

"Well, let me see if he signed into Pettigrew's that day," my friend offered. "I'm over in Brooklyn working with Cratchett, the private eye." A short silence ensued while I studiously ignored the snickering bodyguards. "Okay, Cratchett's checked the sign-in list for Pettigrew's, and Armstrong did sign in for a couple of hours in the afternoon, but we don't have any way to tell if he was in the kitchen until we can interview the chef, and the police still haven't found him. We're going to have to check out the kitchen workers who were there. Oh, and Abraham says to tell you that you have to be at Pettigrew's at four this afternoon for a meeting with him, the publisher, and Petey Haverford to discuss the case. And don't forget we're having dinner with Roberto before the opera."

"I'm going to stay here working while Abe's gone, and get this: His mother is trying to marry us off." She laughed uproariously. "I'm not Jewish, and I'm way too old for her son." I could hear voices in the background assuring Luz that any man would love to date her, and Luz saying they must be two hard-up-for-a-date dudes. "So we'll both have to get dressed when we can and get to Casa Guanajuato on our own unless we're at the hotel at the same time."

I sighed and hung up. The opera was tonight! And my silver velvet dress, after being attacked by the party-room sprinkler system, looked a fright. My next call was to Mrs. Ming's cab-driver cousin, and he did arrive promptly, but then I was right in his neighborhood. I directed him to my agent's uncle's wholesale clothing establishment. Jason would kill me for buying two dresses *and* a cell phone, but I couldn't go to the Metropolitan Opera in slacks or a day dress, not after what Jason had paid for the tickets.

My favorite Chinese dishes are the spicy ones, which I first tasted in Washington, D.C., on a trip with my husband and children. In the Midwest town where I lived at that time, Chinese food was tasty but bland, so *spicy* was an eye-opener for me. Even the Mexican food at home was rather bland, until I moved to El Paso and discovered what *spicy* really meant. Thus, when I saw Spicy Chinese Orange Beef on the menu in New York City, I ordered it, compromising on the version with broccoli because my luncheon companion was a vegan. He was not appeased. The broccoli didn't make up for having to see beef on a plate across the table.

Spicy Chinese Orange Beef with Broccoli

- Cut *¾ lb of sirloin or flank steak* against the grain into thin strips.

- Mix *grated peel of 1 orange, 1 tablespoon grated fresh ginger, 1 clove minced garlic,* and *1 tablespoon cornstarch* in a bowl and toss with beef to coat.

- In a second bowl mix *¼ cup dry sherry, ¼ cup soy sauce, 1 cup cool beef broth, ½ teaspoon crushed, dried red pepper, ¼ cup marmalade, 2 tablespoons cornstarch,* and *⅓ cup water.*

- Cut *3 cups broccoli florets.*

- Heat *2 tablespoons corn oil* in a large skillet or wok over medium heat and stir-fry beef in three batches for 2 minutes each. Add broccoli and stir-fry 3 minutes. Pour in liquid mixture; bring to boil, stirring constantly, and boil one minute.

- Serves 4 over rice or noodles.

Carolyn Blue,
"Have Fork, Will Travel,"
Washington, D.C., Times

11
Being Tailed

Carolyn

Uncle Bernie was the same dear man I'd now met twice, first, on my initial trip to New York City to meet my editor and agent and on this trip, when I bought the silver velvet dress—well, the same dear man except that he now had glass in both sides of his spectacles. He'd gotten a deal on new glasses from a cousin—that's the New York way, everything wholesale.

Of course, he was horrified to hear that the velvet dress had been soaked at the party, but he said if I sent it over, he'd see if he could steam it back into usability. At present it was still dripping on the floor in our bathroom. Velvet soaks up a lot of water.

Loretta's uncle did congratulate me on my publicity coup. He had seen at least three news items on my flaming turkeys, and his niece was delighted with my good fortune. Since I considered the party a disaster, I had to wonder how much good sense Loretta had. Possibly none. This was the second time I'd heard her peculiar view of the event at Pettigrew's.

I did find a lovely ice-blue gown that fit me perfectly and provided a hefty discount because Uncle Bernie said it wouldn't sell well in winter. People wanted warmer colors when the temperatures were below freezing. I didn't mind; the price was right, I was in a hurry, and I could brag to Jason about all the bargains I'd finagled from hardheaded New Yorkers.

So Uncle Bernie hung my dress in a plastic bag while I called the cabbie Ming cousin, who didn't speak much English but could find a written address and gave a 10 percent discount, which I had to give back as a tip. The fact that I tipped him at all, when a family member referred me, evidently made him very happy. He displayed a wide smile, revealing several missing teeth. I considered tipping Mr. Ming 15 percent next time toward a visit to his dentist, although Jason thinks 10 is adequate in most cases. He's probably the only person who thinks that these days.

"Looking for an evening gown?" I asked the three Chinesemen as I exited Uncle Bernie's building. I could have taken a subway to Pettigrew's for the meeting, but I wanted to get there early so I could speak to the knowledgeable Mrs. Christopher.

Since the police couldn't find the chef, I hoped that Mrs. Christopher might be able to provide information, and she did. Evidently Franz had not run away from the consequences of his crime; he had simply gone to a chef's conference in Atlantic City. She also told me that he had been very unhappy because the book launch kept him in New York during the first day of his conference. Furthermore, Mr. Claudius Pettigrew had cancelled the company's Thanksgiving dinner for employees because he didn't want to eat turkey again so soon. Franz prided himself on the wild turkey he always prepared for the annual affair and was reportedly very disappointed, even angry.

"Artistic people are so difficult," Mrs. Christopher remarked. "Not that you don't seem to be a sensible woman, Mrs. Blue. I'm sure you're right in thinking that the flaming turkeys weren't just a culinary mistake but rather the work of some ill-wisher."

"So Franz might actually dislike me," I mused. How strange it was that a man who really didn't know me would go out of his way to take revenge for things that weren't my fault. It wasn't fair. I'd have to alert Mr. Cratchett and Luz to the chef as a suspect; not that they didn't know I had considered him one before, but that was for a different reason.

Mrs. Christopher's assistant popped her head into the office and reported that three young Asian gentlemen were sitting outside and wouldn't reveal whom they wished to see. "They're with me," I said nonchalantly and told them, as I passed by, that the chef might be responsible for the coma of Li Cheng Bao's granddaughter, if the culprit wasn't the man with the tricycle, but I was now going to a meeting in another office in the same building to talk to the private detective. They had the good grace to look embarrassed, and why not? They had failed woefully to be inconspicuous in their bodyguard duties, or maybe bodyguards weren't supposed to be. I'd never had one before, much less three.

I then hurried into the ladies' room to change into my new evening dress because I was afraid that I wouldn't have time to attend the meeting, get back to my hotel, change, and arrive at Casa Guanajuato in time for dinner. Luz had accepted the dinner invitation without consulting me. Not that I didn't want to eat at Roberto's restaurant, just not before the opera. And what was I going to do with the clothes I'd worn today, hold them in my lap during the performance? I also hated the idea of going to the opera without first taking a shower. What a traumatic week this was proving to be, and there were the bodyguards, lounging in the hall across from the ladies'. I hurried to the meeting room, already late.

"My dear," said Mr. Pettigrew, "you didn't have to dress for this meeting, although you look quite charming." I explained that I intended to go from here to Roberto's restaurant and then the performance of *Rigoletto*.

"Well, Abraham Cratchett will arrive momentarily. He just called to say there's a subway slowdown where he transfers from Brooklyn to the track that takes him here.

Don't you find his name charming? Cratchett is so Dickensian. It was his name that initially convinced me to hire him when my nephew made the introduction several years ago. It was at a time when we had need of a private detective's services."

I didn't find it very comforting that my fate might lie in the hands of a man chosen for a Dickensian surname.

"An employee was skimming royalties from the authors' accounts. Very disappointing of him. We had to fire the fellow once Abraham ferreted him out. I don't suppose, being a young person, you're familiar with Dickens, but Cratchett was the name of—"

"My mother began to read me *A Christmas Carol* when I was a child," I interrupted. Although it was nice to be thought young, I felt rather insulted that Mr. Pettigrew took me for an ill-read person. "But I became so eager to find out what happened that I took over reading it myself," I continued. "Of course, Mother was there to help me with the Victorian words and to comfort me when the book made me cry."

"Abraham's mother is our editor and proofreader for the Judaica line, which is small, but, I feel, quite excellent," said Mr. Pettigrew. "Mothers are such an important influence, and what a lovely story about your mother reading you Dickens. I do hope you keep in touch with her. Petronius was a terrible correspondent when he went off to Cambridge for his B. Litt. I will admit he took a first, which pleased me."

Petey took a first at Cambridge? Now there was a surprise! "My mother died when I was about twelve," I replied. "My father, who is a history professor, raised me and was more interested in history than Dickens."

"Ah, that explains all the culinary history you included in your book. I found some of it quite entertaining. Abraham!" A young man with rumpled black hair, a heavy five-o'clock shadow, a long black coat, and earmuffs panted into the room. "Mrs. Blue, this is our house detective, Abraham Cratchett."

After the introductions, Abraham removed his winter wear and announced that Petey had briefed him on the case. He dropped into a chair and began to question me. "Do you always flambé turkeys? I've never heard of that."

I said no, I hadn't previously heard of it either, but Roland had insisted.

Did I think that I might have mistakenly included anything that caused the conflagration?

That question was the clue that he intended to blame me. Had the publisher hired him for that very purpose, so all the lawsuits and charges would be directed my way? "Absolutely not," I snapped. "I don't like flambéing, so I tested the cognac before I used it on the turkeys. It was fine. The chef saw me doing that. When he returns, he can tell you." *But will he,* I wondered, *if he sabotaged the turkeys because he missed a day of his wretched conference?* "Mrs. Christopher tells me that he's gone to Atlantic City, but that he might have reason to dislike me, thus making him a suspect."

"Oh, surely we don't suspect Franz. He's been cooking here for more than ten years," Mr. Pettigrew objected.

"I think I'll need to talk to Mr. DuPlessis first," the detective decided.

Claudius Pettigrew frowned. "I doubt that Roland is a suspect. After all, he chose the author, commissioned the book, and even insisted on the book launch. Since it's something we rarely do, I hardly think he'd want it to go poorly. I imagine the fact that he threw the first flaming turkey over the balcony was just a matter of bad judgment, or panic when he perceived such an unforeseen problem."

"Petey threw the first turkey down," I pointed out. "Roland just followed his example."

"I should add that Roland had a heart attack after the police talked to him," said Mr. Pettigrew. "He's in the hospital."

"I didn't know that," I gasped. If my editor tampered with the turkeys, no wonder police interrogation triggered a heart attack. "Is it serious?"

"Not fatal, at least, but not surprising either. Roland does not take good care of his health. He's been warned repeatedly about his eating habits. Perhaps this unfortunate incident will convince him to mend his ways," said Mr. Pettigrew.

"Would Mr. DuPlessis or anyone else that you can think of—an employee, an author, a competitor—have anything against you, Mr. Pettigrew, anything that might move them to sabotage the party?" Abraham asked, busily making notes on the answers to his questions.

After so long a period of thought that I had to glance at my watch to see how late I was going to be for dinner, Mr. Pettigrew said, "I really can't think of anyone, unless some author whose book we rejected took offense, but there must be thousands of those."

"Is anyone trying to buy you out?" asked Cratchett.

What an insightful idea, I thought. If someone managed to burn the building down, the business would take a serious drop in value and could be resituated somewhere less prestigious and less expensive.

Mr. Pettigrew laughed. "I haven't had an offer in, oh, four or five years, and I do believe at this point everyone in the publishing world knows that I would rather close Pettigrew's than sell it out of the family."

Cratchett nodded. "In that case, I'll continue checking the logs of people who entered and left the building on the day in question. Then there are the surveillance cameras to finish monitoring, and I'll need to interview everyone who was in the kitchen after Mrs. Blue prepared the turkeys and left for the day."

Obviously our private detective had more than a Dickensian name to recommend him. "I'll help you," I said promptly. "I've had some experience with detection, and you know Luz, who's already lending you assistance, is an ex-policewoman. I'll be at the opera tonight, but I'll be available tomorrow and until this is cleared up."

"But solving the problem is what Mr. Pettigrew pays me to do," Cratchett objected mildly.

"And no one has more at stake here than I. I'm innocent of any wrongdoing and want it known as soon as possible, so you can count on me." I looked at my watch, which read 5:45 P.M. "I must leave. I'm going to be late for dinner."

"Not to worry, my dear," said Mr. Pettigrew. "My driver will take you."

"Do you think he can get me to Casa Guanajuato in fifteen minutes?" I asked.

"I'm sure he can, my dear." Mr. Pettigrew looked at his watch, a pocket watch no less. He really was a dear, quaint man, now that I didn't suspect him of wanting to shuffle all the blame off on me. He called downstairs to the driver, and I left within minutes, relieved to be free, but wondering if I should have stayed to hear what they had to say. Mr. Cratchett had remained in his seat.

The bodyguards were still in attendance, so I told them that I had a responsible driver to take me to the restaurant where I was to have dinner, and my host would drive us to the opera and home, so they could feel free take the evening off.

"You don't tell us what to do," said the one who had followed me into the jade shop.

12

Flirting in Casa Guanajuato

Luz

DeShawn and I worked till about four at Cratchett's house, comparing personnel photos of Pettigrew employees and authors with the security tapes. Sure enough Jack Armstrong, a big, pudgy-looking guy, had entered in the afternoon, but that didn't tell us where he went, only that he'd lied to Carolyn. I took the subway back to the hotel, had a hot shower, and climbed into my blue cruise dress. Pretty spiffy. And I wasn't wearing those damned feet-killing sandals Babette in the cruise boutique thought were so great. I'd bought some silver flats for six dollars at Payless Shoes. Had to wear my thrift-shop black camel-hair coat, which no one would say was very formal, but it kept me warm. New York was about the coldest damn place I'd ever been. Then Roberto called and offered to send a car for me. Great.

It took a while to get to Casa Guanajuato because the traffic was bumper-to-bumper. I'd probably have made it faster taking the subway, but Roberto Santibanez didn't seem to mind that I was late, and his car was a lot more comfortable than the subway. "So," I said to our cute host, "is Carolyn here yet?"

She wasn't. Obviously still downtown, probably telling

Cratchett how to solve the case, even when he seemed to
know what he was doing. With DeShawn and Carolyn on
the job, maybe I'd have time to get over to the museum I'd
read about that had a ninety-four-foot fiberglass blue
whale and a skeleton of a Tyrannosaurus rex. One of my
sister's kids had cut out a clipping on the whale and asked
me to take pictures.

Roberto and I went to the bar, where he tried to talk me
into a *mojito*, but after all those frigging martinis at the
turkey roast, I needed some tequila, and his place did carry
the good stuff. It went down like silk—instead of that
diesel-fuel tequila they give you in the bars of Juarez. But
then in Juarez, a drink was a lot cheaper. Hell, I could get
two whole meals in Juarez for what a drink cost here.

"*Querida*, it turns me on to see a woman who can drink
her tequila in a straight shot like that," said Roberto in the
kind of husky undertone that makes a woman's toes tingle.

"You like it; I needed it." I shoved my glass toward the
bartender. Why not? I wasn't paying for it.

"You are a very beautiful woman, Luz. *Muy bonita*." He
played with my fingers and gave me a sexy look. "I am getting very hot. You know?"

I turned on the bar stool and looked him in the eyes.
Great eyes. He was one handsome man. "So you're hot for
older women?" I asked. "I figure I got a good ten years on
you."

"What is ten years? Nothing between two like us. We
are of the same blood. No?"

"Probably not. More Indian in my veins, while you, caballero, are pretty pale. Maybe all Spanish. No?"

"Oh, I don't think so, *mi amor*. You call me caballero?
Maybe you have a fantasy about making love with me on
a horse. Eh? I could hold you against me, naked, the
horse's gait jarring us together. *Sí*, I think this is my fantasy, too."

"I think it sounds damned uncomfortable," I said, turning back to my drink. He was getting *me* hot now, and I figured I'd better throw a little cold water on both of us. "And

you're fantasizing about a naked woman with bullet scars and puffy knees. Doesn't quite fit the picture, does it? I don't even have long flowing hair like a romance-cover heroine, just chopped-off, black going gray."

"Let us hope that your pretty blonde *amiga* does not find us tonight." His chuckle was low and rich, as much a turn-on as his voice. "Bullet scars. Now I'm really—"

"One hell of a flirt," I cut in. "I've got to see you try this line on Carolyn, who's coming in the door right now. She'll probably turn four shades of red and hit you, Roberto. Five dollars says you can't turn *her* on."

"*Querida*, you underestimate me." He swiveled to discover Carolyn at his elbow, apologizing for being late, telling me that she was very impressed with the private detective, who was not only smart but also had this great name. "Mr. Pettigrew hired him because of the name."

"Well, shit. There goes the investigation. You'll end up in jail, and I'll have to do all footwork myself. So, Roberto, when's dinner? I could eat a horse."

"*Está en la carta,*" he assured me. "*Caballo todo con salsa chipotle.*"

Carolyn looked horrified.

Carolyn

Casa Guanajuato was definitely a high-end Mexican restaurant, with stone columns holding up balconies where customers were seated, wide stone steps leading to the balconies, and frescoes of what I assumed to be the owner's hometown. They featured colonial Spanish buildings, street scenes, and outdoor cafés. In the first-floor dining room waiters scurried among heavy, carved wooden tables and chairs and well-dressed patrons eating dishes that looked exotically delicious. I could only hope that Roberto had been joking when he said there was whole horse in chipotle sauce on his menu. Imagining such a sight made me queasy.

We sat on the first floor because Luz refused to climb

stairs after her stair-climbing ordeals on subways earlier
that day. We'd hardly picked up our menus when mariachis
surrounded our table and launched into a very loud rendi-
tion of "Guadalajara," especially painful to the ears once
the trumpets joined in. Roberto waved them away after
they finished and Luz refused his offer to have them play
some *Norteño*, which is evidently a variety of cowboy
music that's popular on both sides of the Chihuahua-Texas
border.

Although I saw many dishes I wanted to try, I wasn't
given the opportunity. When the waiter arrived, Luz and I
were ignored while Roberto ordered for all of us. Swallow-
ing my disappointment, I reasoned that he did own the
restaurant and we were his guests; Luz, however, muttered,
"That's Mexican machismo for you. They all think it takes
a man to choose the food. Notice the waiter didn't even
look at us."

Roberto took no offense. He simply said, "As a Mexican male, I am a great believer in machismo." Then turning to me, he asked why Señor Pettigrew needed a private
detective.

Good gracious, hadn't the man noticed the flaming
turkeys and tablecloths last night, the scorched ceilings,
the belated shower from the sprinkler system, and all the
city officials who stormed the room? "My turkeys were not
meant to explode like fireworks," I responded. "It was a
simple flambé, so someone must have tampered with the
sauce or with the turkeys themselves, and I intend to find
out who did that," I declared. "Petey, Roland, and I are
threatened with charges of first-degree assault. Mr. Pettigrew fears civil suits by those who were—"

"Poor Roland," exclaimed Roberto, as a waiter ap-
proached with plates containing greens topped by thin
slices of jicama. "I visited him this morning. He was inspecting the hospital menu and complaining bitterly at the
choices." The waiter drizzled fresh lime juice on the jicama and fanned a light dusting of what I took to be cumin
across the juicy slices. "Evidently breakfast was not to his

liking. He ordered a cheese and mushroom omelet and instead received scrambled egg whites and dry wheat toast."

"You speak English with hardly any accent," I observed.

"Of course I do. Guanajuato is a university town. I was speaking English from a young age. And now I am an American citizen, which makes my businesses here easier to run, but, of course, a Mexican citizen as well." He savored his salad. "I see that you like the jicama, señora. Have you tasted it before?"

"Both in El Paso and Juarez," I replied.

"Eh. Tex-Mex is not the real food of Mexico, as you will see, and places such as Juarez, Nuevo Laredo, and Tijuana make my country look bad in the eyes of the world— so many drug wars and killings."

I agreed with him and remarked that my husband and I rarely went to Juarez. "As for Roland, I fear that he will have to make do with egg whites in the future if he hopes to avoid another heart attack."

"Dear lady, one must live life to the fullest, tossing away fears that will inhibit joy. Do you not agree?" Then Roberto took my hand and kissed it all the way up to the elbow, sending goose bumps shivering up my arm when I had not yet recovered from the freezing wind of the New York streets. I snatched my arm back and stuck it under the table. Blatantly amused at my reaction, Luz chuckled. The waiter whisked away our salads and replaced them with a green soup dotted with bits of hot red pepper, cilantro, spring onion curls, and tiny, dark croutons. It looked luscious—avocado soup with flair.

"Christ, I hope it doesn't have knockout drops in it," said Luz, and we exchanged smiles, remembering how we had once rendered unconscious the whole crew of the *Bountiful Feast* with the chef's avocado soup. "So Roberto, if you had to say who screwed up Carolyn's turkeys, who would you guess?" Roberto looked so bemused that she added, "For instance, did *you* put explosives in the turkeys?"

"Why would I do that?" Roberto was obviously offended.

"Jealous that she got a book launch. Hoping to hurt her sales."

"Señora Blue and I are not in competition, are we, *mi vida*?"

Then he ran his finger across my lips in a most suggestive way. I found it very disconcerting. "Señor Santibanez, please keep your attention on the question at hand, and also keep in mind that I am a married woman, a happily married woman, and do not appreciate gestures of . . . of a personal nature."

"I have embarrassed you, *mi corazón*. Do forgive me," he replied with another melting gaze.

"I know what that means, and I am not 'your heart.'"

Snickering, Luz held out her hand. Did she want him to stroke hers, too? This was really dreadful. He said, "Not yet, dear Luz."

"Sooner or later," she replied.

I feared that she was contemplating another affair, which was, of course, none of my business. Unless she planned to bring him to our room.

"So Roberto, you hopeless womanizer, if not you, who do you think fiddled with the turkeys?" Luz asked.

At first he decided that it must have been a simple cooking accident, but I assured him that was not the case. Then he said, "Señorita Allison Peabody is a bit of a bitch. I wouldn't put it past her. Then there is Annunziata Randatto, the Italian *abuela*."

The main course arrived: a lovely thin strip of white fish, sautéed to a light gold and topped with sauces of many colors. Perhaps fillet Tampico style, I thought, but I was wrong. It was Bandera, decorated with the colors of the Mexican flag. The topping was much more subtle.

"She is a powerful and vengeful woman," said Roberto, "the matriarch of a huge clan who do her bidding. There are rumors that she once poisoned a woman who opened a restaurant in Bensonhurst, which used the Italian grandmother's recipes without permission. The poison devoured the woman's stomach, and she could eat nothing but bread and broth for the rest of her life. Also no one is sure what the real businesses of Señora Randatto's sons are. She says they import food, wine, and liqueurs from Italy, but perhaps other less legal and more lucrative items are among their wares."

While we consumed our fish, which was so delicious I almost wanted to ask for seconds, Roberto regaled us with other sinister rumors about the Italian grandmother, many of which were so ridiculous that eventually I discounted the whole idea that she was behind the destruction of my turkeys and my book launch.

I did want to ask him whether he thought it likely that Franz or Jack Armstrong might be candidates, but we were running late and the opera awaited us. We were deprived of dessert and whisked off in a sporty car that incited curses from Luz because of its effects on her knees.

I've always loved avocado soup, but this version, which I had at a Mexican restaurant in New York City, was so pretty and colorful, and so very tasty. It had its own panache.

Roberto's Avocado Soup

- Croutons: Cut a *dense, thin-sliced white bread* into tiny squares and fry to golden brown or darker in *garlic olive oil*. Spread on a paper towel to dry and cool. Then reserve in covered containers in refrigerator.

- Avocado Soup: Mix in a blender *2 cans consommé madrilène, flesh of one large avocado*, and *1 cup sour cream*. Season to taste with *salt, chili powder*, and *a bit of onion juice or scraped onion*.

- Place in refrigerator until soup jells.

- Serve in 4 bowls, garnishing with small amounts of *chopped cilantro, thinly sliced green onion curls, red pepper flakes (optional),* and *croutons.*

Carolyn Blue,
"Have Fork, Will Travel,"
Baton Rouge Banner

13

An Evening with *Rigoletto*

Luz

Wow! Lincoln Center was a sight, and the opera house sparkled from the end of an open plaza with fountains, though why the water hadn't frozen I don't know. I was certainly frozen. Of course we had to walk a hell of a long way from the street to get to the doors, and the press was there to meet us, shouting questions at Carolyn. How did they know we'd be here? Had someone ratted us out? One guy shoved a microphone in her face, so I told him I was going to knock him right over on his ass if he didn't back off. He said, "Right, and I'll sue you, lady."

"I'm a cop, jerk-off. Wanna see my badge?" He decided he didn't, and I hustled Carolyn through the doors.

"I wouldn't have minded the opportunity to tell my side of things," said Carolyn.

"You're a suspect," I snapped. "You have to keep your mouth shut. Anything you say they're gonna twist up so you don't recognize it and then smear it across a front page."

Carolyn pouted, and I looked around. Very beautiful, I had to admit, but these hellish-looking stairs curved from the lobby to where our seats were going to be. Oh man, and my frigging knees were already aching from the car

Roberto thought was so great. It was worse than sitting on an airplane, flying with Carolyn to Europe, with my knees shoved up against the seat in front of me.

Turned out Roberto had a seat in a box but managed to talk a lady in our row into taking his box seat so that he could sit with us. She was tempted by the champagne he promised would be served during the opera and let him lead her away. Then he came back and sat between the two of us, figuring to put the moves on Carolyn. *This is going to be some fun to watch!* I thought, except the frigging chandeliers, which had been shining into my eyes, suddenly started rising.

"What's going on?"

"It happens every night," said Roberto.

"Yeah? Well, some night they're going to fall right onto the heads of the people downstairs, who probably paid a lot of money to get their heads smashed in."

"Shush," Carolyn whispered. "They've been going up and down for forty or fifty years without falling on anyone's head, so don't make a fuss. Did you notice the panels on the backs of the seats? They translate the opera from Italian."

I looked and then pressed some buttons. Nothing happened. Wouldn't you know I'd end up sitting in the seat where the screen didn't work. Carolyn's probably worked, and she wouldn't need it. For sure she knew every damn thing that was going to happen. Me, I was here because my mother wanted to hear all about Rolando Villazon. When we handed in our tickets, the woman gave us programs and little CDs, but mine had the Russian soprano Netrebko on the cover, not the Mexican tenor Mom was interested in. I asked Roberto and Luz if they'd trade, but they both had Netrebko, too.

"You can buy a CD of Villazon," Roberto whispered while Carolyn shushed us again because the orchestra started playing.

Pretty soon the curtain goes up, and I see Villazon for the first time. Roberto even has opera glasses, and the tenor is pretty cute, not as big as you'd think to have a voice like that, but very masculine. He's singing this song, in an off-hand way, hardly ever even taking a breath, about women being fickle. Right. First clue that the duke, his role, is a jerk. Then this Rigoletto comes in—big bald head, which the stage lights bounce off. Carolyn's already told me the guy is a jester, but I know what a jester's costume looks like, and this guy's wearing burlap. He doesn't even have a cap with bells on it that would have covered the head. And he doesn't like anyone—a mean S.O.B., but with a good voice.

After some more singing and clapping and scene changes, Gilda, Rigoletto's daughter, comes in. The Russian woman, Anna Netrebko, sings that role, and she's thin with boobs, beautiful, and she's got a great voice, too. I thought sopranos were supposed to be fat. So she looks good, she sounds good, but she's dumber than a donkey. She's in love with a student, who's really the badass duke in disguise, and the old man, Rigoletto, who hates the duke and everyone in his court, adores his dumb daughter and doesn't want any guys getting near her.

Of course he doesn't give a rat's ass about anyone else's innocent daughter and gets suckered into a plan to help kidnap some nobleman's. He holds the ladder, but it's Gilda who gets kidnapped and hauled off to be raped by the duke, who, by the way, has this scene where he sings about how maybe he's finally in love, even if he's lying through his teeth to Gilda about who he is. He almost fooled me for a minute there. Carolyn said the kidnapping was a moment of terrible "irony and hubris" for Old Burlap. I thought he deserved it, and Gilda was too stupid to live, but you wouldn't believe how much stupider the two of them could get.

The best part so far, besides the singing, was the curtain calls. The story sucked, but Villazon and Netrebko came out after whatever act and fooled around like two kids. She skipped across the stage, hauling him after her, with him swinging her hand and holding it up like he'd just won the spelling bee. Carolyn said, "Aren't they charming?"

I said, "I hate those frigging screens with the translations." Mine had finally come on with the music. "You watch the translation to find out what's going on, and you can't see what's happening. You watch the performance, and you don't know what's going on."

Roberto said, "Let's get some champagne." So we did. Then he wanted to know what I thought of the opera.

"I think someone ought to cut the balls off the duke. What a scumbag. And then there's Rigoletto's daughter. How stupid can you get? She still loves him after he raped her? Women like that ought to be locked up for their own good."

Roberto laughed so hard he snorted champagne up his nose. That was real sophisticated. Carolyn handed him a Kleenex to wipe his nose. While we were talking, I'd been looking around, something every cop does, even retired, crippled ex-cops, and I'd spotted these three Asian guys trying to look like they belonged here but not dressed for it. I'd swear they were staring at Carolyn. "Look to your left," I whispered. "Do you know those guys?"

She spotted the Asians and waved. They sneered. "Sort of," she said. "I'll tell you about them later. Surely, you liked the singing."

She was looking kind of disappointed, maybe with me, so I had to say something nice. "Hell, yes," I replied. "Who wouldn't? But that doesn't mean it's not a frigging disgusting story. I can tell already it's going to end in a mess. I just wish the CD had more than stupid Gilda on it. My mother wants to hear the Mexican tenor."

"I know a place you can buy her one, and you're right about the opera ending in a mess," said Carolyn, sighing, "but it *is* a tragedy."

Tell me about it. Rigoletto hires some guy to assassinate the duke, but the killer's sister, who's supposed to lure the duke to his death, falls for him. You should have seen Villazon. He was all over the sister; no wonder she asked the assassin to save the duke's life. The assassin says he does what he gets paid for, being an honorable scumbag, but if some stranger knocks on the door, he'll kill the stranger and put him in the bag instead of the duke.

So, okay, airhead Gilda hears all this and, disguised as a boy, knocks at the door, gets stabbed and stuffed in the bag, and ends up with Daddy, who can't wait to throw the bag in the river—until he hears the duke singing about fickle women upstairs at the assassin's house. Then he looks in the bag and discovers his dying daughter, so he's singing about his misery, and all the scumbags are happy. How's that for a real upper?

While all this was going on, Roberto linked arms with Carolyn and tickled the palm of her hand. She told him to stop it and let her watch the opera, and when he didn't, she elbowed him in the ribs. Roberto went, "Umph!" and I started to laugh, which I figured no one could hear because there was this big thunderstorm going on onstage. But I was wrong, because everyone around me said, "Shhh!"

Anyway Gilda dies, Rigoletto cries, the audience jumps up clapping, and Carolyn says, out loud, mind you, "Here I've heard a superb cast singing a lovely opera that would have brought tears to my eyes if I hadn't been accompanied by an oversexed Mexican restaurateur and a philistine female friend." That's when Roberto had to admit he'd lost the bet and handed me my five dollars, and Carolyn said, "I'm not even going to ask what that was about."

"At least, señora, I hope you liked the dinner."

"The dinner was excellent," she admitted.

"And you will forgive me for my amorous behavior?"

"I will not," she replied firmly and headed for those frigging stairs with us tagging behind.

14
The FBI Comes Calling

Carolyn

I did not want to wake up early the next morning after such a late night, so naturally the telephone rang at nine, Allison Peabody inviting me to join her for dinner at Daniel. What could I say? Several people had indicated that she might have sabotaged my turkeys, and the dinner would give me a chance to question her. And Daniel—a famous restaurant with two Michelin stars and a reputation for wonderful food, ambience, and service.

On the other hand, she extended the invitation by saying that if I hoped to write about "real" gourmet food, I did have to eat some, and that many of the restaurants I'd praised in New Orleans, if they weren't already victims of Hurricane Katrina, weren't what she considered "top drawer." I owed it to Jason to avail myself of the Daniel opportunity when someone else was paying, but I got even for the mean remarks by pointing out that I had come to New York with a friend and—

"Oh, yes," trilled Allison, "the unusual Lieutenant Vallejo. Do bring her along. Everyone should eat at least one good meal in her life, and I'm sure her reactions will be very amusing."

I certainly hoped so. For once, I hoped that Luz would be in full foulmouthed, philistine mode.

"I do hope she has suitable clothes for an evening at Daniel."

"She does." Allison wasn't getting out of paying for Luz's dinner that way. "She has a lovely gown she acquired on a cruise we took on the *Bountiful Feast*."

"*Really?* Well then, meet me there at eight. You do know where it is?"

"We'll find it," I purred. I didn't think I'd like Allison, even if she turned out to be innocent of the attack on my turkeys.

"Waaa?" mumbled Luz from her bed.

"An invitation to dinner."

She went back to sleep. Before I could, I had to take another call, from Janet Fong, who asked if we'd like to accompany her tomorrow night to an Asian fusion restaurant she wanted to try. "I have my book signing tomorrow night at 7:30," I said, disappointed. Asian fusion sounded very interesting. No one had suggested that Janet might be the turkey tamperer, although, of course, I'd need to check her out.

"We can eat early. How about five-thirty? It's not chic, but it will get you to Cooks and Books on time and me into bed by ten. My mother will be your friend for life. She thinks real sleep can only be had between ten and six."

I had to laugh. "She sounds like a sensible woman. Between ten and ten is even nicer, but I can't usually manage that." I took down the name and address of the restaurant, thanked Janet for her invitation, and went straight back to sleep.

The next thing I heard was Luz's voice saying loudly and angrily, "The feds are here to see you, Caro."

Groggily, I stumbled out of bed and put on my robe. Two conservatively dressed men were standing in the doorway, obviously, as Detective Worski had predicted, from the State Department. In this case, I thought a good offense was in my best interest, and I certainly had a bone to pick with the State Department. I said, "It's about time," and they looked surprised. "It's been . . . goodness I don't know how long—since I sent you those emails asking for help, and you never answered when we needed you. My husband and the U.S. Navy rescued us. You should be ashamed of yourselves for waiting so long to come and apologize. And how did you know I was here?"

Luz had fallen onto the end of her bed laughing and gasped, "I don't think that's what they've come for, Carolyn."

The two men looked rather befuddled, I must admit, but that didn't pacify me at all. "You *are* from the State Department, aren't you? What do you want? And whatever it is, you should have called first. We were out late at the opera and need our sleep. You'll just have to make an appointment."

One of them frowned and said, "If you're Mrs. Carolyn Blue, who firebombed the limousine of Ahmad al Hafiz, the Benamian ambassador, we need to interview you."

What *was* he talking about? I wondered, feeling befuddled myself. "I've never heard of Ahmad whatever or his country. What did you say it was? Bon Ami? That's a household cleanser. I'm going to call hotel security."

"May we come in?" asked the shorter of the two men. "I'm Special Agent Horace Figgis from the FBI." He flashed an identity card. "And this is my colleague Special Agent Merton Holliwell."

Now I was really embarrassed, but still . . . "I'm afraid you can't come in," I replied more politely. "This is our bedroom."

Luz got off the bed, looked at their identification, and said, "We'll meet you at the free breakfast downstairs."

"We'll wait for you in the hall," said Agent Holliwell, "and if you try to get away, Mrs. Blue"— He gave me a stern look —"we'll find you. Every police officer and agent in the city will track you down. Wouldn't you rather talk to us now than—"

"I'd *rather* go back to sleep." However, Luz quietly closed the door in their faces and suggested that we get dressed.

"If a turkey hit some diplomat's car, it's like bombing his country," she said, "so we better get this straightened out."

"Tomorrow should be soon enough."

"Yeah, right. First you get us to shoot down a Moroccan helicopter on the cruise, and now you firebomb another Arab country's limo. I'm surprised it wasn't the State Department. You're a magnet for international incidents."

"Well, it's probably a very small country," I said as I started to dress. "I'll bet you've never heard of it either."

Agents Figgis and Holliwell stood waiting in the hallway and escorted us downstairs, where we headed for the free breakfast. Luz and I visited the buffet, then took a table to eat our rolls while the agents, when asked for their room keys by the woman who poured coffee, were told sternly that only guests of the hotel could eat here. They bullied the waitress into letting them sit, but they had to pay for their own coffee. As we passed through the lobby, I'd noticed the three Wise Dragon bodyguards waiting for me and looking perturbed when they saw that we were escorted by two obvious feds, as Luz had called Figgis and Holliwell. I rather hoped the Dragons would follow us and be lectured by the room-key checker, too, but I was disappointed in that respect.

However irritated, I decided to be polite to the FBI. "How can I help you?" I asked Agent Figgis. Although I did find the FBI visit somewhat intimidating, I had reason to be upset because Luz had told me on the way down that I was going to get fat again if we kept going out for big meals, while she, if she had to pay for any of them, was going to go home broke.

"I've lost all that weight from the cruise, and you haven't paid for anything yet. I'm the one who's going to have an angry husband complaining about my credit card bill."

"Oh, stop bitching," Luz had said, after which various respectable people on the elevator, including the agents, looked at her askance. "You're here to write about eating ethnic, right? We should eat at some cheap ethnic places. Sooner or later I'm going to have to pay for my own dinner. Hey, Special Agent Figgis, do you know any ethnic places a retired cop like me could afford?" He had refused to answer.

At the table, instead of replying to my offer of help, Agent Holliwell asked, "What do you have against the Benamians, Mrs. Blue?"

"Would you mind if I had some breakfast first?" I replied sweetly, nibbling on my croissant and sipping my coffee. Then, as if I'd need time to think it over, I said "I'd never heard of the country before you mentioned it, and I've never met a Benamian. But I did hear that the ambassador was Arab, perhaps Muslim. There are Arab Christians, as well."

"He is Muslim, but not a fundamentalist. Do you have ties to any fundamentalist Muslim terrorist groups?"

"You can't be serious." What a really silly question. They obviously knew nothing about me. "I write about food. I live in El Paso. All my friends—well, except Luz—are academics. My husband is a chemistry professor, for goodness sake."

"So he helped you make the bombs?"

"He did no such thing. He's back home in El Paso because there was a . . . a problem."

"What kind of problem?"

"I don't see what that has to do with anything. It was a chemical problem, something to do with metals."

The two men exchanged glances as if I'd just said something significant. Well, I wasn't going to tell them

there'd been a lab accident. They'd assume it had something to do with bombs.

"Does your husband have terrorist ties?"

"Of course not. As I said, he's a professor, and not of Is-
lamic studies or anything even moderately political. We're
a very respectable, academic family."

"Are you *prejudiced* against Muslims, Mrs. Blue, or are
you going to tell us that you've never met a Muslim?"

I thought about that and answered truthfully, "Our
guide in Morocco was probably a Muslim."

"So you've been in an Arab country? How recently?"

"Last fall. We were in Morocco for half a day, and not
a very pleasant one either. Our guide kept shouting at us
and blowing his whistle. I was not favorably impressed.
And some young men on the street in Tangier made offen-
sive remarks, which the guide translated. Again I was un-
favorably impressed and told them so. After all, I didn't
take off my scarf; it slipped, and calling me 'the woman
with the *camel piss hair*' was very impolite."

"Not to mention getting me to help shoot down that
stolen Moroccan helicopter," said Luz, laughing.

"We rescued the pilots," I retorted defensively. She
needn't have brought that up. "And I believe that the chief
steward on the cruise, Mr. Patek, may have been not just
a Muslim, but also a terrorist, not to mention a thief and
a hijacker. That is the extent of my experience with Muslims, less than ten people. One cannot form an opinion of
a large religious group after having met so few, Agent
Holliwell."

"That's *Special Agent* Holliwell," said Special Agent
Figgis.

Goodness, they were sensitive about their titles. "Very
well, Special Agent. I'm sure there are many pleasant, respectable Muslims. I just haven't met any. Does that answer your question?"

"Does your husband have Muslim acquaintances?"
asked Agent Figgis.

"Not that I've met, but if Muslims go to scientific meetings, then he's probably met some."

"The ambassador whose limousine you bombed is claiming that American terrorists attacked him and his vehicle. We have an international incident on our hands, which will be very hard for our State Department to explain."

"Oh, really?" Now I was too angry to be polite. "Well, as little as the State Department did for us when our ship was hijacked, I can't say I care one way or another about their problems."

"Just have them tell the ambassador it was a frigging turkey, not a bomb," suggested Luz, laughing.

"And that its flaming condition was *not* my fault. Nothing I've ever flambéed continued to burn like that. If there was any plot against the ambassador, it was the work of someone else, and I intend to find out who that was. However, I am quite willing to visit the ambassador to apologize on behalf of our country, if the State Department is too busy ignoring the pleas of American citizens abroad to do it themselves. I'm sure the ambassador will understand when I explain the situation."

"Ma'am, I'm sure he won't," said Agent Figgis. "You stay away from him. We'll handle this once we find out what really happened. And you are to keep us apprised of your whereabouts. Furthermore, you cannot leave the city."

I thought about how much trouble and expense that order might cause, not to mention the problem of trying to explain to Jason why I wouldn't be arriving home on time. "I do hope you plan to pay for any extra days at the hotel and extra meals, should they be necessary, and the charges to change our airplane tickets."

"Lady," snapped Figgis, "you're pissing me off."

"And your language is deplorable," I snapped back. That was really the last straw. "I'm going to make a complaint."

"Oh, come on, Caro. Even if he is a fed, he's a cop,"

said Luz. "It's a dirty business, isn't it, Special Agent Figgis?"

She was laughing again, which I didn't appreciate. Neither did Special Agent Figgis.

The FBI left after giving us their cards. I gave the bodyguards a little wave while heading for the elevator, and we went back to the room.

15

Summoned by State

Carolyn

Luz was brushing her teeth and I was flossing when I received a call from the U.S. delegation to the UN, summoning me for an interview about my part in the firebombing of an ambassadorial limousine. I agreed to an appointment in an hour. When Luz heard, she offered to accompany me, but I decided that since the conversation would require some diplomacy, I'd go on my own.

"Right. Diplomacy. You want to tear into them because they didn't answer your emails from the *Bountiful Feast*."

"That, too," I said, smiling cheerfully. I did have a thing or two to say to the State Department, but then I remembered that I should call Detective Worski. I made that call immediately and told him that I'd learned the chef, whom he hadn't been able to find, was at a conference in Atlantic City, which didn't mean he wasn't a suspect anymore, just that he had a different motive for ruining my turkey flambé. "He missed the first day of his meeting and the opportunity to cook a wild turkey dinner because of me," I explained. Detective Worski thought those motives not only hilarious, but also unbelievable, even when I assured him that he obviously didn't understand temperamental chefs. Then I mentioned Allison Peabody, who was jealous of her status as queen of gourmet food writing, and Annunziata Randatto, who might be worried about her status as bestselling cookbook author at Pettigrew's. Detective Worski assured me that I, the person who'd made the turkey bombs, was still his best suspect. "So you get your ass right down to my office, Mrs. Blue. Benitez and I need to talk to you."

Now that was insulting! "I have an appointment today with the State Department, Detective. I think they trump the New York Police Department." I hung up and instructed Luz to tell him I had left if he called again, although I still had to bundle up for my journey into the frigid canyons of New York. Should I be frugal and take the subway, or free-spending and comfortable in a Ming family cab? Frugal, I decided, as I brushed my teeth. All those cabs yesterday? Definitely frugal today.

I hadn't even called Jason, poor man, stuck in El Paso with the DEA, the lab accident, and his unconscious students. I'd definitely call him tonight, and I'd ride subways all day. Mr. Ming might be disappointed; I was, too, but I had yet to tell my husband about the cell phone and the new dress. Goodness, I had to drop the velvet dress off with Uncle Bernie today. So many things to do. I checked the velvet gown for dampness, put it into the plastic bag, and headed for the door.

Luz shouted after me that she'd head for Cratchett, and if I got free of the feds, I could call her there. Then our phone rang, and she answered while I motioned that she wasn't to say I was here. "Cool it," she told me. "Cratchett wants to talk to you."

I took the call, embarrassed that I wouldn't be available this morning to help with the investigation as I had promised. He wanted us to get together to discuss talking to temps who had been employed as kitchen help and waiters the day and evening of the launch party, so I suggested lunch, something ethnic preferably, and we settled on a Kosher-Indian restaurant on Curry Hill, a fusion cuisine the likes of which I'd never heard. He provided directions and I finally got away, with my velvet gown over my arm, to keep my appointment. But by that time I was running late and needed to take a cab after all.

I might as well have taken the subway, since the State Department kept me waiting. After fifteen minutes, I suggested to the receptionist that I return my gown to the store in Lower Manhattan while the State Department was leaving me in limbo. Suddenly I was admitted to the office of some official to whom the lady showed great respect. I think she said he was Assistant something Pratt.

I shook his hand, sat down, and told him all about my unfortunate experience with his agency. He said, "That would make you the woman involved in shooting down a stolen Moroccan military helicopter."

"Not personally. I don't carry guns, but it was a very frightening experience, and I think my own government should have been more supportive. Not that I am complaining about the U.S. Navy. They rescued us when the bomb went off during the Mother's Day dinner."

"You seem to have an affinity for bombs and international incidents, ma'am, which is why you're here today. Ah, Naylor." Mr. Pratt nodded to a man who had entered the office unannounced. "This is Mrs. Blue. Mrs. Blue, Mr. Naylor is here representing the Department of Homeland Security. As you can imagine, two bombs hitting the streets of New York is a matter of concern to his department, even if you do deny being a terrorist."

"I take it that the FBI has been in touch. Very nice to meet you, Mr. Naylor." I shook his hand. "Does the Department of Homeland Security have any particular protocol regarding flaming turkeys striking U.S. streets? It was certainly a shocking and frightening incident, but there were no bombs, just my excellent *Herald-Tribune* turkeys. Because someone sabotaged them, they produced a conflagration instead of the pretty blue-flame decorative effect of a successful flambé.

"Indeed, the volcano turkey with its silver eruption cup on top and lava streams made quite an impression on the guests, who clapped enthusiastically before the whole turkey started spitting fire and scorching the ceiling. Then two employees at Pettigrew's speared my turkeys and threw them over the balconies. Of course, they weren't expecting traffic and crowds at that time of night, but as it turned out, St. Laurence O'Toole's Day was being celebrated, so—" I stopped because both men were staring at me as if I were mad.

"He was an Irish bishop of Dublin, if I'm not mistaken."

"Mrs. Blue, your . . . missiles . . . blew up a car."

"It was illegally parked."

"And hit a diplomatic limousine, causing an accident resulting in injuries."

"I've already explained and apologized to the grandfather of the unfortunate young woman who is in a coma."

"Causing an embarrassing international incident. The Benamians think they were attacked by Muslim fundamentalist terrorists who resent the Benamian alliance with our country."

"Well, they're mistaken, Mr. Pratt. I am not a Muslim fundamentalist. I'm a food and travel writer. Tell them I wrote a nice column about desserts in Morocco, which will probably help their share of the American tourist market since I didn't mention the whistle-blowing guide or the impolite Arab youths who made nasty comments about my hair. I have never seen a camel urinate—well, possibly when I was a child visiting the St. Louis zoo—but I'm sure my hair is not the color of camel urine. How would you feel if someone said something like that to your wife?"

"Your experiences in Morocco are beside the point, ma'am," said Mr. Naylor. "You've caused us to consider raising the national security alert level, and you brought back all the trauma of 9/11 when you—"

"Those were airplanes, not turkeys," I retorted, "and any consternation I may have been partially responsible for causing New Yorkers, I shall apologize for immediately. You, however, should be very relieved to know that Thanksgiving turkeys, not bombs, fell into the city streets.

An unburned turkey, which I myself managed to rescue, was turned over to the fire department. I suggest that before you accuse me of being a terrorist, you call them and find out what foreign substance was added that caused the problem. I am a respectable housewife and mother who writes educational food columns."

"Educational?" mumbled Mr. Naylor.

"I include culinary history. Would you like an example? Louis XIV of France—"

Assistant Pratt gave a loud sigh before I could mention the king's problem with strawberries and said none of this would pacify the angry Benamian delegation, which was threatening to take the matter to the United Nations.

"Oh, for goodness sake! This whole diplomatic fuss is incredibly silly. Neither the ambassador's limousine nor any of his party were injured that I'm aware of. I'll go over this afternoon and explain the situation to the ambassador."

Mr. Pratt sighed again. "I'll have to go with you, and please don't call their concerns silly or mention that you were involved in shooting down a Moroccan helicopter or were insulted by Moroccan youths."

"Naturally not," I replied. "I'll be at Madras Mahal in Curry Hill, or technically Murray Hill, from twelve to one. You can pick me up there." I scribbled down the address of the Kosher-Indian restaurant.

Mr. Pratt ordered his secretary to set up the appointment.

Glancing at the scruffy velvet evening dress I was holding, Mr. Naylor asked me if I was planning to dress formally for my lunch date. "The food there is pretty hot. If you're not used to Southern Indian cuisine, you might consider dressing down. People have been known to make rush trips to the bathrooms."

"I'm from El Paso. I'm accustomed to food that is *muy picante*." I threw in the Spanish phrase so that he'd know I wasn't a country bumpkin.

"Well, it's your ulcer," he retorted and asked if I knew the name of the person in charge of the third turkey. I did and gave him the name, asking that he call me if he found out what had been done to my turkeys. Then I gave him my card. Mr. Pratt confirmed an appointment with the Benamian ambassador at two and reluctantly agreed to have his driver pick me up at Madras Mahal.

Once freed from that unpleasant interview, I got rather confusing instructions from the receptionist on how to travel by subway to Uncle Bernie's. She was very interested in seeing the water-damaged dress and didn't think it could be refurbished, but I had confidence in Loretta's uncle, more than I had in Loretta. Thinking of my agent reminded me that I had a book signing tonight that was bound to be a flop. My first and possibly last book signing.

My bodyguards were with me again—I'd forgotten to look for them at the hotel—but here on the street, I walked right up to them and asked the name of the leader. I might have known. It was Mr. Li, so I told him that if they were going to follow me all day, they might as well take the lead because I wasn't at all sure that I could find my way to the discount clothing establishment or even to the restaurant. Following an angry argument in Chinese, they agreed, reluctantly, but they wouldn't sit with me in the half-empty subway car. Evidently I'd embarrassed them in some unforeseeable way.

16
Kosher-Indian Cuisine

Carolyn

Uncle Bernie did think he could resurrect my velvet gown, bless him, and then my bodyguards got me to Curry Hill and trailed me up the street to Madras Mahal. What a wonderful neighborhood! The restaurants and shops were Bangladeshi, Pakistani, Chinese, Japanese, and Indian. One of my favorites was called Curry in a Hurry, but I didn't have time left to investigate. I had to find Madras Mahal before my ears froze off. I did find it but saw no one inside except some waiters, so I asked for a table for four and sat down to study the menu. The cuisine was Southern Indian, no mention of Kosher, and no gefilte fish or blini. I hoped that Mr. Cratchett wouldn't be disappointed.

After a few minutes on the freezing street, the body-guards strolled in and took a table not too far from me. The least important was sent over to ask, "How long you here?" I told him until one o'clock at least, so they ordered all kinds of things, which somewhat appeased my waiter. Since I had five minutes, I called Jason, who would be in his office doing computer things relating to chemistry, it being midmorning in El Paso.

"Where are you?" he demanded as soon as I identified myself. "I can hear people talking Chinese and—"

"—and some Southern Indian dialect," I finished help-
fully. The chef and the waiter were arguing in the back.

"And they let you call long distance on their telephone?"

Whoops. Caught with a cell phone. I explained my purchase and got a lecture. "I'm waiting to meet Luz and . . .
friends," I finished lamely.

"Friends who have something to do with an article on
the front page of my morning paper? 'El Paso Author Firebombs Lower Manhattan. Terrorism Suspected.' I believe
that was the gist of the headline. My name was mentioned
as your husband. And a DEA agent arrived fifteen minutes
after I got to work to question me. As if I don't have
enough trouble because of the lab accident."

"You don't know yet what happened?"

"Nate came to, but he went back to sleep before I could
question him early this morning. Now please explain what
happened up there, and why you didn't tell me about it."

I sighed, my eyes skipping nervously across the scary
masks that were tacked to bright red backgrounds and
hung on the walls of the restaurant. "I didn't want to worry
you, Jason, when you have so much on your mind. I didn't
firebomb anything, obviously. When I flambéed the
turkeys, they pretty much exploded and burned the tablecloth and the ceiling, and then the publisher's nephew and
my editor panicked and tossed them over the balcony into
the street, which caused—lots of problems. But I'm investigating, Jason. I'll find out who tampered with my turkeys
and—"

"Don't investigate," he shouted in my ear.

"I have to. You don't want me to go to jail for first-
degree assault, do you?"

Jason groaned. The waiter came back and frowned at
me. Luz, Mr. Cratchett, and a large black fellow entered
Madras Mahal, slapping their hands together and rubbing
their ears while they took off jackets, caps, and gloves. I
said, "They're here. I have to go." And I hung up.

"Who was that?" Luz asked. More menus arrived in the

hands of the smiling waiter, hot tea and Indian beer were ordered, DeShawn introduced, and I explained that Jason had found out about the turkeys. "Oh boy," said Luz and opened her menu. I suggested that we order hors d'oeuvres first while we chose entrees. Our waiter nodded approval, and soon we were eating Machu Vada (fried lentil donuts) and Kachori (green pea balls: crisp beany-tasting turnovers filled with spiced potatoes and green peas), and all sorts of things we dipped in a sweet red sauce and a very good green cilantro sauce while my fellow investigators read me newspaper articles I'd rather have missed.

Luz had found one that said the police were protecting the main suspect in the firebombing in Lower Manhattan. "That's me, the police, and you, the suspect," she explained. DeShawn had found one in a supermarket scandal sheet entitled, "Pettigrew Author Flambés Illegally Parked Cars."

Mr. Cratchett told the waiter we'd have a four-person serving of Madras Ravi Dosai. I warned him that it might not be Kosher, but he assured me that he knew where to get Kosher and that we needed to discuss parceling out the interviews with the launch party's rent-a-kitchen-worker people.

"They're a mixed lot, kitchen helpers and waiters, mostly black and Puerto Rican." DeShawn muttered something about people of color getting the "shit jobs," not that he didn't like being a private eye. Mr. Cratchett told him that he wasn't one yet; it took a license, for which he'd have to study. "I thought Mrs. Blue and Lieutenant Vallejo might take the more timid female workers, while DeShawn and I interviewed the felons."

"Felons?" I asked nervously. *Pettigrew hired felons?*

"The just-outta-jails get the shit jobs, too, no matter what color they are," said DeShawn, who had pretty much cleaned up the hors d'oeuvres platter and even licked some sauce from the cilantro bowl, not to mention emptying two bottles of beer, which Luz had ordered for him, ignoring my protest that he might be underage. "He's got ID," she'd

retorted. Mr. Cratchett advised DeShawn not to let Rachel
Cratchett see him licking bowls or he'd never be invited to
lunch again at the Cratchett house.

Then a giant platter of Dosai was served: large, irregu-
larly shaped, crispy, spiced wheat and rice crepes filled with
potatoes, onions, and really, really hot peppers. They looked
so tasty that I took a big bite, chewed twice, and gasped. My
throat was on fire. I ordered beer before I took a second bite,
a nibble. That worked better, and I was happy.

"I figured you and DeShawn could question the respectable blacks, while Luz and I took the respectable Hispanics. Her Spanish is better than mine."

"You ever talk to a homeboy, lady?" DeShawn asked
me. "You gonna fall over if some brotha say *mothafucka* in
front of you? Abe's mama didn't like it."

"I'm sure she didn't, and I don't think I'd fall over, Mr.
Brown," I said, "but I might well wash the brother's mouth
out with soap."

"Don't think she's kidding, DeShawn." Luz took another piece of Dosai and told Mr. Cratchett that if it was
Kosher, she might just convert and marry him, which
would make his mother happy. He grinned. Then she
turned to our young black colleague and added, "Carolyn's
calling you Mr. Brown to show she doesn't like *your* language. My advice is to take any brothers or sisters who
might offend her aside and warn them to watch their
tongues. She's a woman known for slapping guys in strip
clubs when they get fresh with the dancers, and berating
Muslims in their own countries for bad manners."

So that's how the conversation went, and Mr. Cratchett
was very unhappy to hear that I had an appointment at the
Benamian Embassy and couldn't begin the interviews immediately. Luz said in that case she'd go with me so we
could chase down Jack Armstrong later and strongarm him
about lying to me yesterday. "Call us when you get the interviews set up, Abe. You getting the check?"

"It goes on the Pettigrew bill," he said.

I noticed a governmental limousine waiting outside so I

began to gather my coat and scarf and wonder if I was going to survive the Dosai. My second helping had induced a noticeable burning sensation in my stomach. "If you're coming with me, Luz, we have to go. The assistant diplomat's car is here."

We remuffled ourselves and went outside, but there was a problem. The assistant diplomat wasn't in the car. The driver said we'd be picking Mr. Pratt up next, but I couldn't be sure that was true. What if this man planned to kidnap us? He might be from the Benamian embassy, taking revenge for—

"For God's sake, Carolyn, get in the car. I'm freezing my ass off here, and so are you. If the guy isn't Kosher, as Abe would say, I'll knock him out."

The driver said, "The hell you will," and opened the door for us. I was still unhappy with the situation, but Luz all but shoved me in.

"The *felons* probably tampered with the turkeys," I whispered to Luz as my bodyguards came tumbling out of Madas Mahal. Unfortunately for them, they didn't have a driver to pick them up, and there wasn't a cab in sight.

I had Southern Indian food in a restaurant on "Curry Hill" in Manhattan, a restaurant that was billed as Kosher, which meant perhaps no meat and milk, but in fact, meant no meat at all. The following recipes are as near as I can come to what I had, which was very tasty but so hot it gave me indigestion. I've cut back on the peppers a bit.

Potato Mixture for Dosai

- Peel, dice, and boil *24 ounces of potatoes*.

- Chop *3 medium onions* fine.

- Heat *3 ounces vegetable oil* in frying pan, and fry ¾ *teaspoon black mustard seeds*. Add onions, and fry until nearly done.

- Add potatoes, ¾ teaspoon turmeric, ¾ teaspoon chili flakes, salt, and pepper. Cook for 5 minutes or until dry. Set aside for stuffing dosai.

Rava Dosai

- In a medium bowl combine 1 cup rice flour, 2 tablespoons all-purpose flour, ½ cup farina (cream of wheat), 2 tablespoons minced onions, 1 teaspoon minced ginger, 1 teaspoon minced green chili (Serrano or jalapeno, seeded), 10 coarsely chopped curry leaves, ½ cup plain low-fat yogurt, 1¼ teaspoon salt, 2 to 2½ cups water. Mix to form a very thin batter. Cover and set aside for 1 hour.

- Heat a small amount of vegetable oil over medium heat in an 8 to 10 inch, nonstick griddle or frying pan until a bit of sprinkled water sputters on surface.

- Stir batter thoroughly before frying each dosa. Batter should be thinner than crepe batter and spread easily on griddle.

- Ladle about ⅓ cup onto hot griddle in circular motion starting from outside and moving in to make a very thin pancake which develops little holes as it cooks. If your first dosa is gummy and thick, experiment with a thinner batter produced by the addition of water.

- Sprinkle ghee (if available) or melted butter on top liberally. When bottom turns golden brown, turn over and fry other side for 30 seconds.

- Remove dosa from pan with golden side down, spoon 3 tablespoons filling on one half, fold over

like an omelet, and slide onto a warm platter. Keep
in warm oven uncovered and not stacked while frying more dosai.

Carolyn Blue,
"Have Fork, Will Travel,"
Manhattan (KA) Herald

17
An Afternoon with Annoying Males

Carolyn

The first thing Mr. Pratt said when he got into the car with us was, "You can't visit the ambassador without a head covering." Then he wanted to know who Luz was and why she had accompanied me. Luz claimed to be my chaperone, since my husband wouldn't want me to be alone with two men, one of whom probably had several wives and liked blondes. Mr. Pratt was not amused but I was, so when she insisted that we stop at a sporting goods store so I could get a proper head covering, I agreed. Mr. Pratt didn't think the store would have anything nice enough to impress a Benamian sheik.

We got our way on the basis of Luz's argument that, as we were doing Mr. Pratt a favor, he shouldn't insist that we buy something in an expensive store. I was thinking how much fun Luz was, until she picked out this awful hat that had earflaps. It looked like something men wear deer hunting.

"You've been bitching about how cold your ears are since we got here. This will keep them warm, and the black in the plaid matches your coat."

Reluctantly, I tried on the hat and found that my ears no longer ached; I just looked silly.

"Besides that, the press will never recognize you. You look like a kid instead of a turkey bomber."

Very funny, I thought, but I purchased the hat and wore it out to the car, where the chauffeur burst out laughing. Mr. Pratt did not.

He didn't think it was appropriate. I told him that it was, however, practical, covered my hair completely, and would be perfect for wild-turkey hunting the next time I had a chance to go. I'm not sure what got into me. Mr. Pratt glared, looking as if he thought he was being made fun of.

Luz gave me a thumbs-up behind his back and said, "What? You don't think we hunt wild turkeys together? Too bad they wouldn't let us provide them for the Pettigrew party. Maybe they wouldn't have blown up, or whatever they did. Though I have to say, I like hunting javelinas better. Those little bastards are mean!"

Mr. Pratt now looked distressed; perhaps he didn't approve of hunting wild javelinas, whatever those were. When the car stopped in front of a building that didn't look like an embassy, Luz asked suspiciously, "You're not planning to sell us to some Arab white slaver, are you?" After that Mr. Pratt insisted that she stay in the car with the chauffeur and that I mind my manners when we were admitted to the ambassador's apartment.

"If you're not out in a half hour, I'm calling the police," said Luz, "and as a retired cop myself, I know just who to call."

A very nervous Mr. Pratt fidgeted during the elevator ride upstairs and through the presentation of photo IDs to the ambassador's bodyguards. My bodyguards had not managed to catch up with me, which was a shame. They'd have made a nice addition to our entourage. The ambassador's first words to me after the introductions were, "What is that on your head?"

"My head covering," I replied sweetly. "I didn't want to offend you by exhibiting my hair, and it does keep my ears warm. I am a desert dweller and am most uncomfortable in cold climates, as no doubt you are, Mr. Ambassador. Also I was not allowed to bring my chaperone with me for this visit, so I feel more comfortable with my head and ears covered.

"However, I'm sure you are not interested in my husband's feelings about chaperones or my hat. You want to know about the seeming attack on your limousine. Let me assure you that although a flaming object did hit your windshield, it was not a bomb, or indeed a weapon of any kind. I am interested in food, not terrorism. Ah, tea. Please pour mine from this high." I gestured to the servant who was hovering with the silver teapot. "The sound will bring pleasure to the ears of Allah, something I learned on a visit to Morocco, which has very delicious pastries.

"But back to my turkeys. Are you familiar with turkeys, Mr. Ambassador? They are a fowl from the Americas, but have become popular elsewhere. What hit your windshield was a turkey that I flambéed for the party introducing my book on New Orleans cuisine."

"You set fire to your food?" asked the ambassador.

"Yes. I was under the impression that many nomadic cultures do. I'm astonished at your astonishment. Surprisingly, two of the three turkeys flamed up to unfortunate heights, frightening the guests and panicking the employees, who promptly threw them over the balcony, causing one to hit your limousine. I do apologize for any inconvenience you may have suffered. Of course there would have been less inconvenience to others on the street, not to mention the serious injuries, had your chauffeur not been intoxicated, as reported in the newspapers. Intoxicated driving is not allowed in our country, and I was under the impression that alcohol was forbidden entirely to the followers of Islam."

Oh good, I thought. *The ambassador is embarrassed.* "Excellent tea by the way. Mint, is it not?"

"Er—yes, mint. Would you care for a pastry?"

"Ordinarily, I'd have been delighted, but I just had a

lunch of Indian food." I didn't mention that it was Kosher-Indian. "And I'm suffering from indigestion. Your delicious tea has soothed me somewhat, but I think it will be some hours before I can eat again, although I do appreciate your kind offer. Now about your chauffeur."

"He has been returned to our country and will be dealt with by the proper authorities," said the ambassador grimly.

Oh dear. What do they plan to do with the poor man? Stone him to death? I wondered, sorry I'd brought the matter up. "Perhaps I could offer you a gift, so as to express my deep sorrow for having caused you so much distress the other night. It must be terrible to think that extremists are attacking one wherever one goes. I could come here and cook you one of the turkeys for which I am renowned, although I would have to bring my chaperone with me for propriety's sake. I'm sure you understand that, although Mr. Pratt did not."

"I do accept your apology, Mrs. Blue," replied the ambassador hastily. "And I wish that I could accept your charming offer to cook for me, but with the United Nations in session I have so little time and so many social and diplomatic engagements."

"I quite understand and will leave you to your many undertakings. It has been an honor to meet you, Mr. Ambassador." I stood up, still wearing my earflap hat and my winter coat. "Mr. Pratt, shall we go?"

Poor Mr. Pratt, who had squirmed through the whole conversation, was very happy to leave. He and the ambassador exchanged pleasantries, and we were out the door. I even persuaded Mr. Pratt to let his driver take Luz and me to visit that lying Jack Armstrong.

Luz

"So how did it go?" I asked when they got back in the car.

"I have no idea," said Pratt, looking bedeviled.

"He didn't like my hat," said Carolyn, obviously pleased with herself, "but he accepted my apology and refused my offer to cook him a turkey."

"Probably thought you'd set him on fire." Pratt got out first, and Carolyn directed the driver—how did she manage that?—to Armstrong's apartment in Chinatown.

"You'll have to make this a quick interview," said Carolyn as we went upstairs. "I have the worst case of heartburn imaginable."

"Okay. Quick and mean," I agreed and grabbed Armstrong by the throat as soon as he opened his door. He was so big I had to reach up. "So, you lying piece of scum, what's the idea of telling Carolyn you weren't at Pettigrew's the day of her book launch? I saw you on the sign-in list and on the security tape. What did you do? Stuff landmines in those turkeys? If you don't explain right now, I'm going to knee you in the balls, and when you're on the floor, I'll kick your head until you confess or die." Both of us had to help Armstrong to his recliner because he was too scared to get there on his own.

"I was never in the kitchen," he said. "I swear. I didn't do anything to the turkeys." Tears leaked out of his eyes. "I'm sorry I lied," he whimpered. "I need a glass of vegetable cocktail. I feel ill." When he tried to get out of the recliner, I shoved him back. "I make it myself—the cocktail. You must both have some. You'll love it."

"Shut up and tell Carolyn where it is." He did, and she came back with three glasses. I took a sip and spat it out on his carpet. "That's disgusting! Now start talking, Armstrong. Why were you there? Who did you see who can alibi you for the two hours?"

He bolted his glass of liquid vegetable swill and vomited up the whole tale. He'd gone there to see Roland, Carolyn's hospitalized editor, and when he couldn't find him,

he cornered Petey Haverford and followed him around—
but not into the kitchen—demanding a book launch for *his*
next cookbook. Petey had said no, and they'd argued back
and forth until Armstrong went home.

"Doesn't mean he isn't guilty," I told Carolyn after we'd
left Armstrong in tears. "Motive: jealousy." Carolyn
thought he'd probably complain about my threats and
rough treatment, maybe even bring charges. "No, he
won't," I replied, "because I whispered in his ear that if he
tried to make trouble for either of us, I'd come back and get
him."

Carolyn

We were accosted in front of the hotel by a reporter who
wanted an interview. Forgetting that I was now in disguise,
I said, "They were turkeys, not bombs." Luz told me to
shut up and rushed me inside, where I bought a packet of
Tums in the hotel gift shop and chewed up three as soon as
I got into the room, then lay down and waited for results.
The first result was not relief from pain, but a call from
Paul Fallon, who instructed me to immediately write an
article describing the launch party and the turkey fire, in-
cluding the turkey recipe.

"Are you out of your mind? I can be charged with first-
degree assault, and you want me to call attention to that
disaster? I won't do it."

"Carolyn, that wasn't a request. That was an order.
Loretta and I agree that I can sell the rights to thousands of
newspapers and magazines, considering that the party's received nationwide coverage. The articles will help sell
thousands of books. I want it faxed to my office by five tomorrow afternoon, so start writing immediately and make
it charming, seriously charming." Then he hung up, and I
was left to wonder what anyone would find charming
about ruined turkeys and a young Chinese woman in a
coma. I told Luz what he'd said.

"Well, that's the third annoying male we've had to deal

with this afternoon. But he's probably right. People will read anything, so get out your computer."

"My tummy hurts."

"Oh, don't be a crybaby, Carolyn. Take some more Tums."

18
The Deadbeat Gourmet

Luz

Carolyn was still bitching about her stomachache and what a shame it was to visit Daniel when she wasn't well enough to enjoy it. I made her take another round of Tums after we'd dressed up in our evening gowns, and wouldn't you know? Allison What's-her-name, the frigid blond fashion plate, was wearing a short black suit with a few sparkles and four-inch high heels when we got there. She looked us over with raised eyebrows, plucked and penciled, and said, "Goodness, this isn't a night at the opera. I didn't mean you needed to come absolutely formal."

Narrowing her eyes, Carolyn plunked herself down in the chair the waiter was holding. "We're wearing flats, Allison. How casual did you expect us to come?"

"My," said Allison, "aren't we touchy this evening? Feeling a bit nervous about the book signing, by any chance?"

Looked like a bitch-slapping evening to me, and you should have seen the menu. I had no idea what half the stuff meant. As for the restaurant, it was downright intimidating—very elegant, very hushed, and crammed with waiters. The head guy was hanging over us, discussing the specials with Allison and acting like she was the queen of

England, while other guys, one for each of us, all of them in tuxes, were putting our napkins in our laps and filling water goblets. What the hell was I going to order? I wondered, remembering with nostalgia our comfy lunch with DeShawn and Abe.

"I can see the menu is beyond your understanding, Lieutenant. Let me recommend the Pennsylvania Squab Duo for your main course," said Allison.

Before I could defend myself by choosing something else, Carolyn said, "Luz hates Brussels sprouts and probably won't like the foie gras." Then she turned to the maitre d' and announced that she'd eaten Southern Indian food for lunch and needed something very soothing for dinner, something on the three-course prix fixe menu.

"Really, Carolyn," said Allison, "don't feel that you have to skimp, especially not at Daniel. That would be an insult to my taste and to the chef."

"Luz, you'd probably like the veal dish," Carolyn continued. "Roasted tenderloin, braised cheeks, sweetbread ziti, and pine nut porcini, and maybe the Moscovy Duck as an appetizer, just to pacify Allison."

With no better ideas myself, except that I didn't want to eat anything Allison suggested, especially Brussels sprouts, which taste like a baby cabbage soaked in really nasty cough syrup, I said, "Sounds good."

Then Carolyn looked at the maitre d' and said, "I put myself in your hands. Anything you can do to charm my taste buds and eliminate my pain will, I assure you, receive kind words in my column. I am, I'm sorry to admit, the infamous Incendiary Gourmet."

"Ah madam, I am so sorry for your ill fortune, and I do read your column. Quite charming. Our chef and I shall confer and choose a meal that will overcome even the food of Southern India, which was never meant for a delicate stomach."

Allison, who looked really pissed off because the head guy was smiling at Carolyn, immediately began to order for herself, gushing over every dish, and shooting Carolyn black looks. Then she ordered wine, and the maitre d' suggested other wines for the two of us. More black looks. Evidently she'd picked out something that would taste good with her food and crappy with ours. Finally she told Carolyn that no one would think of eating terribly spicy food before a dinner at a restaurant known for the subtlety of its dishes, then hissed in an undertone what bad taste Carolyn had shown by mentioning her column.

Carolyn ignored the bad-taste crack, and said, "Never having had Southern Indian food, I had no idea what I was getting into. Besides it was Kosher, and I didn't think Kosher food was spicy, while I did think, after living several years in El Paso, that nothing could be spicier than Mexican food. Luz didn't get indigestion."

Allison rolled her eyes as if we were both too tacky for words. A man who looked like trouble circled the guy guarding the door and headed for our table as our appetizers were being served. "Mrs. Blue? May I have a few words with you? I'd like to ask . . ."

He had that pushy look of a reporter, and Carolyn wasn't wearing her earflaps. She'd stuffed the hat into the pocket of her coat before we walked into the restaurant. "Get lost," I said.

"Really, Luz, I do believe this is Mr. Braeton of the *Times*. One does not tell the *Times* to *get lost*," Allison simpered.

Carolyn beckoned to a waiter and murmured that she had been enjoying this lovely soup the chef had chosen for her when some gentleman, unknown to her, had tried to join their party.

The *Times* reporter was politely ushered out, Allison looked ready to chew glass, and the maitre d' hurried over to inquire if there was a problem. "How could there be a problem when I'm eating this marvelous soup with its subtle hint of tarragon. I feel better already," Carolyn smiled sweetly at him.

"I am delighted to hear it, madam."

He glided away while she looked Allison straight in the

eye and asked, "Now how would someone from the *Times* know I'd be here tonight? I certainly didn't tell anyone."

Allison shrugged and pushed her half-eaten appetizer away. "I'm sure I can't say, but the newspapers do love a scandal. Perhaps you should have spoken to him. You could use a little good press for a change."

I had eaten up my duck, which was almost raw, for Christ's sake, and tasted orangey. Still, it wasn't bad. I just hoped it hadn't had bird flu. Moscovy? Was that Russian? And didn't they have wild birds dropping dead of flu over there? Or maybe that was Turkey.

The appetizers were cleared, and the main courses arrived. Carolyn received some kind of fish. God knows what weird thing Allison had ordered. I didn't ask. And my veal and sweetbreads were set down as gently as if the waiter were serving live baby. The two gourmets I was with probably thought I didn't know I was going to eat baby cow, but I'm not squeamish, and I love sweetbreads and pine nuts. None of it tasted like you'd expect it to taste, but it was good, and I was hungry, so I dug in and drank my wine while the waiters kept my glass filled. Good thing I've got a head for alcohol. Carolyn was still on her first glass. Maybe her stomach still hurt, and she was taking notes, which Allison complained about.

"It's so gauche to make notes on your food."

"Tell me, Allison, where were you the day my turkeys were tampered with?" Carolyn asked.

"Are you accusing me of something, Carolyn?"

"Is there something to accuse you of, Allison? Were you in the building before the party? Or in the kitchen?" Carolyn was cutting her fish into dainty little pieces and smiling dreamily over each bite.

"I was not in the building, and I do not cook," came the angry reply. "I'm the editor of *Glamorous Gourmet*, not some little housewife trying her hand at gourmet dishes."

"Goodness, you're very rude, Allison. I wasn't accusing you. I was going to ask if you'd seen anything that might help my investigation. Would you care to try my fish? It's quite lovely."

"I do not eat off other people's plates," said Allison huffily and took her cell phone from her handbag. "I have a call." She rose and walked away.

"What a bitch," I said. "I'll call Abe and have him check for her on the sign-in sheet." I made the call, and sure enough, Allison had been at Pettigrew's the afternoon of the turkey roasting. "Maybe she and Jack Armstrong got together to screw things up for you."

"Now there's an interesting thought. Would you like to try my fish? No? It's really delicious, and I shouldn't eat too much. You wouldn't think Jack and Allison would be compatible, but then I've heard that crime makes for strange bedfellows."

"The idea of the two of them together in bed is more than strange." I grinned. "And where is Miss Bitchy? She's talking a long time. Probably trying to explain to the *Times* why she called them over and you wouldn't talk to them."

"Probably," Carolyn agreed. "Although I didn't even hear her phone ring."

She sure was agreeable for someone with a stomachache and a seriously nasty hostess. Maybe the chef had slipped her some tranquilizers. The waiter came up to take our plates and leave the dessert menus, but before he could slip unobtrusively away, Carolyn asked him to check on Miss Peabody, who had been missing for at least twenty minutes at that point.

He asked the maitre d', who sent him back with the information that she'd had to leave because of an emergency, but had sent her apologies and advice that we stay to enjoy our dinner.

"Did she pay the bill?" I asked suspiciously.

"I don't believe she did, ma'am." Now the waiter looked worried. Probably thought we couldn't come up with the cash or credit. I sure as hell couldn't.

Carolyn ordered two desserts: a hot chocolate soufflé with pistachio ice cream and a something or other with hazelnut bitter chocolate ganache and cinnamon cappuccino and java coffee ice cream. She knew I liked chocolate. "We'll share, unless you're averse to eating off someone else's plate," she said smiling.

"You realize she's a deadbeat. We're stuck with the bill, and you've just ordered dessert. Unless we can convince the restaurant to mail her the bill, we're screwed. And with your stomachache, should you be eating stuff with coffee in it?"

Carolyn gave me that loopy smile again and said, "Number one, I ordered the prix fixe, so the desserts come with it. Number two, I'm going to have to stay up writing half the night no matter how I feel, so I'll need the mixture of chocolate and coffee to keep me awake, and number three, I'll pay the bill, but I'll tell Mr. Pettigrew about this and ask if perhaps Allison meant for the publishing house to pay, knowing that we wouldn't ordinarily have spent so much."

"Great idea, Caro. Sure you can afford this? It could be well over three hundred dollars."

"And it should be worthwhile, given what a horrible impression Allison will leave when I'm through with her. Imagine a knowledgeable New Yorker leaving a simple, innocent El Pasoan like me with a huge bill the likes of which I've never seen, in an expensive restaurant to which she invited me. Very, very impolite, even unkind, don't you think?"

Laughing our heads off, we carved the desserts in two, exchanged halves, and dug in. I'm not sure whether it was the desserts or the thought of what we were going to do to the Glamorous Gourmet that made everything taste so good.

Our waiter was hurt that we hadn't asked him to split the desserts for us. Carolyn told him that no one offered that amenity in El Paso, except occasionally to senior citizens, who couldn't eat a whole helping of anything, and she could hardly wait to write her column about how wonderful the service at Daniel was. She even asked the waiter's name and wrote on a pad of paper a little note of thanks and praise to the chef, which she asked the waiter to deliver.

As we left, she took the maitre d's hand and told him how surprised she'd been when Miss Peabody, who had invited us here, had left without paying the bill, but that it had been worth every penny we'd spent.

Take that, Allison, I thought. *Now your name is mud in this fancy restaurant.* "Maybe New Yorkers will start calling her the Deadbeat Gourmet behind her back," I whispered to Carolyn as we waited for our coats.

"Wouldn't that be fun?" Carolyn giggled, and we took the subway home, two hicks from El Paso.

19

Apology from a Feminist

Carolyn

I **did not** view with pleasure the writing I had to do because I had no idea what I wanted to say. The truth was that I didn't want to say anything. I wanted to go to bed and sleep so I wouldn't have to think about the turkeys and the book signing tomorrow and the huge bill I'd been stuck with tonight. The two $95 prix fixes and Allison's $132 meal, plus the glasses of wine at $12 a piece, plus tip had come to over $400. Maybe it wasn't worth that much to get even with her. Jason certainly wouldn't think so. And I should be calling him, explaining what was going on here.

Before I could decide what to do, the phone rang. It was my mother-in-law, the last person with whom I wanted to talk. "Carolyn, I finally got hold of you. It's Vera. First I wanted to thank you for giving my name to your publisher. The idea of writing a new book is just what I needed, just what the women's movement needs. Women have given up fighting for their rights, and this is absolutely the wrong time to do that. So I owe you my thanks."

"You're welcome, Vera." I really meant that, as long as she wasn't here in New York.

"By the way, Lavinia Haverford has invited me to stay at their place. What a piece of luck that she's a feminist.

She has all sorts of plans for my visit, not that I can stay long. I have my classes in Chicago, but now I'm sure I'll feel more enthusiasm for them."

"Um-hmmm." Why was she telling me all this? She'd been so hateful on the cruise, accusing me of having a fling with a Welsh thriller writer, and I hadn't heard from her since, not even the usual distasteful birthday present. "When will you be arriving?"

"I'm here now, calling from my bedroom in her New York mansion. Lavinia wants you and your friend Luz to come over for dinner while—"

"Can't do it, Vera. I'm all booked up."

"Nonsense, one night—"

"Dinner out and book signing tomorrow night—"

"You're still angry about the cruise," she said accusingly. "I apologize. I was depressed after the heart attack, and I foolishly refused to take the pills that would have—"

Now I really was angry. "Depression or even a heart attack doesn't explain why you accused me of adultery."

"I said I was sorry, Carolyn. You really have to come to dinner at Lavinia's. It's in our honor, yours and mine. And she says she has a big surprise for us afterward. The woman's mad for Carolyn Heilbrun, who was a friend of mine. Maybe she's going to give us both complete first-edition sets of Heilbrun's books. I hope you've read them. *The Gift of Years: Life After Sixty.* It's an inspiring book."

"I'm not sixty," I replied, feeling sulky.

"All right. I realize you're touchy about your age, Carolyn, but there's nothing wrong with age, as long as you're still alive. I can't imagine why she killed herself. Only in her seventies. No doubt she had much more to say. And of course the surprise isn't necessarily Heilbrun books, or any feminist books, for that matter. Not that some of them wouldn't do you a world of good. If you like, I can lend you one of mine."

While Vera went on talking, it occurred to me what the surprise was: a séance. Lavinia had thought Vera would love to attend a séance calling up some dead anarchist. Suddenly I grinned and agreed that Luz and I would attend the dinner. The thought of my mother-in-law having a séance sprung on her was just too good to miss.

"If I'm not in jail, I'll come," I agreed. Then of course I had to explain about the turkeys and all the fuss and my investigation and the fact that Detectives Worski and Benitez wanted to arrest Petey, my editor, and me for terrorizing the streets of New York.

"Benitez and Worski, you say? Let me talk to them. You saved me in San Francisco from that ridiculous murder charge; it's the least I can do—"

"Stay away from them, Vera. You'll just make things worse, and I don't need any more trouble. If you want me to come to that dinner—"

"All right, all right, Carolyn. Seven o'clock. Day after tomorrow." After she provided the address, I settled into my writing with a smile. Vera at a séance. It would be priceless. Luz thought so, too, when I told her, and the idea of a dinner that neither of us would be expected to pay for made her even happier. Poor Luz. That $400-plus bill had shaken her up more than it had me.

I took out my laptop and began to type.

When I was first married, my aunt from St. Louis gave me this recipe, as she did every niece and nephew in the family who married. She said she thought she'd clipped it from the *New York Herald-Tribune* in the late 1950s, and she recommended it highly for those who had the time and patience to prepare it. I have used it for dinner parties and for family Thanksgivings, although not every year. Then I put it into my column, and it was very popular among a new generation of gourmets.

As you may have read in the newspapers, when my publisher gave a party in New York for my first book, *Eating Out in the Big Easy*, this turkey recipe caused, with help from someone who wished me ill, a disaster in the streets of Lower Manhattan. I was called the In-

cendiary Gourmet and accused of being a terrorist,
and all because my editor thought that flambéing the
turkeys would add extra panache to the event.

I gave in, reluctantly, and I must admit, the first
turkey I flambéed was very pretty, with blue fire spurt-
ing from the bowl on top and running down the sides
in a volcano effect—very pretty until it spat fire, flamed
toward the ceiling, and caused panic among the
guests, not to mention frightening me half to death. I
was, at this time, flambéing a second turkey and
dropped the pitcher of what I thought was cognac. The
flames and sparks from the first turkey set fire to the
second and the soaked tablecloth.

Employees hoisted the flaming birds on forks and
threw them over the balcony. In the street below a car
blew up, and when a turkey hit a windshield, accidents occurred causing injuries, one very severe. On
our floor, the guests escaped to the balcony, while employees and firemen put out the fire. The police arrived. Various federal agencies subsequently accused
me of terrorism, of creating an international incident,
of traumatizing the citizens of New York, of arson, first-
degree assault, and goodness knows what else.

And I was innocent. Someone had substituted a
powerful accelerant for my innocuous flambéing
brandy. So take my advice. Don't flambé this or any
other turkey you may cook. No good can come of it.

The Fateful *Herald-Tribune* Turkey
Do not flambé this turkey!

- Purchase a *16- to 22-pound turkey, frozen and
  dressed*, and follow the instructions for defrosting it.

- Rub your turkey both outside and inside with *salt
  and pepper*

- Pour *4 cups water* into a pan and add *chopped*

neck, liver, heart, and gizzard from the turkey, 1 bay leaf, 1 teaspoon paprika, 1 clove garlic, ½ teaspoon coriander, and salt to taste. Allow to simmer while you make the dressing.

- In a bowl put 1 diced orange and 1 diced apple, 1 large can crushed pineapple, 1 can drained water chestnuts, 3 tablespoons chopped, preserved ginger, and rind of ½ lemon, grated.

- In second bowl place 2 teaspoons mild mustard, 2 teaspoons caraway seed, 3 teaspoons celery seed, 2 teaspoons poppy seed, 3 teaspoons oregano, 1 large bay leaf, well-crushed, 1 teaspoon black pepper, ½ teaspoon mace, 4 tablespoons parsley, well chopped, 5 cloves garlic, finely minced, 4 headless cloves, well chopped, ½ teaspoon turmeric, 4 large well-chopped onions, 6 stalks celery, well chopped, ½ teaspoon summer savory, 1 tablespoon poultry seasoning, and ½ teaspoon marjoram.

- In a third bowl place 3 packages bakery bread crumbs, ¾ pound ground veal, ¼ pound ground fresh pork, ¼ pound butter, and all turkey fat you can remove from the turkey, rendered.

- Mix all bowls together vigorously and completely with your hands. Then fluff and toss so that the dressing is no longer a sticky blob.

- Stuff dressing in turkey, stuff neck and tie off, skewer other end and tie strings, set oven on high, and put bird in a rack, breast-side down.

- In a cup mix 2 egg yolks, 1 teaspoon mild mustard, 1 clove minced garlic, 1 tablespoon onion juice, ½ teaspoon salt, 2 pinches cayenne pepper, 1 teaspoon *lemon juice*, and enough *sifted flour* to make a thick paste. Have a pastry brush handy.

- Put turkey into hot oven to brown all over. Remove turkey. Turn oven to 325 degrees. Paint turkey all over with paste and return to oven. Let paste set (several minutes) and remove turkey from oven. Paint every inch of turkey again, return to oven to set, and continue until paste is gone.

- Add *1 cup cider* to simmering giblet gravy, remove from heat, stir well, and keep warm on stovetop to baste turkey every 15 minutes.

- After bird has cooked until last half hour, turn back side up for last ½ hour. The turkey should cook 4 to 5½ hours depending on weight.

- Remove turkey, now black, from oven and tweeze off paste coating to reveal golden brown, delicious meat. Remove dressing from bird. Skim and thicken gravy. Enjoy. *But do not flambé this turkey!*

Carolyn Blue,
"Have Fork, Will Travel,"
Boston Clarion

20
Interrogation Without a Lawyer

Carolyn

Having worked on my article until one-thirty, I woke up exhausted when the phone rang. A strange female voice said, "You poor woman! What a thing to happen, and on your special night! Is not every book receives a book launch, Signora Blue. And now the poor Chinese girl is dying from your turkeys. What a thing to happen! And poor Signor Pettigrew. He worries about the lawsuits, no doubt."

"Who is this?" I asked sharply, thinking some nosy reporter was trying to catch me early in the morning when my guard was down. I'd had flaming-turkey dreams again last night.

"Is Annunziata Randatto. We meet before the . . . fire. I wake up thinking of you this morning and decide a home-cooked Italian meal is a fine thing to cheer you up. You come over to Bensonhurst, and I cook you the best Sicilian feast you ever taste."

"That's so kind," I said in a wobbly voice. Home-cooked Italian sounded marvelously soothing. But still. "I don't know how to get to Bensonhurst, Mrs. . . . ah . . . Signora Randatto." Wasn't that where Abraham Cratchett lived with his mother? If we were going to interview the felons and other temporary workers at his office after I finished my article, I could just pop over to the signora's for lunch. It wouldn't hurt to find out where she'd been on turkey day.

"I put my granddaughter on telephone with directions. So easy on subway. There is a subway near your hotel? Yes?"

"I think so. I'm on Broadway, uptown, but Mrs. Randatto—"

"You come and bring your friend, the policewoman. We have a nice lunch, some good red wine. Now I put on granddaughter." I could hear her shouting for someone named Rosaria. Then a girl with no accent whatever—Mrs. Randatto had a delightful Italian accent—gave me directions that seemed to go on forever. I accepted them without mentioning that I might be in Bensonhurst anyway. I'd have to find out.

"Who the hell are you talking to at this hour?" asked Luz when I'd hung up. "And when did you get to bed?" Her black-and-gray hair was mussed, her eyes puffy, her expression irritated.

"Signora Randatto," I replied. "She's invited us to lunch. Maybe you don't remember her. She's the—"

"Yeah, yeah. The old Italian lady in the black dress at your flaming turkey party. Built like a friggin' tank."

"She's probably a wonderful cook. She's had lots of cookbooks published."

"Who am I to pass up free food?" Luz looked at the clock and cursed. "We better get cracking. First we need to call Abe. You do it." Luz creaked out of bed and headed for the bathroom.

I sighed and took out my cell phone, but before I could pull up the number, the hotel phone rang again. This time, Detective Worski was on the other end. "Well, finally," he said. "I'll expect you down here within the hour."

"I can't do it. Sorry, Detective. I have to proof an article for the newspaper syndicate, then have lunch with a cookbook writer, followed by an appointment with the private detective, so there's no way—"

"No problem. I'll get a warrant for your arrest," said the detective.

I sighed. Obviously the article would have to replace Mr. Cratchett. "I'll be there in an hour if I can finish with time for lunch and an afternoon for working on my article."

"Sure," said Detective Worski. "If we don't arrest you while you're here."

"You are *so* mean." I hung up and told Luz when she emerged wrapped in a towel, that I had to go to the police station.

"Okay, but this morning we're eating the free breakfast, and I'm going with you to the station after I've had enough coffee to drown the headache I got from the wine and Allison Pissface." I reminded her that the name was Peabody, thanked her for offering to see the detectives with me, and tactfully refrained from protesting her language.

"Yeah, yeah, and I appreciate your getting me invited along for lunch." She picked up the telephone to call Mr. Cratchett and explain our problem, and I went to the closet to choose something appropriate for both Detective Worski and a visit to the home of the famous Italian grandmother. What kind of house would she have? A historic brownstone? A condo? Considering how popular her recipes were, she probably made a lot of money. I had several of her books myself. Too bad I'd never make money on my own book.

Then I remembered: I was having a book signing at a big New York bookstore tonight. No one would come, and I'd be sitting there all by myself, feeling sad and self-conscious. It was going to be absolutely awful. I'd have gone straight home if I hadn't been ordered to stay in New York City until the police put me in jail or found someone else to blame for my turkey disaster. If only Mr. Li's granddaughter would come out of her coma and recover.

"Abe is really ticked off. He says he and DeShawn will interview the felons today, but we'd better show up tomorrow to help with the others," Luz informed me when I was dressed.

The bodyguards were back, but peeled off when we arrived at the police station. They probably thought I'd be safe there. "You have a new suit," I said to Detective Worski after we'd climbed the stairs to the detectives' enclave. At least it was new since I first met him several years ago. "It's very handsome, Detective." We were in a ratty old building that needed a better heating system. Neither Luz nor I had taken off our overcoats, and I was surprised that he had.

"Hey, Benitez, get in here," he yelled and then asked if we wanted donuts.

"No, thank you," I replied. "We just had breakfast." I remembered the nasty donuts the last time I'd visited his station house. Before I could protest, he was pouring coffee, and Luz was accepting a donut.

Detective Benitez arrived, wearing the tightest black slacks and turtleneck I'd ever seen, and although she was slender, she had ample breasts and a large rear end, which the pants emphasized. And she was scowling at me, as if I were some hardened criminal she hoped to arrest. Detective Worski smoothed the lapels of his suit, looking pleased by my compliment. "I got married. The new wife bought me this suit for the wedding, and my kids from my first marriage gave me the tie. Spiffy, huh?"

"I wouldn't tie that rag around the neck of my dog," said his partner. "And who has his first wife as his best man? Never saw a weirder wedding in my life."

"That's cause you're Puerto Rican," retorted Worski. "What the hell do you people do when you get married? Shimmy under sticks and get drunk on rum?"

"That's the Haitians. And they're black, man."

I was taken aback by the conversation, although admittedly the tie was dreadful. Pink dogs and purple birds scrambled all over it. Maybe his children didn't like him, or perhaps they were very young and had bought it at a

Disney store. "I believe you wanted to interview me, Detective, but first let me ask: Have you located the chef? And what did the fire department find inside the turkey? Also have you thought to interview people who worked in the kitchen that day? They may have seen who put flammable materials in or on my turkeys."

"We're the ones who ask the questions, and your friend can wait for you downstairs." Detective Benitez had returned to scowling at me.

"Absolutely not," I retorted. "We have been and will continue to investigate, so Luz needs to know everything I hear."

"Look, if you want a lawyer—"

"I don't need a lawyer. I haven't done anything wrong."

"I stay, or we both leave," said Luz.

"What the hell." Detective Worski stood up and indicated that we should all follow him to the interrogation room, which was not intended for four people. Detective Benitez leaned against a wall, and Luz complained that her knees were jammed against the table.

"First off, Mrs. Blue, you're in serious trouble. The Li kid has about a hundred broken bones, but the worst of it is, she's in a coma, and nobody expects her to regain consciousness. Even if she does, there'll probably be brain damage."

My heart ached to hear this more detailed explanation of the poor girl's prognosis.

"As for you, you're facing the same charges that turkey tossing kid on Long Island faced: first-degree assault, reckless endangerment, and criminal mischief. Unless you stole the turkey, you don't have to worry about possession of stolen property, but if the Li kid dies—well—"

"But I'm not responsible for any of these things," I cried. "And I intend to find out who is. I've already told you that. So, Detective Worski, since you don't have the actual remaining turkey, I've brought the recipe for you. I made the dressing, the paste to bake on the skin, and the basting sauce myself, so anything that's found on or in the bird or on what's left on the tablecloth, even in the roasting pans, if they're still in the kitchen, and that isn't in the recipe, will be a clue."

"I'll be damned," said Detective Worski, who had been looking over the recipe I'd handed him.

"There's no need to swear," I replied.

"Yeah, I remember how you didn't like swearing. My mother was that way. But this is the same recipe she got from her mother and made one Thanksgiving."

"Really? My aunt gave it to me. She got it from the *New York Herald-Tribune*, which is no longer in existence. She said that was a great shame. Anyway, it's a lovely turkey, isn't it?"

"We all hated it," said Detective Worski. "The dressing is full of weird stuff, and the gravy's the pits. She never fixed it again. Didn't speak to any of us for three days because the recipe had been such a pain in the ass to make, but damned if we didn't have to eat every last bite of it. That took the whole three days."

I could see from the corner of my eye that Luz was laughing, and I could hear that the female detective was, too. "The readers of my column loved it," I said coldly.

Worski passed my recipe to Benitez, who looked it over and said, "Jesus! Look how long this sucker is!"

Then, obviously having paid no attention to my defense, they asked me what I had against my publisher—I didn't mention the long delay in publishing my book; whether my chemist husband had suggested things in the recipe—which was nonsense, of course; where I'd been after I left the publisher's kitchen, and who could vouch for me—that would be Luz, with whom I'd taken the subway in the wrong direction on our first try, which neither of the detectives seemed to believe; what I had really been doing during the time I claimed to be lost and afterward—purchasing an evening dress from my agent's uncle, both of whom, with Luz, could vouch for that period of my day; Loretta and Uncle Bernie's addresses and telephone numbers—I had to get out my address book and write those down; and so many other things, not the least of which was: Had I been trying to kill anyone in particular down on the street? I was quite exhausted by the time the interrogation was over. Luz then started an argument with Detective Worski over his "stupid" idea that I, who had not thrown the birds onto the street, had dreamed up a plot to kill someone with a flaming turkey.

"So she used the fat guy in velvet and the blond goth to do her dirty work? That makes it conspiracy to commit murder," said Detective Benitez smugly.

"What a load of crap!" snarled Luz, and pulled me out of my chair. "You don't have anything on Carolyn, and we've got a date for lunch in Bensonhurst."

"Why Bensonhurst?" asked Detective Benitez. "What a dump! Bunch of old wooden houses, with tacky shops down a street in the middle. You're not gonna find fancy food there."

"Hey, I got family in Bensonhurst," protested Detective Worski.

We left them to their argument and headed for the door.

21

In the Parlor of a Sicilian *Abuela*

Luz

Because Carolyn had these directions from the Italian grandmother's granddaughter, she thought maybe we could find our way there even if we were starting from a different place. "I've already been to frigging Bensonhurst. Let me find it, and then we'll look at her directions." I discovered a Spanish speaker behind a bulletproof-glass ticket cage in the subway station and got directions from him. Carolyn sulked while we climbed down more stairs, and my knees started to ache. I wouldn't be doing any volunteer detecting this afternoon. I'd go straight back to the hotel with Carolyn and lie down with capsaicin cream rubbed into my knees.

I don't know what Benitez had against Bensonhurst. Once we got off the main drag and followed the directions on the paper, we saw some more neat old houses with fancy woodwork but better paint jobs than Cratchett's place. Some had yards with grass, bushes, flowers—even in November with the wind like to freeze my nose off—and shrines to the Virgin. Now there was a surprise. Catholics with shrines in their yards in New York City—well, this was Brooklyn, not Manhattan, but still . . .

I was limping, and Carolyn had forgiven me for not

letting her be the trailblazer by the time we got to the Italian *abuela*'s house, which was attached to other houses, most of them brick with tiny fenced yards and steps up to tiny porches. There was a whole street of them; some even had little iron balconies on the second floor, and all those houses contained members of the Randatto family, although I didn't find out about that until later. The next big surprise was the old lady. She came to the door herself, wearing cropped striped pants, no socks, and sneakers. Her legs looked like a road map of Italy. Wow! I'd expected another black dress and grandma shoes, so my mouth dropped open. Carolyn elbowed me while we both stood on her doorstep with our teeth chattering from the cold.

"Ah, you are here at last," said Annunziata Randatto. "I was afraid *la polizia* had put you in their jail." She laughed heartily and dragged us inside. "And you are so cold. New York is not Sicilia, sad to say. Rosaria, are you cooking? They have come."

The last was shouted at a skinny kid with long black hair, who was hovering in the hall. Pretty girl, but she didn't look very happy as she scuttled through a swinging door that let out a whoosh of great food smells. And the place was hot, really hot. First, I'd been freezing. Now I couldn't wait to get out of my fifteen-dollar St. Ignacio thrift-shop coat, which I'd bought back home. One of the good Catholic ladies who put in time there told me it had been donated by a guy who came down from the north to run a *maquila* over in Juarez, and they'd had it for three years because no one needed a coat like that in El Paso. Carolyn had said it was camel hair and complimented me on it. I didn't tell her it was a man's coat I got cheap.

"Signora Randatto, it was so kind of you to invite us," Carolyn was saying while she reluctantly gave up her own coat. Hers was left over from when she'd lived in the Midwest.

"Is nothing," said the old lady and served us cups of *caffè correcto*, or words to that effect. Really strong coffee with, probably, 300 proof alcohol in it. Carolyn coughed. I managed not to, and the old lady beamed at us. *"Espresso con grappa.* My son Luigi imports grappa. Good, *sì?* Warms the insides." She drank hers down and patted her big stomach. The woman looked like a rhinoceros in capris. My grappa burned all the way down to my knees, and they were happy about the whole thing.

"Very tasty. And so warming," said Carolyn, looking as if she might faint.

Café Correcto is tasty, but it's half grappa. Unless you have a good head for alcohol, don't have more than one. I do wish someone had told me that when my hostess in Brooklyn kept offering me seconds.

Caffé Correcto

- Prepare *espresso* in your machine. Powdered espresso and hot water is *not* the same, according to aficionados.

- Optional: Place *1 teaspoon sugar* in bottom of double espresso cup or double shot glass.

- Pour *one shot of espresso* into each cup.

- Pour *one shot of grappa* on top of espresso.

- Top with whipped cream (if you're not Italian).

Carolyn Blue,
"Have Fork, Will Travel,"
Philadelphia Telegraph

"So what do *la polizia* say to you? So much fuss for just a kitchen accident. Should be no problem, I think."

"One person in a coma, several injured on the street. Cars trashed. They're investigating," I reminded her and accepted another *caffè correcto*. The cups were really little.

"Ah, but you are *polizia*, too." The *abuela* nodded wisely. "You would not see is very foolish."

"That's just what I said," Carolyn agreed. "And obviously someone did something dangerous to my turkeys, but it wasn't me. I'll just have to find out who did it. I suspect the chef."

"Franz?" Signora Randatto nodded. "German. They are bad people. It took the mafiosi to get them out of Italy in the war. Everyone remembers the Americans bring in la Cosa Nostra, Sicilians and their American cousins, to do the job. This is the old war. In the forties, sì?"

"So you have Mafia connections, Signora?" I asked.

The old lady glared at me from her gigantic chair with a whole wall full of pictures behind her, guys with mustaches, women with big busts and pulled-back hair, kids dressed in a century's worth of styles. "The Randattos are never Mafia. We come here to get away from them, those thieves and murderers. Then they follow us." She made a spitting sound. Rosaria came in, still scowling, and announced lunch.

Fun family, I thought and followed her to the kitchen. We'd passed a dining room with virgins, saints, and grisly crucifixes on the walls and a table big enough to seat all of Bensonhurst. I guess only the family got to eat in the dining room. Rosaria served us at a table that looked like someone had been hacking up whole hogs on it, but did we eat! First we had cauliflower with *perciatelli*, which is big pasta shaped like long, thin tubes. If you'd asked me what I was eating, I couldn't have said. It sure as hell wasn't Mexican food, but it was the only time I ever thought cauliflower tasted good, which was because it had all sorts of tastes that *weren't* cauliflower. Carolyn seemed to know what was in it. She was talking about garlic and sardines and other stuff while Mrs. Randatto kept interrupting her by saying, *"Sì, sì,"* and asking what the police were going to do about the case.

"Not arrest me, I hope," Carolyn said glumly.

"They're going after someone for aggravated assault," I added, "murder if the Chinese kid dies, and the fire department is talking about arson." Next came the stuffed squid. Christ! Can you imagine eating something that has all those wiggling arms? Of course the squid were dead, not wiggling, but I didn't appreciate being told by the granddaughter that the tentacles had been chopped up and put in the stuffing. Not that they didn't taste good, and they'd been cooked in tomato sauce, so I just had to keep my mind off the frigging tentacles.

Signora Randatto, who kept making her poor granddaughter jump up from the table and bring something else to eat, accompanied the squid and zucchini—the squash had raisins and vinegar, as far as I could tell—with the opinion that if it hadn't been some bad cognac—Carolyn got upset about that—it was probably Franz, the German. But if it wasn't him, it was probably Jack Armstrong.

We both blinked at that one, since we suspected him ourselves. He hadn't been at the party, which was suspicious, didn't we think? And he was a vegetarian who wrote diet cookbooks. Signora Randatto thought diet cookbooks were the work of the devil. Furthermore, he was a man who played practical jokes, so the flaming turkeys were probably his idea of a joke. I could see that Carolyn was taking all this in, probably planning to call Worski and give him more information on the vegetarian.

We drank red wine with the meal, sweet wine with the fried cottage cheese donuts, which she called *Frittelle di Ricotta*, and then we were invited back to the wall-of-mustaches room for biscotti and more spiked coffee while Rosaria got to clean up and do the dishes. I figured one of us better stay sober or we'd never get back to the hotel. Hell, we'd never even find our way to the subway station, so I offered to help the kid. *Abuela* didn't like that much, but I insisted, so off Carolyn went for biscotti. I had that once and nearly broke a tooth on it until Carolyn told me I should dunk it in coffee. Go figure. Hard to believe

Carolyn would approve of dunking anything in anything. She'd given me the evil eye when I dunked my donut in Worski's interrogation room.

Over the dirty dishes, I got an earful from Rosaria. Of course, I told her she was a great cook, and she said she hated cooking. Her grandmother had made her stay home from school to cook the meal, and she'd had an important math test. She loved math. She wanted to go to college and become a big wheel on Wall Street, but her grandmother, who made all that money from the cookbooks, forced Rosaria to do the cooking and probably would for the next fifty years. Her grandmother ran everyone in the family— sons, daughters, cousins, grandkids—and Nonna thought all women were supposed to cook. It was God's plan for women—food and babies. The poor kid burst into tears.

I told all this to Carolyn once the Sicilian *abuela* announced that it was time for her nap and we headed home. Reasonably snockered, Carolyn just giggled. The Chinamen were still tailing us, and people were staring at them. Not that there weren't Asian stores in Bensonhurst, but the store guys weren't wearing suits like Carolyn's guys. I kept looking back at them, and one of them kept looking back at the Randatto house, where Rosaria was standing on the doorstep. What was that about?

Then I spotted a shop with a big picture of Rolando Villazon in the window. We had to stop. I'd never hear the end of it from Mom, who'd first decided I should take a tape recorder to the opera to tape the great Mexican tenor. Turns out that's a no-no. I bought a CD. Carolyn bought two, and the Chinese guys didn't buy any. "Maybe they don't like opera," I whispered to Carolyn.

"Small wonder." She giggled. "Chinese opera is *awful*."

Thank God we got seats on the subway. My roommate would never have managed to stay upright all the way to the hotel. The Chinamen had figured out that she was in bad shape and were sneering, which seemed to be their natural expression. Great bodyguards. I didn't believe it, but I wasn't sure what was going on with them. Maybe they'd just liked blond hair, but now that she was wearing the earflap hat, they should have given up.

So I'd had to get Carolyn sobered up in time to finish her article before five, get my knees in shape for the Asian Fusion, whatever that was—another subway trip, I figured—and for the book signing. Carolyn had promised she'd get a chair for me at the signing table and advised me to bring a book along because no one was going to show up. Because she was so wigged out about the signing, I felt sorry for her, but sorrier for me. Pain is worse than being a book-signing wallflower, no matter what she said.

Home-cooked Sicilian food is so delicious, even if the hostess plies you with grappa in the parlor after lunch and gives you bad advice about book signings. Here are two recipes you can try in your own kitchen, especially if you can get fresh squid in your supermarket. Sicily is an island in the Mediterranean. Not all of us are fortunate enough to have such easy access to fresh seafood, but then not all of us like squid, especially encountered on a beach. Does that happen? Not to me, but as a child I once worried about it during a seaside vacation that included a mean male cousin.

Sicilian Tube Pasta and Cauliflower

- Soak ¼ cup raisins in warm water for 20 minutes.

- Cut a large head of cauliflower florets into bite-size pieces.

- Steam cauliflower six minutes and set aside while bringing a 6 quart pan of salted water to boil for pasta.

- Rough chop 1 large onion and cook in ¼ cup olive oil over medium heat until beginning to brown. Add 3 cloves finely minced garlic and 1 can (8 *anchovies)* rinsed and chopped. Break apart anchovies with a spoon.

- Cook *1 pound perciatelli* (also called bucatini; use green linguini if preferred) in the boiling, salted water 10 to 12 minutes, or until al dente, drain in colander, and pour into serving bowl.

- Pat dry drained raisins. Add raisins, cauliflower, and *4 tablespoons toasted pine nuts* to onions. Pour in *½ cup water,* no more. Cook 10 minutes, mixing to coat cauliflower with pan juices.

- Sprinkle cauliflower with *¼ cup minced parsley* and lots of *fresh ground black pepper.* If pasta is not yet ready, keep cauliflower warm over low heat.

- Spread cauliflower sauce over cooked, drained pasta.

Stuffed Squid

- Buy *ten 4 to 6 inch (not counting the tentacles) squid* (also called calamari), cleaned. If they're not cleaned, you'll have to do it yourself.

- Chop tentacles fine. Pit and slice *5 large Sicilian green olives.* Set both aside.

- In *2 tablespoons melted butter* sauté *½ cup finely chopped onion* until soft and add *2 finely minced cloves garlic.* Continue sautéing until onions are translucent. Cool.

- Mix *¾ cup fine breadcrumbs, 1 tablespoon each grated Parmigiano and Romano cheeses,* chopped tentacles, and olives. Add to cooled onion-garlic combination.

- Break up *1 egg* with fork and mix into bread mixture with a light hand.

- Stuff each squid half full, no more because the dressing will swell to fill the extra space. Close open end with toothpick.

- Heat *2 tablespoons olive oil* in a heavy pan; brown squid on both sides over medium-high heat. Add *16 ounce can chopped plum tomatoes* and cook 15 to 20 minutes. Serves 4 to 6.

Carolyn Blue,
"Have Fork, Will Travel,"
San Diego Call

22
The Wrong Restaurant

Luz

Three reporters hustled toward us in the lobby when we left the elevator. Carolyn scuttled into an office to have her article faxed, while I tried to stare down the press. Fat chance. They came right over and asked if that had been Carolyn Blue who ducked down the hall.

"Yeah, right. Like Carolyn Blue wears a hunting cap with earflaps. She's gone back to El Paso. That was my little brother. His English isn't great because he grew up with my dad in Mexico, but I guess you could try interviewing him when he gets back. Don't know why you'd want to. He's not an illegal alien."

"Blue's left town? I thought she was a suspect in—"

"Right. Wouldn't you leave town if you were a suspect and hadn't done anything but flambé some turkeys? Say, do you know where the museum is that has the whale?"

They didn't even bother to answer and had left before Carolyn got back. "Well, Paul will get the article almost on time. Shall we go? I can hardly wait to try fusion cuisine." But she had to wait a while. We had one hell of a time finding this restaurant the Asian-fusion lady invited us to. Took the subway way uptown, still got off too early, and had to walk for blocks. With the wind in my face, it felt like my cheeks were freezing off, and Carolyn kept saying she was so glad she had the earflaps, but her fingers ached, and the shuttered stores and dark neighborhoods made her nervous.

"Christ, Carolyn, you got four people guarding you, not that those three guys behind us look all that friendly to me. You sure they're bodyguards?"

"Of course, they are," she snapped. "Oh, thank goodness, I think this is it."

We stumbled into a place with woven grass walls, wooden floors, a bamboo hammock with cushions in the window along with some sofas, and a naked-lady altar on one side—and she sure wasn't the Virgin. A blue ceiling with crystal chandeliers that looked as out of place as a mariachi guitarist in a string quartet, pictures of funny-looking musical instruments on the wall, and a sushi bar that I said right off I wasn't visiting completed the picture. But don't think I'm complaining. It was warm enough in there to take my coat off.

The bodyguards followed us in, wearing black leather coats with fur collars and ears red from the cold. They did not look happy when they sat down two tables over and started muttering in whatever language. Pretty soon a slim Chinese girl came in, all muffled up, and introduced herself as Janet Fong. She looked around quizzically before she sat and whispered, "I don't think this is the right place."

"It's the address you gave us," murmured Carolyn, who had been studying the menu, "but everything seems to be Thai."

Janet Fong studied the menu handed to her and agreed. Thai, not fusion. "I can't imagine how this happened." She looked pained. "Unless I mixed up printouts from the Internet. This is not the menu I chose."

"But it does look interesting," said Carolyn, always the diplomat. She'd hardly closed her mouth when a huge roar rattled the restaurant and my teeth.

"What the hell is that?" I'd been scared to death, which was irritating.

"The subway," shouted Janet, nodding her head toward the window, where I could see, beyond the hammock and across the street, a train thundering along raised tracks.

The waitress didn't seem to notice the fact that the chandeliers were jumping on their chains. She'd just taken orders from the bodyguards and come over to us, pen held over order pad. "We have Thai dumpling with pork, shrimp, and chicken. Very popular." So we had that. The meat was ground, the dumpling part was like a wonton skin, and the sauce wasn't even spicy.

After that came the golden triangles, which were tasty. They had crab and chopped-up vegetables inside, with a crispy fried outside and a bright red chile sauce that was sweet, but really hot. I figured Carolyn might be gobbling them up with the idea of getting herself another bellyache so she could skip out on the signing.

Then with our main courses we had beer, which Carolyn said tasted just like German beer and Janet insisted was Thai beer. Carolyn and I both ordered duck, me because mine last night had been great, and Carolyn because she hadn't been able to eat anything that rich last night. Mine was called Ped Paradise Crispy Duck and it was just okay, nothing *picante* and hard to chew. Carolyn's was Ped Choo Chee Crispy Duck and turned out to be fish, so she complained. The waitress said, "Is very popular. You try it," and disappeared. Janet apologized for the mistake and the waitress and offered whatever she'd ordered, but of course Carolyn wouldn't think of taking Janet's order, so she hacked off pieces of the fish, which required some muscle; it must have been fried into stone.

"Those men are staring at you," Janet whispered.

"Oh, don't pay any attention to them," Carolyn replied, chopping off another piece of fish. "Mr. Li Cheng Bao, to whom I paid a consolation call because my turkey was partially responsible for his granddaughter's injuries, sent them along to protect me." Janet looked alarmed, while

Carolyn, oblivious, pushed some rice with mushrooms into her curry sauce. "Delicious, but very spicy." She sighed. "I hope I don't develop another round of heartburn."

"Don't chance it," I advised and scraped her rice and sauce onto my plate. I never get heartburn.

"Mr. Li is . . . is a very powerful man," said Janet in a shaky voice. "If he has sent men after you, I do not—"

Shots rang out, glass broke, and I grabbed both of the innocents and dragged them to the floor. "What are you doing?" Carolyn cried. "It was just the subway train again."

"It was just someone firing a gun," I snapped. "Your bodyguards recognized the sound and ducked out the back."

"Were the Lis shooting at Mrs. Blue?" asked our nervous hostess.

"I think the shots came from outside."

"Maybe the Wise Dragons were being shot at," said Janet.

We were still under the table, or as much under as I could get the three of us. It wasn't that big a table. "Maybe it was the frigging Sicilians. I didn't like that Italian grandmother much."

"She is a frightening woman," Janet agreed. "Can we get up now, do you think?"

"What a ridiculous conversation," said my clueless friend Carolyn, and she pulled away from me and stood up, noticing, for the first time, holes in the window and the hammock. "Oh, my goodness. And the Wise Dragons ran away. Mr. Li will be ashamed of them."

"I'll pay the bill," said Janet, "and you ask for a cab to be called. We'll all take the cab for safety." She was shaking.

"Call Mr. Ming, Carolyn," I ordered. "I'm calling Worski and Benitez."

"I haven't finished my dinner," Carolyn complained, but then she looked at the stone-hard fish and the place where her rice and curry sauce had been before I took it, and she dialed Mr. Ming.

I couldn't get Worski or Benitez so I called Abe and told him what happened. Like the good guy he is, he offered to recruit DeShawn so the two of them could come to protect us at the book signing.

"I hope you have a gun," I said. He did, but he didn't plan to bring it along. Instead he'd bring a portable metal detector so we could keep anyone who was armed from getting into the store. "According to Carolyn, there won't be any customers," I retorted, "but don't let me stop you. If we find an assassin, we can club him with a metal detector." Carolyn didn't hear my conversation because another train rumbled by, so the metal detector was a surprise to her later, and not a pleasant one. I moved my charges away from the bouncing chandeliers and kept my eyes open for gunmen and taxicabs.

I had the most delicious appetizer, Golden Triangles, in a Thai restaurant in New York. Although I couldn't find a recipe, this one for spring rolls comes close and isn't that hard to make.

Thai Rock Crab Spring Rolls

- Shred ¼ head green cabbage, 1 medium-sized carrot, 2 medium stalks celery, and one small onion or two shallots. Slice 1 oz. shitake mushrooms.

- Put a little *vegetable oil* in a large wok over a low heat and add vegetables, mixing until cabbage starts to wilt.

- Add 1 tablespoon oyster sauce, 6 ounces precooked minced rock crab or lobster, ¼ teaspoon black pepper, ¼ teaspoon salt, sprinkling of curry powder, and toss well.

- When vegetables have wilted, place mixture in strainer and strainer in refrigerator. Leave for 2 hours or until cool to the touch.

- Using *1 package spring-roll skins*, place 2 ounces of stuffing in corner end of each skin, fold bottom forward and over top, roll full turn, tuck sides in while continuing to roll forward.

- Mix *4 ounces tempura powder mixed with water*. Place a dab on tip of skin. Roll over tempura mix to seal closed.

- Preheat *vegetable oil* to 350 degrees. Place several rolls in at a time and fry until golden brown (2 to 3 minutes).

- Serve with *Thai sweet red chili* sauce for dipping. The sauce can be purchased on the Internet, in an Asian grocery store, or maybe in your supermarket.

Carolyn Blue,
"Have Fork, Will Travel,"
San Francisco Bay Times

23

Book Signing of the Year

Carolyn

After Mr. Ming let Janet off, I confessed to Luz that I'd had a call the day after the turkey party from the owner of Cooks and Books, canceling the originally proposed repeat of my turkey flambé (I was to have brought a cooked turkey and flambéed it there) and the reading of some culinary history bits. The signing was still on, but it was obvious to me that neither of us expected anyone to come.

"Probably afraid you'd burn the bookstore down," said Luz.

"Store just around corner," said Mr. Ming.

We looked out our windows—nothing was happening on my side of the street, but Luz whistled and scared Mr. Ming. He slammed on his brakes, causing a chorus of car horns. "Think they're waiting for you?" Luz asked. I peered out her window and saw a long line of people snaking around the corner.

"There's probably a movie theater in the area," I replied glumly.

"Here is," said Mr. Ming. He pulled up in front of the store, which had two stories with food and cookbooks in every window and a horde of people clustered around the door, some pushing and arguing with one another.

"Oh, my goodness," I groaned. "It's probably a protest demonstration."

Luz opened her door, saying, "Pay the man. You're not going to wimp out of this." Then I saw Mr. Cratchett and Mr. Brown plowing through the crowd in our direction, with long metal wands in hand. People evidently thought they were going to be attacked and made way. The detective and his new assistant didn't hit any of the protestors, although I think DeShawn used reprehensible language. Some of the women looked offended. I certainly was, if I'd heard right. I gritted my teeth and followed Luz to the curb, where the women were welcoming her. "*She's* the author," said Luz, nodding at me.

My cover was blown, although some ladies and several men looked dubious, perhaps because of my hat and earflaps. Still, they didn't look unfriendly as Cratchett and Brown hustled us inside, where there were more people lined up in front of a table stocked with *Eating Out in the Big Easy*. Hovering there and looking anxious was a tall, gaunt woman with short gray hair. She wore a fuzzy, multicolored wool suit. "If one of you is the author, may I ask why these men are using metal detectors on my customers?"

"She's the author," said Luz, pointing at me and pushing me around to the seat behind the table. "And Detectives Cratchett and Brown are here to protect her. I'm an ex–police lieutenant myself. Someone put bombs in her turkeys, or haven't you heard?" Luz hadn't even given me a chance to take off my hat and coat, nor did the first woman holding my book.

She shoved it into my hand and said, "I read about you in the paper. Could you sign my book 'To Marilyn Levine from the Incendiary Gourmet, Carolyn Blue'?"

I opened my mouth to protest, but the wooly-suit lady said, "Of course she will," and shoved a pen in my hand. Then she sat down beside me and whispered in my ear,

"They're asking for copies of the recipe for the flambéed turkey. If you have one with you, I'll have a clerk start photocopying. We'll charge an extra five dollars for a signed recipe, but only if they've bought the book. And then we'll split the profits fifty-fifty."

I handed her my purse and told her to look inside, but specified that she could not copy the first page of material, which was part of a column and copyrighted by my newspaper syndicate. What a piece of luck that I hadn't had time to clean out my purse since I'd faxed the recipe to Paul.

"Excellent!" she exclaimed and rummaged around, dropping half the contents on the table while I signed more books. "But the way, I'm May Summersoon," said the owner, "and don't comment on my name. My parents had a peculiar sense of humor. When the line started forming at six-thirty, and in this weather, mind you—it's fifteen degrees out there and dropping—I called around to some other bookstores to round up more copies of your book."

"Could you write, 'To Michelle, this book is a blast, happy cooking, Carolyn Blue'?" asked a young woman wearing jeans and a pea coat. Poor thing. Both her lips and fingernails were blue. "I thought your turkey flambé was a real hoot. Can I get a copy of the recipe she asked for?"

"Of course you can, young lady," said Ms. Summersoon, who had been waving wildly to attract the attention of someone on her staff. "Why don't you stop by the coffee shop and warm up while we're getting copies made? Mrs. Blue, could you sign right here?"

She pointed to the end of the recipe, and I signed that, saying, "Would you mind giving your seat to or finding one for my friend, Lieutenant Vallejo? She has bad knees."

Ms. Summersoon stood up promptly and grabbed the arm of a man carrying another armload of my books to the table. Because she'd caught him by surprise, he dropped the top book on Luz's knee, and Luz muttered, "Son of a

bitch," rubbing the bruise and grimacing. An elderly lady
stepped out of line, offered my friend three Advil tablets,
and advised her to get her knees replaced. Advil did wonders, as the lady claimed to know, since both of her knees
were made of Teflon at this point.

Ms. Summersoon had glared at Luz for swearing and
then whispered to the book-carrying man. Had the backup
boxes arrived yet? He shook his head. Frowning, she
shoved the recipe into his hand and told him to copy all of
the pages but the first, put them in the copy feeder, and set
the machine on continuous copy. And to get someone else
to help him staple.

Then, while I was dutifully writing into a book, "Happy
Birthday from Carolyn Blue to a fellow glutton," the owner
was calling for quiet and announcing the availability of
signed copies of the infamous turkey recipe for five dollars
at the cashiers' stations shortly, not to mention coffee,
sandwiches, and desserts for sale in the adjoining coffee
shop. "We're featuring desserts by cookbook writer Con-
nie Collins tonight. I'm sure you're all familiar with her
wonderful recipes."

A fellow glutton? I thought handing the book to the
man who had asked for that signature. I wasn't a glutton,
and I had a mind to tell him, but he gave me a huge grin
and waddled off while the Advil lady stepped into his
place. She and Luz discussed knee problems while I
signed, "To an OLD friend, from Carolyn Blue." She actually asked for that and patted me on the head with the
advice that my hair needed attention after being muffled
up in that "strange hat." "My late husband used to wear a
hat like that when he went out to chop wood at our cabin
upstate." I got out a mirror and comb and tried to re-
arrange my hair.

Mr. Cratchett and Mr. Brown kept wanding everyone
who got through the door, but at least the grumbling died
down after Ms. Summersoon asked over a loud speaker,
which evidently sounded out into the street, that customers cooperate with the security measures set up to

protect tonight's author. "We must remember that an act of sabotage was committed against her turkeys this week, and she was shot at at a restaurant uptown just this evening, so we can't be too careful, and we thank you, Mrs. Blue, for agreeing to be here this evening, under frightening circumstances, to meet and sign books for your many fans."

"Did you tell her about the gunshots?" I whispered to Luz, who had been studying everyone inside as if they might have brought along plastic explosives to escape the metal detectors.

"Yep. And it got her off my back about the wanding, so don't complain."

A girl who looked about eleven stepped up and confided that her mother was teaching her to cook. Her mother said, "She saw the article in the paper about your flaming turkeys and asked for your book for her birthday."

"It was so cool," said the child. "*Food writer bombs street with flaming turkeys.* I read about it after I got home from school."

Very cool, I thought grimly and rubbed my hand, not that I didn't see Loretta's point now: Even bad publicity sold books. And where was she? She'd promised to attend. Then it struck me that perhaps *Loretta* had sabotaged my turkeys. As I was writing "To Patrick from a red-hot writer, Carolyn Blue," and nodding while Patrick told me about his wonderful recipe for beer-basted hamburgers, which I might like to include in my next book, May Summersoon got on the loudspeaker a third time to assure her customers that they were perfectly safe because not only was my personal security detail on duty inside, but she'd also called in uniformed officers to protect those outside.

While the owner was making announcements, my Ming-family cell phone rang. With a cacophony of sirens and horns in the background, my agent admitted that she'd been involved in an accident on the parkway, the name of which I didn't catch, but that she was keeping abreast of my "knockout signing" on a radio station while the police and ambulances untangled the cars and drivers.

The store became more and more crowded as those who'd come through the line wandered around waiting for the five-dollar recipes to show up at the cash registers, chose more books, and got coffee and pastries in the coffee shop. Ms. Summersoon arrived at the table, beaming, to tell me that boxes of my book were being unloaded in back even now and she'd decided that she should send clerks out to people on the street with trays of coffee and cocoa for sale.

"Now there's a woman who knows how to make a frigging profit," Luz muttered. "My knees are killing me. You keep signing, and I'll take a walk around just in case there are any scumbags in here that I missed."

The lady whose book I'd just signed asked Luz to sign as well, and pretty soon people were trying for signatures from Mr. Cratchett and Mr. Brown, the latter of whom was delighted. It turned out that he was signing *Big Black Rapper*. Later I heard that Mr. Cratchett was tucking his business card in my books. The evening was beginning to take on the quality of a hallucination, not that I've ever had one, but still . . . and my hand was really hurting. If only I'd taught myself to write with my left hand, but there'd been no need up to now.

"Stop rubbing your hand," hissed a woman who dropped into Luz's vacated chair. "And smile." I'd never seen her before. "And don't let your employees sign your books. I've never heard of such a thing."

"Who *are* you?"

"Eveline Warren, Pettigrew publicity. We met at the launch party." She glanced around. "It seems to be going well. I'd have been here earlier if my five-year-old hadn't jumped off the bathtub and broken the pipe to my bidet."

I was bemused to hear that she had a bidet, not to mention a five-year-old. "Was he injured?"

"That's not the point. You can take a child to the emergency room, but try to get a plumber after hours in Manhattan."

Eveline Warren wandered off, cell phone in hand. Maybe she was still trying to find a plumber.

The signing was supposed to end at nine-thirty, but there were many people on the street waiting to get in, Ms. Summersoon wouldn't let me go, and Mrs. Warren returned to back her up. The owner brought me coffees and lattes and cappuccinos and pastries and reports of how many books and recipes we'd sold. Mrs. Warren made calls to pass the numbers on. I'd begun to wonder whether it was legal to sell a recipe my aunt had cut out of a newspaper, even if that paper was no longer publishing.

And I kept signing books, but only with my name, since Ms. Summersoon announced that the author couldn't keep writing in messages because of all the people waiting. Then she reminded them that they were buying first editions of what would prove to be a classic cuisine book and it would be worth more with just the author's signature. Classic? The woman was crazy. I felt a little crazy myself. I couldn't believe my first, and maybe last, signing—although people did write books from prison—had been so well attended.

On the other hand, prisoners didn't visit wonderful restaurants to gather materials for books, and prison libraries probably didn't have much culinary history on hand. Which brought me back to the thought that Loretta might be responsible for this huge scandal/triumph. She'd told me not to worry. So had Petey. He'd loved the party, and he and his uncle were making profits off my book. Even Roland had thought the book would do well, regardless of Hurricane Katrina. And he'd had a heart attack. Perhaps because the flambé had turned out to be so dangerous. Or was I just paranoid?

At eleven-thirty the last half-frozen, jumped-up-on-coffee reader staggered out of the store; Mrs. Warren shook my aching hand and brought tears to my eyes; then

Ms. Summersoon locked the front door behind her, pulled me out of my chair, and gave me a hug. Oh my goodness, I'll swear her fuzzy wool suit left a rash on my arms and cheek.

"Now you just sit down and sign the rest of these," she said, pointing to the box of forty that was left. More tears came to my eyes, which she took to be tears of joy. They were tears of agony and dismay because I didn't think my right hand was up to forty more signatures.

24

Trolling through Temps

Luz

Abe was seriously pissed off when I showed up at the temp agency and Carolyn didn't. "Her frigging hand was swollen and as hot as a brush fire," I replied. "I had to pack it in ice, give her painkillers, and send her back to bed."

"So what happened with her," asked DeShawn. "She bash someone an' bust up her knuckles?"

"Don't be an asshole, DeShawn. You were there. She signed so many books and shook so many hands she got arthritis or something. So let's start questioning the temps."

"What about my plan?" asked Abraham, looking bad-tempered. He must have stayed up past his bedtime wanding all those scandal-suckers and would-be chefs who wanted to meet the woman who'd turkey-bombed New York. "You and Carolyn were supposed to do the women," he reminded me. "Carolyn and DeShawn the blacks, and you and me the Hispanics, and DeShawn and me the felons."

"I thought you two did the felons yesterday."

"Couldn't find them," said Abe with disgust. "You put a Jewish detective in a place like Bed-Stuy or Harlem, and everyone's on the side of the felon. But I got them here this morning. The agency called them in for jobs."

"I hope you got a gun on you, Abe," I retorted. "They're not going to be happy. Maybe all three of us better take the felons. Then we'll divide up the women, blacks, and Hispanics." I thought a minute about that. "Well, however it turns out."

As we went off to start on the felons—there were only three of them—DeShawn said, "I see in the paper this article that says maybe some Chinese tong guys are following and trying to shoot the flaming-turkey lady because some Chinatown girl is gonna die from the turkey accident."

"Nah. They were in the Thai place with us when the shots were fired. They took a runner, and we hid under the table. Coulda been someone shooting at them, not us. Who the hell knows?" Then we went in to question the first felon, a black guy hired as kitchen help.

"How come a man who knows his way around a kitchen ended up in prison on an assault-with-a-deadly weapon conviction?" Abe asked, sounding mildly sympathetic.

The guy shrugged, a flush highlighting a scar on his cheek. "Took an onion chopper to a man told the chef I spit in the soup. What you want with me? I suppose to git a job here, not answer questions."

"We're investigating the turkeys that caught fire where you were working," I threw in.

He claimed he "didn't do nothin' to no turkeys." He was at the fry station.

"So who did you see messing with the turkeys?" I asked.

The only person he saw opening the turkey-oven doors was "some skinny little gal from Puerto Rico."

I interviewed her later, after we had lunch at a Kosher-Mexican restaurant Abe recommended—fish tacos, for God's sake, and you could tell the tacos had never seen a drop of lard—not the tacos, and not the boring-as-hell refried beans that came with them.

The girl had been the turkey baster and burst into tears when I told her they'd turned into firebombs. She swore on her *abuela*'s grave she never put anything on them that didn't get taken out of the roasting pan with the baster, but she couldn't swear someone else hadn't got to them while she was on break or busy putting little stuff out on plastic trays.

Abe and I talked to a couple of other girls who insisted they couldn't even see the turkey ovens, which were in an L off the main kitchen, where they were working. The second felon ratted out the third, said number three had messed with the turkey. Then number two asked us to tell his probation officer he'd cooperated. Turns out both of them were polishing silver and loading and unloading dishwashers after lunch was served to the publishing house employees. Neither one could have seen or gone into the turkey-oven L.

DeShawn, after talking to a black guy who had been carrying supplies up from the service entrance, told us the chef didn't even let the "brotha" into the kitchen, just the pantry. A Puerto Rican waiter who came in early to set tables claimed he'd been banging a female bartender in the unisex john and hadn't seen anything in the kitchen, just the flaming turkeys in the dining room. His bartender girlfriend backed him up. The last three, two women and a man, who were there doing whatever they were told in the kitchen, hadn't seen anything and didn't recognize any of the Pettigrew employee pictures, even the picture of Franz.

Which is to say that we spent most of the day getting nowhere and scaring a bunch of people who probably hadn't done anything and were living hand to mouth. At ten dollars an hour tops and no benefits, how the hell did they live and eat in this city? Well, maybe the kitchen jobs provided leftovers now and then. One of the Puerto Rican girls confided in Spanish that she'd been able to take home some of the dressing that didn't get burned up or hit by the fire extinguishers because no one wanted to eat anything that had been in those turkeys. Her *perro* ate it first, and when he didn't get sick, the family finished it off.

My God, illegal immigrants in El Paso do better than that, although not all of them have indoor plumbing. When the girl saw me limping, she wanted to give me a recipe her grandmother used for arthritis—guess what was in it? Hot chile peppers, just like my capsaicin cream, but her *abuela* made her own.

"So what we do now? Ain't none of those brothas know nothing," said DeShawn, which was true enough. Or else some of them were lying, which was also possible.

"If you've got any more ideas, Abe, you're on your own for today. I've got to get back to the hotel. Carolyn and I have to eat dinner at Petey Haverford's crazy mother's house."

"Strange woman," Cratchett agreed. "She asked me once if I was a follower of Kabbalah. I told her that was for people like Madonna, that the Jewish side of my family is more into scholarly pursuits than mysticism. She seemed offended, but I didn't know at that time Mrs. Haverford held séances. If you see any ghosts at the dinner table, let me know." He started to laugh. "And don't let anyone hold hands with you around a table. No telling who'll show up."

DeShawn said, "Ghosts ain't nothing to laugh about, man. All the old women in my family seen 'em. I never forget when my granny say there was one behind my chair at dinner, looking hungry at Mama's fried chicken."

Abe advised DeShawn to keep in mind that his granny may have *thought* she'd seen the ghost, but DeShawn hadn't.

"How you know? No way I was turning around to look."

The conversation reminded me of the stories my grandmother told me about *La Llorona*. Scared the shit out of me, listening to hear if that wailing lady was going to sneak into my bedroom at night, grab me, and drown me in the Rio Grande. Ghost talk didn't make me feel much like going to dinner at Haverford's, but I figured I could count on Vera to get us out of any séances we might be invited to join. Maybe I ought to suggest that Mrs. Haverford call up one of the turkeys and ask it what had happened. I caught the subway, laughing to myself at how well that suggestion would go over.

25

Chasing Publicity Hounds

Carolyn

Luz had been so good to me, numbing my hand in the ice bucket, which she set on the floor beside the bed, and feeding me pain pills and croissants from the free breakfast buffet. Those pills were her own antiinflammatory prescription meds. I probably would have slept the morning away if it hadn't been for the phone calls. First, Loretta called me with congratulations on the wonderful success of my signing and the two-thousand-plus sales of the article to newspapers and magazines. It was really an I-told-you-so call; she reminded me that the night of the flaming turkeys she'd told me her motto: Any publicity is good publicity.

"Did you put something in my turkeys, Loretta?" I demanded angrily. "I know you were there early that afternoon."

"Think what you want, Carolyn, but I was at Pettigrew's on behalf of another client," she snapped, "and to see how you were doing. And what did I find? *You* weren't there. If you thought your turkeys were in danger, you should have guarded them yourself." She sounded so self-righteous that I almost apologized until she added, "You have more luck than you deserve, my girl. Don't think I don't remember when you came here the first time whining about not wanting to write the book at all after I got you an excellent contract, and you a complete unknown."

She hung up on me, which might be a sign that I had placed myself in the bad graces of my agent. By then I was wide awake and quite agitated. I might as well have gone with Luz to help quiz the temporary employees, one of whom might have seen the dreadful move against my turkeys. I pulled my hand out of the ice bucket, where the ice was melted, but the water was still blessedly cold, and got dressed. There was still something I could do to help my own cause: I'd visit Roland in the hospital. He was another publicity-hound suspect and needed to be questioned.

Getting bathed and dressed with a puffy, painful hand was not much fun, but I managed and then stopped on my way to the subway at a discount drugstore to ask if they had anything that would render my hand at least partially usable. Of course the white-coated, flush-faced druggist wanted to know what was wrong, saying loftily, as if I were some idiot, that different medical problems required different medical solutions.

When I explained about signing my name so many times that I'd disabled my hand, he identified me as the Incendiary Gourmet he'd read about in the papers and for whom hundreds of people had stood in the cold to get signed copies of *Eating Out in the Big Easy*.

"I'm a bit of a chef myself," he said proudly. "My specialty is beautifully colored drinks filled, of course, with specialty alcohol."

Which explain his red nose, I thought uncharitably.

In exchange for promising to come in and sign his copy, as soon as he got one, I was fitted with a glove that circled my hand and wrist. Velcro immobilized them. I did feel better, although it was hard to get my winter gloves over the orthopedic contraption and even harder to sign the charge slip. The pharmacist agreed to call Mr. Ming for me. I'd decided that a taxi was in order for the ride to the hospital since my poor hand had required medical attention from two different people, one of whom was more or less a professional.

I stopped at the drugstore's paperback shelves, bought Roland two books that he probably wouldn't like—I couldn't visit his sick bed empty-handed—and arrived outside to find Mr. Ming waiting. He always arrived so quickly that I wondered if he was following me, too. The Wise Dragon fellows had been lurking one aisle over the entire time I was in the drugstore. The question was: Had they been at my signing last night or cowering in Chinatown after the shooting at the restaurant?

Roland was still hooked up to machines that I assumed monitored his heart rate. He was eating his lunch from a tray and complaining about the salt-free soup, the low-fat spread on his supermarket bread, and the sugar-free Jell-O presented to him as dessert. I asked how he was feeling, only to be told that a decent meal was all he needed to prepare him for release, but as such a meal wasn't available in this hospital, he was afraid he'd be tied to this bed for the rest of his life. When I gave him the books to cheer him up, he grunted at the book covers, thanked me with no enthusiasm, and pushed them off the other side of the bed.

Not a cheerful patient, I thought, *but undoubtedly in less pain than I am.*

"How was the book signing?" he asked.

"Dreadful," I replied. "I signed thousands of books and did damage to my hand," which I displayed in its orthopedic shell.

"Thousands?" His face brightened. "You wouldn't fool a sick old man, would you?"

"They had to send all over town for more books, and people were lined up out in the cold buying coffee from Ms. Summersoon's café waitresses to keep warm while waiting to get in, and all because there were so many articles about the turkey-bombing and the Incendiary Gourmet in the papers."

"Ha!" said Raymond. "Didn't I tell you? A success. I

hope Claudius is happy. Or course he is. The loss of a tablecloth or two and a few smudges on the ceiling are nothing to worry about."

"What about the lawsuits and the prospect of being arrested? That may happen to you, too, Roland."

"Nonsense. You should thank me, Carolyn. I've made your career."

"I knew it! You were the one who made the turkeys turn into huge torches. First, you insist that I flambé them, then you sneak into the kitchen and— well, don't think we won't be able to find someone who saw you doing whatever you did, you . . . you terrorist."

Roland's face turned an unhealthy shade of puce while he snarled, "I was checking in the kitchen all day, but that's because I am a gourmet, not a terrorist." His machines began to beep and then shriek a warning.

Oh dear, what had I done? Was he having another heart attack? Nurses and doctors rushed in, dragging carts of high-tech equipment, pushing me out of the room, and surrounding Roland. I stood around in the hall until a nurse came out and told me to go home. "Mr. DuPlessis won't be having more visitors for some time."

"But how is he?" I asked.

"As well as can be expected," she snapped and bustled down the hall in her ugly white shoes, while I slunk away to the elevator.

Back at the hotel I filled my ice bucket at the ice machine, not an easy task one-handed, returned to the room, and lay down, dropping my hand into the ice and water, which I'd carried to the bucket, glass by glass, from the bathroom. To take my mind off what I'd done to Roland, I thought about the bed, which was about the most comfortable I'd ever slept on. The hotel had a whole brochure on their beds, pillows, and sheets, which I'd read when we first arrived here. I'd even attempted to read at least the high points to Luz, who wasn't at all interested and fell asleep in the middle of the paragraph about the various layers of things that made these beds so comfy. I remember

thinking that her rapid decline into sleep was perhaps a tes-
tament to her bed. In fact, I was feeling drowsy, except for
the fact that my hand was turning into an ice cube with fingers, albeit a relatively pain-free ice cube.

As I drifted, almost on the verge of a much-needed nap,
the phone rang, and I reached across with my good hand to
answer. It was Jason, asking how things were going. I told
him I thought I'd killed a man this afternoon. Silence on
the El Paso end of the line. "I mean I upset him, and because he was in the hospital recovering from a heart attack,
he seemed to be having another one." All this I said in a
calm, sleepy voice. And then I began to cry. "I killed my
editor."

Once my husband ascertained that I didn't *know* Roland
was dead, he suggested that I not jump to conclusions and
asked if the police had yet realized that I was innocent in
the turkey bombing, which the local paper had been covering on a daily basis. I wept more tears and managed to
relay that I was not yet exonerated and had only suspi-
cions, no solid suspects.

Jason sighed and said at least he had good news, well,
better news than the last time we'd talked. His student
Nate, once fully conscious, had told him that Jose had
pulled off his safety mask to answer his cell phone and,
while talking to his girlfriend, had turned his back on the
experiment. Then he'd failed to replace the mask when he
went to the hood to look at the experiment, which more or
less fumed into his face. "So it's not good news for Jose,
but I'm off the hook with the DEA," said Jason. "So that's
partially good news, don't you think? And how was your
book signing last night?"

"Crowded," I sniffled.

"But that's wonderful."

"Not really, Jason. All those books I signed last night
for four hours made my hand swell up and hurt, so I had to
spend the rest of the night with my hand in an ice bucket."

Jason advised me to go to a doctor, and then, noting

how long we'd been on the phone, said goodbye. *Men are so insensitive*, I thought, and cried some more.

When Luz arrived and found me all soppy about having killed Roland, she called the hospital, identified herself as his sister, and demanded to know how he was.

"Oh well, he had a little anxiety attack this afternoon, probably brought on by all his complaints about our food," said the floor nurse, "but he's fine, Miss DuPlessis. Asleep at the moment. Do you want me to wake him up or have him call you back?"

"No, no," said Luz. "Just tell him for me that if he doesn't watch his diet and eat the heart-healthy food you give him, I'll fly in from Phoenix and make him eat oatmeal four times a day." Ever so relieved, I got the giggles, imagining Luz forcing oatmeal into my editor's mouth.

26

Dinner in Magnificent Style

Carolyn

When Luz and I were ushered into the Haverford's brownstone monolith by a maid, I whispered, "This is absolutely baronial." The entry hall was paved in stone and hung with shields and swords with suits of armor lurking in the dim, far corners.

Lavinia Haverford rushed out from a door on the left and explained that every artifact had been owned by or was a copy of something owned by a famous warrior, military history being an avocation of her husband's. One sword had belonged to a woman with whom Lavinia had been in touch, "But don't tell your mother. I've been saving our séance for a surprise. Vera's such a dear eccentric. I never know what she's going to say."

"I can believe that," said Luz, while Petey, who had followed his mother into the entry hall, was trying to give me a kiss on the cheek. I ducked so nimbly that he found himself with his head over my shoulder within kissing distance of Luz, so she leaned forward, kissed him on the cheek, and patted his head. "Good to see you, too, kid. Thrown any more flaming turkeys into the streets? Had any visits from the police?"

I was happy to see that he looked discomfited. Lavinia

said blithely, "Petey is not allowed to speak to the police without our lawyer present. What a silly to-do over a few turkeys gone wrong. I'm sure you had nothing to do with their unexpected behavior, Carolyn."

I would have said something irritable had we not entered a library with a lovely fire crackling in the fireplace, ceiling-high bookcases stuffed with well-worn books, and ladders that slid along a rail so that readers could get at them. Most of the books were old, but the chairs, tabletops, and sofas were all of leather. Vera hoisted herself out of one, spilling her drink on the carpet in the process, and gave me a hug. Then she hugged Luz. Then she told a man wearing rather baggy clothes that she needed another drink. He turned out to be Professor Haverford, who called a butler to get the drink and a maid to mop up the carpet. The husband wore wrinkled khaki trousers and a tweed jacket with leather padded elbows and smoke coming from one patch pocket where he'd stuffed his pipe while rising to greet us. The butler whisked the pipe from the pocket, said, "Excuse me, sir," and gave the smoking pocket a few hard slaps.

"Did it again, did I?" said the professor amiably and greeted us both. "So have you ladies been troubled by bedbugs since you arrived in New York?"

I'm sure we both looked taken aback, but he informed us that American cities, especially New York City and Atlanta, were under attack by a veritable army of foreign bedbugs. "At least that's my theory. In my youth bedbugs were almost extinct here, but now travelers are bringing them back in their clothes and luggage. Very interesting phenomenon."

"Now Brian," said his wife, "can we have at least one evening without mentioning bugs? Brian is an entomologist," she explained to us.

"Heard the joke about the famous entomologist who refused to learn the names of any more colleagues and students because for every human name he learned, he forgot the name of an insect?" Dr. Haverford laughed uproariously.

My mother-in-law joined in and asked him if he'd heard the joke about the feminist who refused to learn any more names at all because when she did, she forgot the name of another male chauvinist pig. They both thought that was funny, and I could see that Vera was quite at home here, at least so far.

Luz and I were provided with drinks, and a Mrs. Carlton, a friend of Mrs. Haverford, arrived with the news that she was divorcing her husband because he made demeaning remarks about her feminist beliefs. Petey then remembered that his uncle couldn't be here tonight because he was attending a lecture on a recently discovered manuscript by the Pearl Poet.

I nodded in a more friendly fashion. Dear Mr. Pettigrew. You had to be fond of a man who liked *Sir Gawain and the Green Knight* and "The Wanderer." Or had it been "The Wayfarer"?

"I don't know why I bother to invite my brother," said Mrs. Haverford. "He always accepts and never shows up."

"I love the Pearl Poet myself," I remarked. Goodness, my drink tasted good. I accepted a second one because it was warming me up. I don't think Mr. Ming liked to turn on the heater in his car. Maybe he didn't even have one.

"All about men, aren't they?" said Vera. "You'd think there weren't any women around in those old times, except for the stupid ones who were worshipped from afar by knights who otherwise were out raping the peasant girls in their spare time."

"Here, here," said the lady planning to divorce her husband.

"Uncle Claudius probably wants to get his hands on the new text and sell it with more commentary than poetry," said Petey gloomily, "as if there's any profit to be made on medieval poetry. Not that I don't like it myself, but we *are* in business."

"Don't be a philistine, Petronius," said his mother severely.

"And speaking of profits," said Petey, "Uncle Claudius was very pleased to hear the sales figures from your signing, Carolyn. From everywhere, for that matter, where the story of the turkeys was picked up."

"You're the one who put something explosive in my turkeys, aren't you?" I asked, angry all over again. "I know you were in the kitchen. One of the felons saw you duck around the corner to the turkey oven. You probably snuck in while the turkey-basting girl was arranging canapé trays."

"Felons?" echoed Lavinia, looking shocked.

Vera, who had sat beside me on a leather couch, gave me a rap on my injured, Velcroed hand, and asked her hostess, "How did you happen to be named Lavinia? I don't recognize it as a feminist name."

"Unfortunately, it isn't," said Lavinia sadly. "My mother was more interested in getting people to donate great works of art to our museums. In fact, she was on the board of several. A good woman, but not enlightened. Lavinia is just part of the family tradition of Roman names. I was named after the daughter of the wise king Latinus and his wife Amata, who committed suicide when her husband gave Lavinia in marriage to Aeneas. I have my doubts about that story since I've never been able to get in touch with the Roman Lavinia."

"I beg your pardon," said my mother-in-law. "Did you say—"

"I didn't do anything to the turkeys, Carolyn. I don't know how you could say that," Petey butted in, sounding very hurt.

"Dinner is served, madam." The butler bowed, and we straggled into the dining room, which looked like a medieval banqueting hall, maybe even a mead hall from Anglo-Saxon times. It had rafters and stone walls, another fireplace, and a huge table with huge chairs. Vera looked like a midget perched on hers, and my feet barely reached the floor. There were antlers and hunting horns, shields and coats of arms on the walls, and I kept sneaking looks to see if the Venerable Bede's allegorical sparrow would fly through the warmth and light of life out into the dark of death. Or had that been a swallow?

When Petey tried to sit down beside me, I scooted away and took a seat by Dr. Haverford, who, I'm happy to say, had knocked the embers out of his pipe and left it in the library. Vera sat down beside me, and Petey got stuck between Luz and the guest feminist.

I loved the dinner. It wasn't exotic, but it was warming and hearty, and I hadn't had lunch. Over the oxtail soup, which was actually French onion but particularly rich, Professor Haverford told me about the mating habits of some Tasmanian insect. I didn't mind. I told him about the Australians' success growing truffles in Tasmania and New South Wales. What I did mind was spilling soup hither and yon while trying to eat with my left hand. I should have stayed home. But goodness, the professor was fascinating on butterflies, so I suggested that he read Barbara Kingsolver's wonderful novel *Prodigal Summer*, in which one of the characters was an expert on moths and a lot of the metaphors had to do with them.

"Oh, don't try to talk Brian into reading a novel," warned Mrs. Haverford. "If a book isn't about insects—"

"I resent that, Lavinia," said the professor. "I intend to get a copy of this book immediately. Would you write down the title and author for me, Mrs. Blue?" Delighted, I did so and went on to tell him about the main theme, as I saw it: the interdependence of species from plants to humans.

"Unfortunately, I can't get Carolyn interested in feminist books," said Vera. "She's always reading novels, cookbooks, and history."

"Well, what would we do without cookbooks?" said Professor Haverford diplomatically. "We all have to eat, and I must say I do love a good history book. Lavinia decorated the first floor of the house as a surprise for me."

That explained the historically gloomy ambiance. We went on to discuss the recent and excellent book about the American revolution, *1776*, a biography of John Adams, and the story of the Lewis and Clark expedition, which had been mostly about Lewis and Jefferson. I had never realized that Lewis was probably bipolar and had killed himself. Also, I was somewhat embarrassed about the professor's comments on the prevalence of venereal disease among the men who were members of the expedition.

At the other end of the table Lavinia was telling Luz that she preferred to think she'd been named after Lavinia Fontana, a famed painter from Bologna, who lived from the mid sixteenth century to the early seventeenth, bore eleven children, and left the house, children, and management of her career to her husband.

"Every woman needs a house husband," said my mother-in-law in high good humor. We were eating rare roast beef, which our host carved with a short sword, lovely browned potatoes with gravy, and green peas with mint leaves, followed in the French style by a salad with apples and walnuts. If I'd thought the soup was difficult, the roast beef was impossible. Vera finally shoved her plate into the center of the table, moved mine to her place, and cut my food into small pieces.

"Thank you," I murmured, embarrassed because people were staring at us.

"What happened to your right hand?" she demanded, evidently having noticed for the first time that mine was bound and incapacitated.

"Writing my name on books for hours, " I replied softly.

I did manage to eat quite a bit of the entrée once Vera pitched in. I should have asked her in the first place. Then there was the wine: It was exquisite, nothing Jason and I could have afforded. The butler brought it in for Professor Haverford's inspection, with a cobweb or two trailing. I wondered if the professor was rich, too, or if all this wealth had devolved from the Pettigrews.

We had trifle for dessert, and the professor confessed to

me that he did like English cooking, which he supposed I
found rather mundane since, according to Petey, I wrote
about more exotic foods. I wondered if I could consider
English food ethnic for the purposes of my book. Probably
not in New York, where ethnic meant people who had
come here well after the Dutch and English. However, I did
say I'd loved every bite, and the wine as well.

He laid his hand on mine in a fatherly way and beamed.
"Good girl," he said. I noticed Vera eyeing us suspiciously.
I'd have to keep away from her for the rest of our time in
New York. She'd probably accuse me of having designs on
the professor. Why couldn't I have had a sweet mother-in-
law who would have made up, to some extent, for the death
of my own mother? I was feeling rather tearful when
Lavinia tapped her spoon against her wineglass.

27
A Difficult Guest

Luz

That had to be the world's weirdest frigging family. After meeting the parents, I sort of agreed with Carolyn; Petey probably did put explosives in the turkeys. The food was good, not spicy, but pretty good anyway, and although I'm not usually crazy for wine, unless it's mixed up in Carolyn's sangria, these were great, as long as I was drinking them with the food. Did that mean I was getting fancy tastes? My mother would be disappointed in me.

Then it all went to hell when Lavinia tapped on her glass. "And now for my surprise. It's just for ladies. You gentlemen aren't invited."

"Just because I brought a martini in when *Mater* got hold of that woman who used to take axes to saloons," said Petey, grinning, "I never get to take part anymore."

"But we ladies," continued his mother, ignoring his complaint, "are going to embark on a fantastic feminist journey. In fact, I just received the signal that the medium and the other ladies are waiting for us."

"Medium what?" asked Vera, who hadn't been paying attention. "Feminism is an all-out effort. Medium enthusiasm doesn't come into it."

"I know what you mean, dear Vera, and we're so proud to have someone of your stature join us tonight. I know you've read with admiration about the good work of Emma Goldman, the famous labor organizer. As I have, you've probably always wished you could have met her. And tonight you will."

"How are you going to do that?" Vera asked, as if Lavinia had just said she was going to flap out of the room and fly to Europe under her own power.

"We're going to call upon her spirit to join us," said Lavinia. Vera just stared at her. "A ceremony organized in your honor, Vera."

Vera raised an eyebrow and said, "The woman's dead, Lavinia. Dead is dead. How much of that wine did you drink?"

"No one is dead to those of us who have a spiritual connection with the other side," said Lavinia. "Through a medium I've used for years, we're going to hold a séance to contact the spirit of Emma Goldman. I decided on her because of your work here with Latina police-women."

"What work?" asked Carolyn suspiciously.

"I got in touch with your Detective Benitez," Vera answered, "a very interesting young woman. We're having a meeting for Latina policewomen tomorrow night."

"Detective Benitez thinks I'm guilty of first-degree assault," Carolyn snapped.

"She's just doing her job, Carolyn," said Vera soothingly. "That doesn't mean she shouldn't receive equal pay for equal work. We have at least 105 women coming tomorrow night."

My God! Vera was going to take the Latina cops out on strike, I thought. *They'll get fired.*

"And please stop this nonsense about Emma Goldman, Lavinia."

"With you in the circle, dear, she's sure to attend. And I know you'll have questions for her, given that you're holding a labor-organizing meeting yourself. Oh, Brunhilde!" She waved to the maid, who was clearing the dessert dishes. "Would you bring Dr. Blue paper and a pen so that she can write down her questions for Emma?"

Vera flung down her napkin, slid off her chair with a thump, and said, "That's it. I thank you for your hospitality, Lavinia, but I don't do séances. Carolyn, Luz, I'll have to stay with you. They can bring in a cot for me. Just wait here while I run upstairs and throw my clothes in my suitcases. I won't be a minute."

Silence descended like a desert dust storm, bringing on coughs and hands clapped over mouths, at least over mine. You had to appreciate Vera. No one was more likely to make you laugh at the wrong time, unless it was Carolyn. You'd think the two were blood relations. The maid brought in the pad for Vera's séance questions and handed her a pen, which Vera stuffed in her handbag as she was leaving the room.

Lavinia looked devastated. "The ladies are going to be so disappointed, Carolyn, that your mother can't come. Couldn't you prevail upon her to—"

"My *mother-in-law*, not my mother," said Carolyn, "and I'm sorry, Mrs. Haverford, but I've never been able to convince Vera of anything."

"Not to worry, my dear," said the professor, patting Carolyn's hand. "We can't all be as interested in séances as Lavinia is. In fact, I've never been to one myself and don't intend to start in my graying years."

"And here I thought you never attended because you weren't interested in feminism," said Lavinia sharply. "I even asked the medium once if it was possible to get in touch with a bug, but she said she couldn't speak to one. Carolyn, I do hope you can convince your mother-in-law to give her talk to the Carolyn Heilbrun Memorial Book Club tomorrow afternoon. My reputation as a feminist will be ruined if she doesn't attend either event."

"And be sure she comes in to sign her contract tomorrow morning," said Petey. "I can feel it in my bones: She's going to make a big splash in commercial publishing."

"I'll do what I can," Carolyn replied as all of us heard the *bump, bump, bump* of Vera's luggage being dragged down the stairs.

"Gracious, someone help her with her suitcases before she knocks off pieces of the slate stairway," cried Lavinia.

"We'll do that, Mrs. Haverford, and thanks for a great dinner." I grabbed Carolyn's arm and pulled her out of her chair.

"It's been lovely," said Carolyn as I dragged her toward the door.

"She going to stay with us?" I hissed into her ear. "There's no room."

"Did you hear me invite her?" Carolyn hissed back.

Vera, having reached the bottom of the stair, thrust one bag at me and one at Carolyn, and hustled us out while the butler held the door for us.

That left us in the street, with Mr. Ming and his taxi God knows where. Vera insisted that we take the subway, so we arrived at the hotel hauling her bags, my knees aching, Carolyn moaning about her hand, and all three of us half frozen. I never intend to visit a cold place in the middle of winter again. Ever.

Vera scared some poor bastard at the desk into providing a cot when he insisted they didn't have any. Then she apologized to us for moving in without notice and added that it wouldn't be all that inconvenient because she'd be leaving day after tomorrow, but all the time she was apologizing, she was taking her clothes out of the suitcases and stuffing them onto the rack, which wasn't big enough to hold even our clothes.

Carolyn looked somewhat relieved at the promise her mother-in-law made to leave quickly and passed on the messages about attending the contract signing and the book club. "Lavinia's very worried that you won't—"

"What a foolish woman! Believes in séances and thinks

I'd give up the chance to talk about Carolyn Heilbrun. Here her husband knew Carolyn, but Lavinia never met her, although Brian teaches at the same university. And she calls herself a feminist! As for her son, why would he think I'd skip signing the contract? I'm delighted to sign the contract. My goodness, my joints are aching. I believe the weather here is harder on me than the weather in Chicago."

"Well, I'm not giving up my bed to you, Vera. My arthritis is worse than yours, and you're the one who insisted on taking the frigging subway so we all limped into the hotel on legs like frozen tamales."

"Did I ask to take your bed, Luz?" she retorted and stared at Carolyn.

So guess who ended up on the cot? Carolyn, who loved the beds. And believe me, that cot didn't look like it had more than an inch and a half of padding. For sure it didn't have a whole brochure full of advantages. Even through the blanket, you could see the butt depression in the middle.

Jason called her before she went to bed, something to do with his graduate students. Then Vera asked to talk to him and told him all about the séance she'd had to get out of and how she was now sharing a room with us, and how his sweet wife had given up her bed and got Vera a book contract with her publisher, and how she was going to organize a group of Latina policewomen tomorrow because the city was screwing them over (well, she didn't put it in those words). Then she gave the phone back to Carolyn, climbed into Carolyn's bed, and went straight to sleep.

Carolyn told me the next morning that Jason had apologized because she'd gotten saddled again with his mother, not to mention the cot, but she didn't seem much placated because she got out of bed groaning. Evidently the cot wasn't any more comfortable than it looked. Of course Vera didn't even notice. She was leaving when we woke up, heading downtown to sign her new contract. I offered Carolyn some of my capsaicin cream, but she wasn't about to rub hot pepper oil on her skin. She thought the skin would peel off. So we both went back to bed and slept another hour, Carolyn in what was now Vera's bed.

"Aren't you afraid of catching feminism?" I asked. She told me to shut up.

28

The Return of the Chef

Carolyn

I've never hurt so much after a night's sleep. The hotel brought the cot and shoved it in between my bed—the one I gave up to Vera—and the outside wall, which was as cold as the cot was lumpy, so I tossed and turned, trying to find a comfortable position, until I realized that moving around made me colder. Then I fitted my bottom into the depression created by other bottoms, and, hoping to create a warm if uncomfortable nest, tucked the scratchy covers and sheets (which were *not* those described in the brochure) around me as best I could, and I finally slept.

Unfortunately, awakening was agony, as was moving from the cot to the now empty, comfy bed for another hour's sleep. Even taking a long, hot shower hurt, but Luz insisted that we get up and start investigating. Since our efforts had produced nothing so far, I wasn't excited about spending another day at it. The beds in jail couldn't be worse than that accursed cot.

Luz told me not to be a wimp and chose clothes for me, rumpled by Vera's attack on our closet, and forced a Mobic pill down my throat. Since that was her own painkiller, when she ran out, she'd have to fly home and leave me here. When she dragged me down to breakfast, I wasn't hungry, but she waltzed me into the coffee shop and ordered as if I hadn't eaten in days, rather than missing one lunch and replacing it with a huge dinner. She bought papers from the hotel gift shop and tried to get me to read. She cut up my bacon, as Vera had done my beef last night at the Haverfords', and I think Luz would have fed me if I hadn't given in and made the effort to eat, but I acquiesced only because the Mobic was beginning to kick in.

"Says here that members of a Chinese tong have been seen in Bensonhurst, probably trying to put the squeeze on Asian shopkeepers. Think that's our guys?"

"How would I know?" I responded grumpily as I ate some scrambled eggs left-handed. "They weren't in front of the Haverfords' when we left."

"They'd have turned into icicles if they'd stayed outside the whole evening. You know, I've never seen an icicle? Not in El Paso. How come New York doesn't have any? Does the city knock them down so they don't fall on pedestrians?"

I picked up a piece of bacon with my fingers. Left-handed, I couldn't seem to spear or slip a fork under one.

"Say, Caro, here's an article comparing you to that teenager who threw a frozen turkey through a woman's windshield. He hurt her so bad that they really piled on the charges, expected him to get twenty-five years. Then she came out of the coma, forgave him, and talked the judge into giving him six months in jail and probation."

"Thank you for sharing that Luz," I retorted. "Unfortunately, no one expects poor Birdie Li to survive."

When my phone rang, I ignored it. Luz got it out of my purse, turned it on, listened, and said, "It's for you. Mrs. Christopher."

While Luz started reading another newspaper and stuffed pancakes into her mouth, I held the phone to my ear, but there was nobody on the line.

"This paper says rumors are going around that Chinese gangsters are trying to move in on the Mafia in Brooklyn.

Wow! Maybe our guys are moving in on Mrs. Randatto and her guys."

"She's not Mafia." I hung up and put my cell phone on the table, then made a mess trying to spread jelly on my toast. Luz had to take it away from me and do it right.

Then her phone rang, so she wiped jelly off my hand and picked up, telling me afterward that Roberto knew this great little Peruvian restaurant in Queens that he wanted to take us to tonight.

"What's the use of going? I can't make notes," I replied peevishly. Now I was hungry, but it took forever to get anything into my mouth.

"Too bad. Maybe for once you could eat something without writing about it. Anyway, I accepted."

Then my phone rang again, and I picked it up myself, getting some sticky, residual jelly on the keypad.

Mrs. Christopher wanted to know why I'd hung up on her. "I'm one-handed," I muttered. "Who knows what keys I might have hit trying to pick the phone up. I got jelly on the talk key this time."

"Really?" Mrs. Christopher sounded disapproving. "Well, I called to tell you that Franz has returned to work. If you want to talk to him, I suggest you come over here."

I thanked her unenthusiastically because I'd just spotted jelly on my blouse. Then I passed the information on to Luz, who said, "Finally a break. Can't you eat a little faster? We need to get over there."

"I'd like to see *you* eat left-handed," I retorted. "At least if you hadn't cut up my bacon, I could eat it with my fingers." I continued to fumble bits of bacon, toast, from which the jelly tended to slip off, and evasive bites of scrambled egg to my mouth. I'd have to change my clothes before we could set off for Pettigrew's, and frugality no longer meant anything to me. I called Mr. Ming when the time came.

"Look at this," said Luz as Mr. Ming maneuvered his cab through midmorning traffic. "It's on the book page."

I accepted the folded section with reluctance, expecting

a review of my book, probably a bad one. The headline read:

INCENDIARY GOURMET BODYGUARDS HASSLE BOOK BUYERS

Texas writer, Carolyn Blue, who bombarded Lower Manhattan with flaming turkeys at a well-attended book-launch party, went herself one better by arriving at a Cooks and Books book signing with bodyguards to run metal detectors over her fans.

Would-be readers showed up by the hundreds, standing out on the cold street, buying coffee from cookbook proprietor May Summersoon, in order to purchase signed copies of *Eating Out in the Big Easy*. The signing, scheduled to end at 9:30, closed at midnight with only three customers being turned away for carrying weapons. They disappeared before they could be interviewed.

"I told you they were bodyguards," I said to Luz.

"The paper didn't even put our names in, and we were the ones risking our lives," Luz retorted.

Mr. Ming, who may not have been armed or faster than a speeding bullet, was still faster than the subway that morning. Before we could clamber out at Pettigrew's, he asked, "You are flaming turkey gourmet?" to which I nodded. "You sign my autograph book? I have autograph of Jackie Chan and many other famous people." I couldn't oblige him because my hand was still strapped up.

"Maybe when my hand recovers, Mr. Ming. Or else I'll send you one."

He promptly wrote down his address. "And one for Auntie Ming, please. She not know you famous."

The Pettigrew Building had better security today, a guard with a weapon, who looked as if he might know how to use it. He called Mrs. Christopher before he'd let us take the elevator upstairs to the Pettigrew floors. Mrs. Christopher met us and congratulated me on the success of my book signing while looking at my hand like a woman who wanted to tend to the wounded, but she said nothing about it; she just called the kitchen and sent us on our way with an admonition to Franz to answer any questions we might have.

"Could you tell me which of the writers was in your kitchen that day?" I asked, although I think Luz had planned to ask the questions. We were in a cubbyhole that served as the chef's office, sitting on two stools that had been dragged away from a prep table. Evidently visitors ordinarily weren't invited to sit down.

"Everyvun vas in mine kitchen dat day," he said angrily. "Like dey tink I'm a bus station here. Mr. Haverford comes in tree times. Mr. DuPlessis comes in four. As if I can't put on der party vitout interference from people don't know cooking. You come in." He glared at me. "You unt your turkeys. I don't need voman from Texas to cook der turkey in mine kitchen. Look vat happens. You burn two all up, unt ven I save der last von, you grab away. Crazy people."

"Hey, Franz, did you lose at the tables in Atlantic City?" Luz asked. "You're pretty grumpy this morning."

"I am gut gambler. I vin. I am gut chef. Should leave me alone in mine own kitchen."

"Did Petey or Roland look at the turkeys?" I asked.

"Petey? Petey! He don't come near food. Might get der clothes splattered. Roland make me open door, he look, he say they very brown for so early, unt I close der door. Vy you order domestic? Vild turkey ist better."

"So what about the writers?" asked Luz, who wasn't interested in varieties of turkeys. "Allison Peabody? Was she here?"

"Not in mine kitchen. Dat one don't cook, don't come in here. If she come here, I trow sauce on her. I tell her dat ven she say she have better vild game dan mine in Hungary. Hungary! Land of peasants." His face had turned red.

"What about Roberto Santibanez?" I asked.

"He send girl vit fancy nakos. More peasant food."

"You suspected Roberto?" Luz gave me a black look.

"Annunziata Randatto?"

"She send girl with crostini. Granddaughter maybe."

"Jack Armstrong?" I was losing hope.

"Dat one don't like no kitchen vit meat cooking. He ist not here."

"Janet Fong?"

"She ist bring in French-Vietnamese tings to put in microvave unt wery hot sauce for dipping. Not bad, but too spicy."

"But what about the turkey?" Luz snapped. "Did she have access to the turkeys?"

"No interest in turkeys from China voman," said Fritz. "Now I cook haddock, vich ist lunch today."

Desperate, I grabbed his arm with my good hand before he could leave. "Wasn't there anyone in here that day who didn't belong here or who could have done something to my turkeys? Did *you* sabotage them because you were mad about missing the first day of your conference, or because—"

"You tink Franz ist dumkopf. Make mine kitchen looking bad vit exploding turkeys? I am busy chef. No time for ruin food. Only time I look at your turkeys vas ven open oven for Roland. Go avay, Texas voman. Cook for cowboys, not in mine kitchen."

"There had to be someone here who . . . who had an opportunity to—"

"Ya. Der gas man." Franz laughed uproariously. "Der gas man come about der gas leak. Ve all must leave in case stove blows up. Mr. Pettigrew like old gas stoves from time of der Grandfater Pettigrew. Okay vit me. Dey cook gut. Just need repairs. Ve leave, gas man come out quick, ve go back."

"How do you know he was a gas man?" Luz asked.

"He got der gas-man uniform."

"Did you call him here?" I asked, almost holding my breath.

"*Nein.* Maybe someone downstairs. Has happened before. Maybe pipe downstairs leak, vun dat go into mein kitchen. Dey come vit sniffer, find, maybe close us for fixing, maybe not. Dis time not."

"What time?" asked Luz.

"Two-tirty, maybe tree."

Luz and I exchanged glances, thanked Franz, and hurried away while he called after us, "You tink gas man put bomb in turkeys." Loud laughter followed us, but Luz had her cell phone out before we exited the kitchen.

"Abe? Luz," she said. "Look at the tapes around two-thirty or three for a gas man coming in one of the doors. He wasn't called, but he had the frigging kitchen to himself for a while that afternoon." She listened, and then said, "Franz, the missing chef, got back from Atlantic City. Carolyn and I are on our way to Brooklyn."

29

Working the Case in Bensonhurst

Luz

Mrs. Cratchett let us in again with a pencil stuck behind her ear and glasses hanging on a chain. Snow was spitting on the Victorian houses and into the neighbors' little front yard shrines, sending tears dripping down the faces of Virgins and saints. I hated to think what the weather would be like later in the day. Carolyn was so wired she wouldn't even stop for lunch before we hit Bensonhurst, so I had to hope Mrs. Cratchett would provide some. Pastrami maybe, but not the chicken and dumpling soup.

She was bundled up in a thick sweater the color of a red plum. It looked like she might have knitted it herself and dropped a few stitches. "They're downstairs," she said and gestured toward the door to the stairway.

Man, that office was frigging cold, only one little electric heater glowing red to take off the chill. I'll swear there were two the last time I came. Both Abe Cratchett and De-Shawn Brown had sweaters on and scarves around their necks while they compared Pettigrew personnel pictures to a printout of the gas man. They passed us copies of the printout and divided their piles in half.

"The chef says no Pettigrew people got near the turkey ovens except Roland, who just peeked in and said my turkeys looked too brown," Carolyn told them while she tried to get out of her cold-weather woolies. First, she pulled the black glove off her good hand. Then she blew on the naked fingers sticking out of the gray Velcro support on the right hand. Finally she was ready to attack her coat buttons. Christ, I'd be through my pile before she even got started, but I kept looking at the photos. The printout of the gas man wasn't very good, blurry, eyes and forehead obscured by a baseball cap. Too bad he wasn't one of those guys who thought he looked cool wearing his cap backward with the bill on his neck.

Even in a heavy winter jacket, he looked like he might be skinny and young. *Woman wearing man's clothing?* I wondered, and fished out pictures of Janet Fong and Allison Peabody. I didn't think so, but the gas man sure hadn't been Roland or Jack Armstrong, that pudgy puke. I should have choked him a little harder.

"Help," Carolyn cried. I glanced up to see that she'd managed to unbutton her coat and shrug part of it onto the electric heater. Scorched wool smells kind of like skunk. Both Abe and I grabbed for the coat. Carolyn looked close to tears, and DeShawn said, "The coat's okay. Only burned on the inside, Miz Blue."

How come she got called Miz Blue and I got called Luz? Had I asked him to call me by my first name? Hell no. Not that I minded, but she's younger than I am. I should have—

"You wanna take off your scarf?" DeShawn asked her. "I wouldn't, I was you. It's cold down here."

Carolyn fell into the last chair and took a deep breath. "I'm ready to start," she said. "How long do you think my coat will keep smelling like that?" Nobody hazarded a guess.

"You'll have to sit here at the computer desk," said Abe. "Unless you can do anything with that hand."

"Not much," Carolyn admitted as he handed her the printout. She took DeShawn's chair, and Abe put the keyboard onto the top of the printer to give her room.

"Just compare your pile of personnel pictures to the printout," Abe told her. "We don't even know if it's a real gas man because the uniform's covered by the jacket, and the security camera only takes black-and-white so we can't tell if the pants are the right color. The time's right: two fifty. The guy signed, but his name is illegible. The rest looks like Gas Company, but anybody with a clipboard and a tool box can claim that."

We all went back to work except Carolyn, who kept staring at the gas man, tilting the picture as if maybe she could see under the hat if she looked from a different angle. "It's not a very good picture, is it?" she remarked.

"Like I said, cheap camera at the tradesman's entrance," Abe replied.

"But he looks sort of . . . I don't know . . . familiar," she persisted. "Couldn't you sharpen it up somehow? I thought computers did that."

"It's not a digital photo," said Abe.

"Do you have a magnifying glass?"

Our private eye was beginning to get a little impatient. DeShawn said, "I maybe could make it better." Cratchett looked as if he doubted that. Carolyn, meanwhile, hadn't done a single comparison.

"Knock yourself out," said Abe, and DeShawn moved Carolyn out of the computer chair and at the same time away from the dinky electric heater. She sniffed at her coat, examined the scorch marks, and sat back down in the original chair, still studying the picture. Big help she was.

"I thought private detectives always had magnifying glasses," she complained. I bit my lip to keep from laughing, and Abe, who looked really irritable, started tossing stuff out of his desk drawer until he found a magnifier.

"It's scratched," said Carolyn.

"Live with it," was Abe's reply, and then there was a tense silence while DeShawn messed around with the computer and the printer.

Luckily Mrs. Cratchett called down the stairs that lunch was ready, so all of us, except DeShawn, trooped upstairs for Reuben sandwiches—that's corned beef and sauerkraut between two slices of weird bread—a heap of dill pickles, a bowl of soup, and this disgusting-looking stuff called *schmaltz*. I asked the mom what it was, and she said *chicken fat*, as if everyone served chicken fat instead of butter.

"We don't eat meat with milk products," she said. "'Stew not the kid in its mother's milk.' Aren't you familiar with the commandment?"

I passed on the chicken fat, but I figured the two of them, plus the cop dad, were heart attacks on the hoof. Of course, so was I. My mother uses lard. I did know Jews didn't eat pigs, so I didn't mention lard. No use making them sick, just because she'd made me sick. Jeez, chicken fat. How disgusting was that?

DeShawn came bursting into the dining room, carrying a new printout of the gas man, which he gave to Carolyn. Then he said, "Oh man, look at those sandwiches. Miz Cratchett, you are one cool mama, except you ain't black, but I don't hold that against you." He helped himself to three sandwiches, four pickles, pulled his soup closer, and eyed the *schmaltz*.

"Chicken fat," I said. "You spread it on your bread."

"Yo, *mama*! I do like fried chicken. Bound to like this," and he dumped a spoonful on his bread, then scooped soup into his mouth with the same spoon.

Abe took the printout from Carolyn, studied it, and asked, "How did you manage this, DeShawn? You been printing money at home?"

DeShawn grinned. "I did say I know a thing or two 'bout computers. So Miz Blue, that help you any?"

Carolyn had stopped eating to stare at the new gas-man picture. "I think I've seen him before. No baseball cap, no heavy jacket, but . . . I wish I knew the color of his hair."

Abe picked up the magnifying glass, looked closely, and said, "Black, probably curly. Look at the sideburns sticking out from under the hat on your left. The collar covers them on the right. He could be Jewish, but the nose is wrong."

"As if we all have the same nose," said Mrs. Cratchett, laughing.

"Most of us don't have that one," her son replied.

"I'm going downstairs for a minute," said Carolyn. "Please, excuse me." She took the latest printout, the magnifying glass, and a whole Reuben with her, each between fingers of her left hand. As far as I could see, she hadn't eaten anything but some soup and a slice of bread without chicken fat.

The rest of us ate our lunches and talked about what the hell we were going to do next, since the gas-man angle didn't seem to be panning out—unless Carolyn came up with something, and how likely was that? She was always seeing people she thought looked like other people or who just looked familiar. I'll never forget the time we were eating in a burrito place when she decided some guy in jeans and a work shirt reminded her of her gardener. She just had to go over to check. Poor guy shot out of there like someone had set fire to his pants. Probably illegal. For sure didn't speak English.

"All right," said Carolyn, reappearing with half a sandwich, the magnifying glass, and papers stuck between her fingers. She let them loose one at a time on the table, and the interesting thing was, the sauerkraut was missing from the sandwich. Had she flushed it? Abe had a john in the basement. She passed a photo, the printout, and the magnifying glass to Abe. "Compare these two pictures."

"The old woman and the gas man?" he asked.

"Yes, look at the noses. Allow some broadening for age, and they have the same nose. Furthermore, I'm sure I saw his picture on the wall at Mrs. Randatto's house. He must be a grandchild or a grandnephew. He's too young to be a son. Maybe he's Rosaria's brother. Did she say she has a brother, Luz?"

"No, she mostly bitched about being a slave to her grandmother."

"Exactly. So this young man probably is, too, and the grandmother sent him over, disguised as a gas man, to sabotage my turkeys."

Abe kept looking from one picture to the other. "I wouldn't give it much credence if you didn't think you'd seen him on her wall, but what have we got to lose? We'll work the computers, track down the relative, and—"

"Why don't we just go over to her house and accuse her?" said Carolyn impatiently.

"Like she's going to confess on no evidence? Get real, Caro," I said. "And thanks for lunch, Mrs. Cratchett."

"You seem to have lost your sauerkraut, Mrs. Blue," said Abe's mother. "Shall I add more to your sandwich?"

"Oh, thank you, but we need to get to those computers," said Carolyn, as if she was going to be any use tracking someone down on a computer.

"There's dessert," called Mrs. Cratchett. She probably thought no one, especially DeShawn, had had enough to eat.

"You flushed your sauerkraut, didn't you?" I whispered to Carolyn as we headed downstairs to the icebox.

"Of course not," said Carolyn indignantly. "It just happened to fall out."

30

Tracking the Unknown Suspect

Carolyn

I could feel the cold climbing my legs as we descended into the basement. How could Mr. Cratchett work here all winter with only that one little heater to keep him warm? Wasn't the temperature bad for his electronic equipment? And as for me, I was new enough to computers that I'd be of no use searching for an unnamed descendant of Annunziata Randatto. Maybe I should offer to go upstairs, where it was warm, and help Mrs. Cratchett wash the dishes. We could have a cup of hot coffee together at her kitchen and discuss the people in New Mexico who still have Jewish customs but have only recently realized they're descended from Jews who came from Spain to the New World to escape the Inquisition and then from Mexico City to New Mexico for the same reason. I'd read a book about it. She'd probably be very interested.

"You can use this computer," said Abe, steering me to a machine that might well have been the first desktop on the market. "It's okay," he assured me. "I just swap out parts to upgrade the old ones. Put the grandmother's full name, or as much of it as you know, into this box. See, it's labeled GOOGLE. It's a search engine. Then you hit GO and see what you get. Look at everything that might have information."

At least I'd used Google before, but this computer was
farther from the heater than I'd been on either of my last
basement postings. I read six hits, about her books, her
work among Sicilian immigrants, and her donations to and
volunteer work at her church, by which time my left hand
was frozen and hitting the wrong keys, even using the ag-
onizingly slow hunt-and-peck system to which I was reduced. Fearing frostbite, I retrieved my glove from the
pocket of my scorched coat and pulled it on with my teeth
so I could read four more articles. The others were calling
out names. There was a Tommaso Randatto, but he was
dead, and a Luigi Randatto in his fifties; he sold the finest
grappas in the country. "He must be Annunziata's son," I
called out, wanting to add something to the search. "Luz
and I drank some of his grappa in our coffee."

All those hits other people were getting, and what did I
come up with? A Maria, who married one Angelo
Calogero, who had been born in Palermo. I'd found a genealogical site. The couple had two daughters and four
sons. I did the math on the boys—sixteen to twenty-five
years old. Should I mention them?

Not wanting the others to think I was napping over here
in my freezing niche, I called out, "Annunziata's daughter
Maria and her husband, Angelo Calogero, have four sons."
I added names and ages, then minimized the genealogy site
in order to put the sons' names into Google. "Look at that!
They had a big baptismal party for the youngest, Salvatore.
He's sixteen now." I felt quite pleased with myself. I was
getting the hang of this.

"I'll take 'em," said DeShawn.

So I went on searching and read an article about
Lorenzo Randatto, a traffic court judge in Boston, who had
been charged with fixing tickets; an Allesandro Maria
Randatto, whose vegetable cart had been knocked over by
the carriage of a wealthy man, who had reimbursed the
angry vegetable vender with the princely sum of ten dollars; and an Ettore Randatto, who had won the prize for the
largest zucchini grown in Bensonhurst at a contest in 1990.

The zucchini had measured twenty-six inches in length, but Ettore's age was not given. Had he been a young urban farmer, he might be our man.

"Ettore Randatto," I called out. "He won the prize for the biggest zucchini in 1990."

"That's Annunziata's husband," said Luz. "He's dead."

Sighing, I got up and put one arm into my coat. "Sorry about the cold," said Abe, helping me with the other arm. "My second heater died yesterday, and I haven't had a chance to replace it."

"Well, get on the ball, man. If you do it before we close the case, you can charge it to Pettigrew," Luz advised.

"I couldn't do that," said Abraham, who had his nose very close to the screen. "If I charge it to Pettigrew, it's part of my income, and I pay taxes on it."

"Crap," said DeShawn. "You gonna take Social Security outta my money?"

"I am," said Abraham. "Have you traced the grandsons anywhere?"

"Yeah, three work for an uncle, and that Salvatore's a student at Brooklyn Science and Technology, an' he got him a website. Nothing but kid stuff on the website, but he don't like his granny much, I can tell you that."

"Okay, I'll take it from there," said Abraham, showing his first real interest.

"How come you're takin' my guy?" asked DeShawn.

"Because you're an impressionable young person, and I don't want to teach you bad habits."

"Huh?"

"He means he's going to do some hacking, and it's between him and his computer," said Luz, laughing. "So can the rest of us quit? The Randattos and Calogeros seem pretty clean except for the usual traffic tickets, public intoxication, and one assault charge that was dropped. I don't even know if the assault guy was one of ours, and he was too old to be the gas man."

I myself hadn't had a real hit since Salvatore, but the genealogy sites were interesting. "I have a few names of people who married into the families," I announced.

"Take a break," said Abraham. "Go on upstairs and make yourself something hot to drink. My mom's probably in her office on the second floor translating ancient Hebrew, but she won't mind you using the kitchen."

I was happy to take his advice, and the other two came with me. Abraham seemed to be impervious to the cold. He was back at work before he finished offering us a break. I took him some coffee, and then we settled in the parlor, warming our hands on the cups and sipping. "What do you think this upholstery is?" Luz asked. "It makes me squirm after about five minutes."

The parlor had a sofa and two chairs covered with the same uncomfortable fabric. "You ever hear 'bout horse hair? My granny, who's dead, had a chair she found left on the street an' got some kids to haul it home for her. Try sittin' on one a them mothahs in short pants." DeShawn shook his head at that boyhood memory.

"It can't be that old," I murmured and stood to look at family pictures on the wall. Conversation languished, and I went to the window. More snow. Getting to the subway would be difficult. Maybe Mr. Ming wouldn't be able to drive to Bensonhurst even if we called him. I wondered what Jason was doing and whether his student, Jose, had come out of his . . . whatever.

"Salvatore Randatto Calogero!" said Abraham triumphantly. He was standing in the doorway with a wide smile on his face. "An honor student at Brooklyn S and T, won the sophomore prize for the best computer-science program, honorable mention for his experiment in a chemistry department contest, grandson of Annunziata Randatto, the famous Italian grandmother cookbook writer. I do think he's our man."

"Why?" I asked, judging it too good to be true. I'd been wondering if I'd ever get home, where it was probably warm, at least in the daytime. It certainly wouldn't be snowing. I'd never seen snow in El Paso, although older

people remember a white Christmas in the middle 1970s
that kept families from getting together for Christmas dinner. Tamales are a big Christmas favorite in El Paso.

"Well, one reason is I was able to trace his Internet traffic. The kid's been reading about flammable liquids.
Maybe he picked out one—like the yellow-brown-colored
one that just keeps on burning if you light a match to it—
cooked it up at school or in his basement, and substituted
it for your cognac."

I found it hard to believe a sixteen-year-old could have
done such a thing. "Where did he get the gas-company uniform?"

"In a uniform store," said Luz. "Or you can order one.
Hell, you can get a nun's habit without proving you're a
nun."

"How would you know that?" I asked, astonished.

"Because there are nun and monk stores in El Paso.
How else? I wanted to go trick-or-treating as a nun when I
was a kid, but my mom said the habits didn't come in my
size."

"Well, how could a sixteen-year-old pass for a gas man
at Pettigrew's?"

"If you saw the five o'clock shadow on this kid's school
photo, you wouldn't have to ask," replied Abraham.

"Then how would he have got hold of this flammable
liquid?" I asked, now hopeful that I might indeed be able
to go home.

"Carolyn, if terrorists can make bombs they put together in airplane johns out of ordinary stuff people pack
in their carry-on luggage, this kid can make anything he
wants," said Abraham patiently. "He's smart, he's scientif-
ically oriented, and he probably needed to get his grandmother off his back. Maybe they didn't even mean for
anyone to get hurt, just to make a fool of you."

A surge of hope washed through me. "So what do we do
now?" I asked. I wasn't going to suggest that we go to the
boy's house and ask him. No one had thought that was a
good idea when I suggested visiting Annunziata Randatto.

"I'm going over to Brooklyn Science and Tech; they're in session, and he doesn't strike me as the kind of kid who would be cutting classes. I'm going to tell the principal that I'm a graduate myself, which I am, and that I'm a private detective working out of Bensonhurst, who needs a computer-savvy kid who'd like to make ten dollars an hour running computer traces for me after school, and I read in the newspaper about one of their students, Salvatore Calogero, who won the computer prize. Then the principal's gonna call the kid in—"

"—and he gonna be peein' his pants to get at that job," said DeShawn gleefully.

"Then you hire him and question him discreetly over a period of days until he confesses, which is unlikely to happen. How long is that going to take?" My hope waned.

"Wrong," said Abraham. "I'm going to tell him I got a kid coming in tomorrow, so if he wants to come over to my house after school to look at the machines and see if he's up to the job, I'll be there this afternoon, or he can get a ride over with me."

"What if he says no? Every mother tells her children not to accept rides from strangers."

"He's not going to say no, Carolyn," Luz assured me, "and if he does, Abraham and I will wait outside for him and drag him over here for questioning."

"That's kidnapping," I protested.

"It'll work," said Abraham. "It would have worked on me when I was sixteen. And your coming along is a good idea, Luz. You'll be a retired police lieutenant coming on board as my partner because business is picking up. Just don't swear."

"Christ, you sound like Carolyn," she snarled.

"Most principals don't like swearing in their offices," said Abraham, who rarely seemed to take offense. "So let's get going and hope the kid isn't on the football team and wired into practice."

Abraham took his coat out of the hall closet while Luz limped downstairs for hers. "You two stay out in the kitchen so he won't see you when he comes in with us. My mother's got bagels in the refrigerator. Microwave some, and help yourself to cream cheese and jam. Then, after we get back, listen at the basement door till he's fallen for my computer setup. *Then* you come on down. The four of us ought to be able to break him pretty quick."

I felt another surge of hope rise as they left. And to think that I'd found Salvatore, the little horror. What kind of boy puts flammable liquids on someone else's turkey? And his grandmother would go to jail, too. Contributing to the delinquency of a minor, conspiracy to commit arson. She'd given me advice about my book signing, bad advice according to Ms. Summersoon with whom I'd chatted while signing the last forty books.

31

Reunion at the Old School

Luz

Abe's old high school looked like a square brick prison. It even had a fence around it with iron spikes on top. Any kid got thrown from the fourth floor onto those spikes, he was dead meat. "Kinda grim, isn't it?" I asked.

He shrugged. "It's a good school. Must be a hundred years old, but they've kept it up. Parents who don't have a dime to waste will kick in when it needs something the city won't pay for. Of course, it may have changed. Used to be mostly Jewish and Italian. The Italians brought the good lunches to school, and we brought the good grades home." He laughed. "A little political incorrectness there."

"Well, I'll admit there's no graffiti and no gangbangers hanging on the corners selling dope or smoking weed."

"Nope," said Abe. "If they're following the old pattern, they still recruit cops' kids for the football team. I wasn't one of them, but I had a friend named Feingold whose dad was a captain on the Brooklyn force. Hymie weighed 220 and played center. Guys from other schools and dropouts looking for trouble tended to stay out of Little Hymie's way. He was an enthusiastic street fighter, and if there *was* any trouble Hymie couldn't handle, we could always count on his dad, Big Hymie, to send cops over to break it up."

He laughed nostalgically. "Those were great times. If they hadn't let me in here for computer science, I'd have been beaten up every day in some other high school full of future criminals who thought any kid wearing a skullcap was fair game. My mom got me enrolled here. Dad thought I should learn to fight."

That conversation took us through gloomy halls with no windows as far as the principal's office, a place that made me nervous because my principals had always been nuns. This one was a short, skinny guy, dark hair, dark skin, and a hawk nose in a little face. "Hi, Mr. Mosticelli," said my detective buddy. "I didn't know you were the new principal."

Mr. Mosticelli didn't look all that pleased about it, but he stood up to shake hands. "Abraham Cratchett, isn't it? You were in my European history class, if I remember correctly. You wrote on a test that the Catholic Church had always had it in for Jews and almost fell over when I agreed with you and gave you a B, even though you seemed to think that Holy Roman Emperor Charles V was a fool for abdicating and going into a monastery."

"Yeah, well, I figured he was the big cheese, so why give it all up for a false Messiah?" Abe laughed. "Turns out it was gout, not piety that drove him to the monks."

"I saw that in the paper, Abraham," said Mr. Mosticelli. "And who is this lovely lady, your wife?"

"You and my mother. Mom practically proposed to her in our living room. This is retired Police Lieutenant Luz Vallejo. I needed a partner who spoke Spanish, and she's my man. I don't know if you know it, but I'm a private detective now. If my dad ever retires, maybe he'll come in with me."

"I wouldn't count on that," said Mr. Mosticelli. "I remember your father. Brooklyn's finest, through and through. So what can I do for you, Abraham?"

I just kept my mouth shut through all this. It was interesting, though. Different from El Paso for sure. Abe spun his story about needing a kid to do computer searches and seeing the name Salvatore Calogero in the paper. "Wouldn't hurt to have a guy who speaks Italian," he added, as if he aimed to hire a little United Nations sooner or later.

"Salvatore Calogero. A good boy with a talent for computers, I'm told. But if you're looking for a linguist, you might want to consider one of the Asian students. The old neighborhood's filling up with them, running us Italians out. My wife wants to move to Oklahoma when I retire. We have two children in Tulsa."

"Well, the Asians are smart, but I think I'd rather stick with one of the old families. The Calogero kid lives in Bensonhurst, doesn't he?"

"He does. His dad is first generation, but his mom is a Randatto. They've been here almost as long as your mother's family. I'm surprised she's still living in the old house. Let me get Sal in here."

I breathed a sigh of relief. An Asian kid wasn't going to get Carolyn and me back to El Paso, and I was sick and tired of cold weather and cold wind and this frigging coat that was so heavy it made my shoulders ache. Just what I needed, to have my shoulders turn as bad as my knees. Even aching hips were better. Hips and knees could be replaced. I'd never heard of a shoulder replacement.

Pretty soon Salvatore Calogero shuffled in, looking like he was heading for a firing squad. Poor kid probably spent his early years being educated by nuns. "I didn't do anything, Mr. Mosticelli," he said right off.

"I know you didn't, son," Mosticelli replied. The boy then proceeded to look as cool as a kid his age could. "This is Abraham Cratchett, one of our earlier computer whizzes, and his new partner, Lieutenant Luz Vallejo."

The boy looked less cool. Had he had run-ins with cops? I wondered.

"She's retired and becoming a partner in Abraham's private detective agency."

Now the kid went wide-eyed. Obviously private detectives rated higher than cops.

"He's looking for a high-school student to work for him after school and mentioned your name."

The kid burst into a wide smile.

"Ten dollars an hour. Three hours a day. You'd be running computer traces on missing persons and persons of interest in other cases," said Abe casually, as if he weren't luring the kid into a trap.

"Wow!" said the kid.

Then Abe mentioned a bunch of computer equipment he owned. Didn't mean anything to me, but the kid's eyes got wider.

"You mean I'd get to use your dual-core?"

"That's the idea. You'll want to come to the office and see the equipment. That is, if you're interested in the job."

"Yes sir, Detective Cratchett. I'm really interested. And I can run any equipment you've got, even if I never have before. I mean, I can read the manuals. I mean, it never takes me any time at all to—"

"Great," said Abe, and handed the kid a card. "You can come over after school, or—" He looked at his watch. "Or if Mr. Mosticelli wants to let you miss a half hour of your last class, I'll give you a ride."

The kid looked pleadingly at his principal. "It's ten dollars an hour, Mr. Mosticelli! My class is shop, and I already know how to use a glue gun. My dad taught me, and he'd really like me having a job. He's always saying I should get a real job that pays something instead of working for free for my grandmother."

"That would be Mrs. Randatto?"

"Yes, sir," said the kid, his face falling. Maybe he was afraid Mosticelli would call her for permission. If he did, we were screwed. She might know Cratchett since he was on retainer to her publisher.

"I suppose you could miss shop," said the principal, "but you do have to call your mother for permission. If she's worried, let me talk to her. Abraham's an old student of mine."

So that's how it worked. The mother took Mosticelli's

recommendation of Abe, which might well be the last one Abe ever got from his old history teacher. In fact, when Abe told her he'd read about her son's prize in the paper and chosen him for the job on that basis, Mrs. Calogero said she and her husband were so proud of Sal, and would love to have him work for a graduate of S and T, especially here in their own neighborhood, where he could walk home. Blah, blah, blah. I could hear her over the phone from where I sat. She had an accent that would take a hacksaw to cut through.

In five minutes flat we had the kid in the backseat, talking computers nonstop with Abe. He seemed like a good enough kid. I just hoped Abe didn't get taken with him and decide he didn't want to send young Sal to jail. Guess I should have known better. We arrived back at Abe's and headed straight downstairs after saying hello to Mrs. Cratchett, who frowned at her son as if he was a child predator. Obviously Carolyn and DeShawn, who were hiding out in the kitchen, had told her the whole story—probably Carolyn, who can't keep her mouth shut, even when she really needs to.

Abe let the kid sit in front of the dual-core, whatever the hell that was, and run a trace on some name. The kid did better than I did. Maybe not better than DeShawn, I couldn't tell. Probably better than Carolyn. I figured she'd just stumbled across Sal because she liked genealogical sites. Hell, for all I knew, Sal might have put himself up where she found him.

Then DeShawn came stomping down the stairs to be introduced. "Hi," said the kid, "I'm going to come in after school to do the trace searches."

"Good for you, bro," said DeShawn.

"And this is Carolyn Blue," said Abe. "She's a client."

The kid first looked puzzled. "Blue?"

"Yeah," said Abe. "You probably read about her in the paper. They're calling her the Incendiary Gourmet because of some turkeys she flambéed."

The kid gulped. He had some Adam's apple on him; I could see it even under the five o'clock shadow. "Turkeys?"

"You know anything about that, Sal?" I asked, pulling up a chair so we were almost knee-to-knee.

"No, ma'am," he said in a little voice. "I don't read the papers much."

"Well, you probably didn't need to read about it. You already knew what was going to happen."

"No, ma'am. I didn't. Honest." He was clutching his elbows, looking really scared.

"You don't have to be frightened, Salvatore," said Carolyn gently. "We just want to know what happened." She was giving him this sweet, motherly look.

Way to go, Carolyn! I thought. We were going to play good cop, bad cop. Young Sal didn't have a chance in hell.

32

The Interrogation in the Basement

Carolyn

I had to feel sorry for the boy. Even needing a shave, he had the saddest brown eyes, and his lips were trembling. "Why would you do a thing like that?" I asked gently.

"It wasn't meant to make a *big* fire," he said. "Just burn up the turkeys. Like a joke, you know?"

"Pretty elaborate joke," said Abraham. "Did you buy the liquid or make it?"

"Made it." He was beginning to look sulky.

"You don't even know me," I pointed out. "Why would you want to burn up my turkeys?"

"Well, you were going to set them on fire anyway," he said defensively.

"Not a fire like that. Just a pretty display."

"It's a silly idea. Why would *you* want to do that?" He looked as if he was regaining his courage.

"Why the hell did *you* care what she did with her turkeys?" Luz snapped. "They'd have been fine if you hadn't stuck your nose in. Where'd you get the gas-company uniform?"

"Borrowed it," he muttered.

"Who'd you borrow it from?"

"Just someone."

"Whose idea was it that you change the flambéing liquid for something that wouldn't stop burning?" I asked, still trying to sound pleasant, although I was losing patience.

"I don't know what you mean. Can I go home now?" He glanced back at the computer he'd been using, then said, "I guess there's no job."

"There's a job," said Abraham, "but I'm not giving it to a liar. If you can explain this—"

"Nothing to explain," the boy mumbled. "I just played a trick. I guess it didn't work out so good."

"*Well*, not *good*," I corrected, unable to help myself. Children never learn acceptable grammar if they aren't corrected immediately.

"Come on, Caro," said Luz impatiently. "We don't care whether the kid knows the difference between *good* and *well*. Who the hell does?"

"I do!" I retorted. "And I do not understand why a boy who's never seen me before today would go to the trouble of using the Internet to concoct something that would ruin my launch party and cause all sorts of damage. It makes no sense at all. Someone put him up to it."

"So he's covering for someone. Wants to take the rap himself," said Abraham. "Happens all the time, but playing stupid isn't going to keep you out of jail, Sal, unless we get the full story. I've got enough evidence to have you arrested for arson and more. They'll probably certify you as an adult, and you'll end up in prison with a felony conviction on your record when you get out. No job with me, no college, no figuring out some great program, starting your own company, and ending up the next Bill Gates.

"Instead you'll be a felon on parole, scrambling for some scut-work job like those part-timers in the kitchen at Pettigrew's, the ones who saw you there when you sent them outside so you could check for a fake gas leak. Between what the police are going to find when they check your Internet searches and the witnesses to your entry at

Pettigrew's, you don't have a prayer of beating this rap. You're even on the sign-in sheet and the security tape. Your only hope is mitigating circumstances."

"You're gonna turn me over to the police?" he asked, as if he'd never foreseen that. "Not only is there no job, but you're gonna get me arrested?" He looked horrified, and added, "That sucks."

Abraham shrugged. "Your choice."

"And it's too bad, too," Luz chimed in. "You were just what we needed if you hadn't turned out to be the arsonist."

"But I didn't mean to be an arsonist." He sounded panicked, and he was gnawing his thumbnail.

"Evidently you did, Salvatore," I said. "You admitted that you wanted to burn up the turkeys."

"Stop calling me Salvatore. You sound like my grandmother."

"I know her," I replied. "I even had lunch at her house the other day. A fine woman."

"You don't know anything. Messing with the turkeys was her idea," he said indignantly. "Like you said, I never heard of you until she told me I had to make up something that would burn your turkeys to ashes. I didn't care about the stupid turkeys."

"Now, Salvatore, why would your grandmother do that?" I asked gently. "Are you making up a story?"

"No way," he protested. "You wanna know who got me the uniform? She did. She got it from a cousin in Queens who works for the gas company, and she made Rosaria, who's my cousin, take it in to fit me."

"I met Rosaria, too," I said, looking doubtful. "Why would a nice girl like Rosaria, who's such a fine cook, want to get herself involved in something like this?"

"Because everyone does what my grandmother says," he replied desperately. "She's a mean old bitch."

I gave him a scandalized look, and he hastily revised his sentence, "Old woman, I mean. Sorry. And Rosaria hates to cook. She didn't want to learn, but our grandmother made my aunt teach her, just like she makes me take care of her garden. Like I care if the Randattos win another zucchini prize like Grandpa did before he had a stroke."

"Rosaria did tell me she hated cooking," said Luz thoughtfully, as if she was finally beginning to take his story seriously. "So the gas-man caper and the fire-bomb turkeys were your grandmother's idea?"

"Right," said the boy, but then he began to look frightened again. "You can't tell her I ratted on her." His face had turned white with fear. "Mother of God! I'll be dead meat if she ever finds out."

"All right, Salvatore," I said soothingly, "but I don't understand why she'd want you to do that to me. She'd never met me before the night of the party."

"You think she'd tell me? She just says do this, do that. No explanation. And we all have to do what she says." He was shivering, but I wasn't sure whether it was caused by fear or the temperature in the basement, which was a bit warmer because of the five bodies crowded near the futile electric heater.

"Hey, kid," said DeShawn, "you're a sucker if you take the rap for your granny. She don't sound like no nice lady to me."

"What do *you* have to do with this?" Salvatore asked disdainfully.

Oh my, I thought. *Racial prejudice rears its ugly head.*

"I'm the muscle in this agency," said DeShawn, looking mean. "And I'm pretty sharp with them computers, too, so don't think Abe can't get along without you. Detective agencies don't hire felons. Right, Abe?"

"Quite true," Abraham agreed. "Your best chance is to tell the whole story to the detective who's investigating the case. Mrs. Blue happens to be a friend of his, and she'll put in a good word for you if you're truthful. You'll probably get off with a misdemeanor charge, suspended."

"And *then* my grandmother will kill me. Or she'll get someone in the family to see that I have a fatal accident."

"Oh, my goodness, Salvatore, believe me, I won't let that happen," I assured him, horrified at the thought that the Italian grandmother might collude in the death of her own grandchild.

"If you tell the truth, Sal, your grandmother's going to jail," said Abraham. "If you don't, you'll be going to jail, which I'd be sorry to see. Mr. Mosticelli thinks you're a student of great promise."

"Who'd believe me?" the boy said miserably. "My grandmother's a famous woman. People all over the country try to make her recipes. According to her, no one can do it except maybe a few Sicilians, but she's still rich and famous."

"What nonsense! I've made a number of her recipes," I said indignantly.

"Who the hell cares about the recipes," snapped Luz. "Either the kid's going to tell his story, or he's going to jail, and there's no worry about the cops not believing him. He's got no motive, and he didn't think the whole mess up. Why would he? So what do you want to do, Sal? Spend twenty years or so upstate with a bunch of hardened criminals who think you're really cute and want a piece of you, or tell Detective Worski what really happened? Your grandmother may not like jail, but they'll probably put her in the kitchen and make her the most popular woman in the woman's prison, where they don't see a decent meal from one week to another." Luz grinned. "It's a great opportunity for her to widen her audience."

Salvatore stared at Luz for a minute as if she was crazy. "You're kidding, right?"

"Right," she agreed. "We heading for the cop shop with or without you. You don't come, they'll come and get you after we've talked to them. Your mother, who sounded like a nice woman, will probably have a heart attack when her son is arrested in her own house. On the other hand, you go with us, you earn points for solving their case like a good citizen, and your mom can stay proud of you. You can go to work for Abe here, and your dad will be happy, too. So how about it, *hijo*?"

The boy looked at me as if I had the answer. "I think it's the right thing to do," I told him. "I'd want my son to be a good citizen."

33

Salvatore Chickens Out

Luz

When the five of us left Cratchett's, the wind was blowing snow in my face. It felt like a rain of needles, and cold! *Hijo!* If I hadn't had that thousand-pound wool coat on, I'd probably have dropped dead on the spot. Add to that that Mrs. Cratchett saw us leaving with the kid, whose face was tear-stained, and demanded to know what was going on, like we were planning to kidnap him and drown him in the river.

Abe took her aside and told her the kid wanted to confess to the police, and we were going along to stand behind him. Then we piled into Abe's car, an old black clunker that ran like he rebuilt it every month, Abe and DeShawn in front, the kid between Carolyn and me in back. He didn't have a word to say the whole ride, but Carolyn held his hand and kept assuring him that everything would turn out all right.

Abe and DeShawn discussed the prospects of the New York Knicks. Great ride. Bad traffic, bad weather, and we had to cross a bridge. I was sure we were going to skid right off into the river, but Abe seemed to know how to drive in snow. If I'd been at the wheel, we'd have been drowning in ice water before we got halfway across to

Manhattan. Still Abe's car had a working heater, which he turned on. So it was a step up over a ride with Mr. Ming, and pretty soon we were looking for a parking place somewhere near the police station where Worski and Benitez hung their hats. They'd be waiting for us because Abe had called to say we were bringing a turkey-case suspect in.

They had to wait a little longer while we found a place to park four blocks away, and then we had to stand around shivering while Abe fed the meter. That was the longest, coldest walk I ever took, and I'll tell you, if you've ever heard the story that hell is cold, not hot, you better believe it. My frigging teeth were chattering after two blocks, and Carolyn kept saying she didn't think it was ever this cold in the Midwest, where she used to live. The native New Yorkers didn't take it so hard, although Sal's lips had disappeared he had them held so tight. Might have been he was scared, but we'd told him the truth: He'd get off light, and Grandmother Randatto would take the rap. Still, the poor kid was caught between a big Sicilian rock and a legal mountain.

We all raced up the steps and through the doors in a burst. Grimy floors and hard benches never looked so good because today the cop shop was *heated*! In fact, it was so well heated, we were shedding coats, gloves, and hats while Carolyn told Sal that she and Abe were going upstairs to tell Detective Worski we were here, and Sal wasn't to worry; it would all be over in a half hour. The kid still wasn't talking, so DeShawn and I sat him down between us, just in case he got any ideas about running. Running is one thing I don't do anymore, and DeShawn didn't have his bicycle with him, so "better safe than sorry," as my *tia* said about a million times when I was in the police academy and she was bent on talking me into dropping out.

Carolyn and Abe were back in about five minutes, and we went up the stairs single file, Sal between Abe and De-Shawn, Carolyn last and sounding out of breath.

Benitez was still in the detective's room, looking pissed off as usual. Her shift was probably over, and she wanted to head home before she got snowed in here. I was worrying about that myself. The introductions were made, while other detectives, who were at their desks instead of working cases out in the miserable weather, stared. And then the shit hit the fan.

Sal launched himself at Benitez, babbling, "They kidnapped me. Help me, ma'am." Benitez staggered, got a hold on him, and shoved him into a chair.

"What the hell?" She looked at Worski.

Worski looked at the kid and said, "*He's* your suspect? He's a kid."

"I'm only sixteen," Sal sniveled. "I'm an honor student at Brooklyn S and T. They fooled my principal by saying they had an after-school job for me so I'd go with them, and then they took me into the basement at his house." Sal pointed at Abe. "It wasn't even heated, and they kept me there until I confessed to something I didn't do. Please, can I go home?"

He managed to look pathetic, the little shit, and the two detectives, frowning, didn't know what to say. I felt like giving the kid a rap on the head but restrained myself because it wouldn't look good when I'd just been accused of kidnapping. DeShawn was muttering the *m-f* word until Carolyn elbowed him and said she didn't appreciate that kind of language, but Abe—well, Abe didn't flick an eyelash. He just readjusted that little cap on the back of his head and shoved his hands into the pockets of his coat. Now that I think of it, we looked like a damn funeral procession, every frigging one of us in black.

"Salvatore," said Carolyn, obviously shocked, "I'm very disappointed in you. You promised to tell the truth, and I assured you that everything would be all right, and what are you doing? Lying to the police and telling a really terrible lie. You know very well that—"

"Mrs. Blue, maybe you better keep you mouth shut,"

said Worski, "since you've got enough at stake here to make you—"

Carolyn started looking mulish, but Abe interrupted. "Detective, my client won't say another word. As for Sal's kidnapping charge, he was delighted to come with Lieutenant Vallejo and myself. His principal vouched for me, and his mother gave permission."

"But you lied to him about why he was going to your office."

"It wasn't an office," said Sal. "It was a scary, cold basement. I want to go home."

"Hold your horses, son," said Worski. "We'll get to the bottom of this."

"Perhaps we should all retire to an interrogation room and listen to the tape I made of Sal's confession. It will explain a lot about why he did what he did and who—"

"You taped me?" he shouted, and then burst out crying. Carolyn patted him comfortingly on the back and passed him a tissue. She's a woman who's always ready to pitch in if someone has a runny nose. Of course, Benitez was trying to get her away from the kid, and Worski wanted Abe to know that the tape wasn't worth shit because the kid hadn't given permission and, even worse, his parents hadn't.

"I'm well aware of that, Detective," said Abe, still as calm as a Valium addict. "But the tape is instructive, and there is evidence against the boy that you can easily retrieve. There are tapes showing him entering Pettigrew's in disguise on the day when the flambéing sauce was switched; he had the opportunity because he claimed to be investigating a gas leak in the kitchen and sent the kitchen staff out; and a warrant will get you his computer search on flammable liquids. I imagine a search of his house will even turn up the chemicals he used. He hasn't been at all careful about covering his tracks. He had means and opportunity.

"As for motive, his grandmother put him up to it, and

evidently Mrs. Randatto is a formidable woman who wanted to sabotage Mrs. Blue's book-launch party."

"Randatto?" Worski looked thoughtful. "In Benson-hurst? Annunziata Randatto?"

"The very same," said Abe.

"I've heard stories about her. Maybe ten, fifteen years ago a buddy of mine in Brooklyn said everyone thought she offed her old man because he retired from the family business to grow zucchini and let the sons take over, and they were screwing it up. He died; she ended up running everything."

"She killed Nonno?" The kid began to cry again. "She'll kill me, too. You can't tell her I—"

"Tell you what, Sal," said Worski. "I think we need to get your parents in here."

"You can't do that either." He accepted another tissue from Carolyn. "If they tell my grandmother, Mama will—"

"Well, the fact is we can't let you go, and we can't question you unless you have a parent or a lawyer present. You got a lawyer?"

"I'll tell you anything you want. Just don't call my mother. What's she going to think? She's so proud of me, and now she'll think I'm a criminal."

"She didn't know your grandmother put you up to this turkey business?"

He shook his head violently. "Nonna said it was be-tween her and me and Rosaria and my cousin in Queens who works for the gas company. Even he doesn't know why she wanted the uniform, just that he'd better get it over to her house. I don't know what she threatened him with. Can you put me in a witness-protection program or something? I've seen that on TV." The kid thought a minute. "But if you do that, I'll never see Mama again, and she'll be scared and sad. Oh boy, I am really screwed. I hate my grandmother!" More tears, poor kid. Even I felt bad for him, the little turncoat. Saying I kid-napped him.

Abe's cell phone rang, and Worski gave him a dirty

look. "You wanna settle this business, or you wanna take calls on my time? I could be home with my new wife, who's probably cooking goulash. Damn, but that woman likes to make goulash."

"How wonderful," said Carolyn. "Is she Hungarian?"

"She couldn't be more Hungarian if she played gypsy violin."

"I have to take this call," said Abe. "It's my mother."

"Oh hell, we wouldn't want you to pass up a call from your mother," said Benitez. "I got plans, but if your mother's calling, we'll all wait until—"

"Thanks," said Abe and pressed the Talk button. "Hi Mom, what's up?"

Benitez, looking seriously pissed off, got her own cell phone out, tapped in a number, and said, "Hi, Vera. It's Juana. I'm stuck here at the precinct. Looks like I could be here all night the way things are going, but the others will be there, unless the snow gets worse . . . Uh-huh . . . Well, at your age you shouldn't be walking on icy streets, if you don't mind my saying so. Take a cab. Lemme give you Sergeant Melendez's number. She'll have a better take on how many are coming."

"Is that my mother-in-law you're talking to?" asked Carolyn.

"Well, her name's Blue," snapped Benitez after hanging up, "and I'd be attending an organizing meeting if it weren't for you and your turkeys. She's a ball of fire, that woman."

"Yes, isn't she?" Carolyn murmured.

"He's with me, Mom. Tell her he'll call her." Abe snapped his phone shut and said, "My mom says Mrs. Calogero just called and wanted to know where her kid was."

"You see? She's worried about me. I gotta go home," cried Sal.

"What you've gotta do, kid, is call her."

"I'd love to have your wife's goulash recipe, Detective," said Carolyn. "And if I publish it in a column, of course I'll give her full credit. In fact, Salvatore, I imagine your mother is a wonderful cook. Maybe she'd like to give me a recipe, too."

"Are you crazy?" the kid exclaimed. "It was your turkeys got me in this mess. My mother's gonna hate you."

"I beg your pardon," said Carolyn huffily.

34

Arrival of the Distraught Mother

Carolyn

Detective Worski returned to the room and announced that Mrs. Calogero was coming to the station. Her son groaned and put his head down on the detective's desk where, speaking to the scarred wood surface, he said, "She'll probably bring Dad—or Nonna. That's it. She'll bring Nonna, and my grandmother will—"

"She's not bringing your grandmother, kid. I told your mom not to tell the old lady you were here. Okay? As for your dad, your grandmother sent him to New Jersey to truck in a load of fruit or something, so he won't be back in the city till later tonight."

"In this weather?" I asked. "Poor man." I was picturing the immigrant father lost in the snows of New Jersey.

"We're sending a car for your mom, and she's getting a sitter for the younger kids, so no sweat."

"No sweat?" said Salvatore, his voice breaking. "She'll have to get one of my aunts, and the aunt will tell my grandmother, and my grandmother will come down here and kill me."

"Not going to happen, kid," Detective Worski assured him. "Now, Benitez and I want to listen to Cratchett's tape before your mom gets here."

"Speak for yourself, Worski," growled his partner. "I don't want to be here at all. I'm off shift. I'm tired. I got a meeting, and it's snowing out there like a son of a bitch."

"Detective, you should watch your language in front of the child," I whispered.

Detective Benitez ignored my plea. "So, Sal," said Detective Worski, "we got to put you in a room until your mom gets here. Who do you want to go in with you? We don't like to leave kids by themselves."

Salvatore studied the three of us and pointed to me. "At least *she* didn't lie to me about a job, and she was up front about why I was really in the cellar."

"I'd be delighted to sit with Salvatore," I said immediately. "In fact, Detective Worski, maybe you could provide me with coffee, and the boy needs something to eat. Teenagers are always hungry, and it's probably past his dinnertime. Maybe a sandwich and a Coke to tide him over until he gets home." I said the last to reassure him.

Detective Worski grumbled something about coffee and donuts being good enough for most guests at the precinct, but he did call downstairs and ask that someone order a sandwich and bring it up with a Coke and coffee to room 210. Then Detective Benitez led us to a nasty little room with hard chairs and scruffy walls and floors. I felt like a prisoner myself sitting in there; nonetheless, I knew that it was incumbent upon me to make conversation with Salvatore in an attempt to take his mind off his troubles.

"I was very impressed with your school records, Salvatore."

"How come S and T let you see them?" he asked. "Isn't that against the law?"

"I suppose I should have said that I was impressed with the article about you in the paper." If Abraham had been searching illegally online to find out about Salvatore, I didn't want to get him in trouble—which isn't to say I approve of hacking. "Honor student, winner of prizes in computer science and chemistry. Very impressive. As it happens, my husband is a chemistry professor."

"I only got honorable mention in chemistry, and I wish I'd never got that. It's no big deal. Three of us got honorable mention, but Mom told my grandmother, and that's probably how she came up with the idea that I could make something to keep your turkeys burning. How come you were setting fire to turkeys anyway?"

"My editor thought that up, so I didn't have much choice."

"Yeah, well my grandmother thought up having a bigger fire, and *I* didn't have any choice. I told her I wasn't that great at chemistry, and she got mad, like I was saying that to get out of obeying her. And look what happened. I must have screwed it up. She said the turkeys burned the ceiling and set fire to the tablecloth."

"They did; two of the turkeys anyway. I expect the tablecloth was my fault. I was so frightened when the first turkey started hissing, spitting sparks, and clawing toward the ceiling that I dropped the flambéing sauce. Then the sparks set the tablecloth on fire."

At least he looked more interested. "Wow, I wouldn't have minded seeing that. Grandma thought it was pretty funny, everyone running out on the balconies and all."

"Did she really?" I muttered angrily. Then it occurred to me that the boy didn't seem to know what had happened on the street. Hadn't she told him? Did he really ignore the papers and the TV news? "The whole debacle got a lot of coverage in the media." I watched him closely.

"What's a de-what?"

"Disaster," I replied.

"Wow! And I'll bet I didn't even get my name in the paper. Or maybe that's a good thing, since they want to arrest me."

"Well, it certainly made you harder to find." Deciding on a change of subject to something that might cheer him up, I said, "I noticed that your father's originally from Palermo. There are wonderful Norman buildings there with gorgeous mosaics."

"I don't know about that, but he came over as soon as

he could get together enough money for passage. That's why my grandmother calls him the just-off-the-boat son-in-law and treats him like shit. Sorry. Anyway, Dad says Palermo is falling apart because of all the graft and the Mafia getting their share of all the money for everything."

"Goodness." I needed to get off that topic, although I wondered if his father had been in the Mafia. Maybe he still was. "If your grandmother doesn't approve of first-generation immigrants, how did your mother happen to meet and marry your father?"

"Oh, that's cause he got a job at the family fruit market hauling boxes and sweeping floors. He met my mom, and they fell in love, and my grandmother had a shit fit. Ah—sorry about that. But they kept seeing each other anyway on the sly, and then they told Grandma they were getting married, and if she didn't like it, they'd just move to another city and never come back since she didn't pay my dad a decent wage anyway. Grandma locked Mom in her room for two weeks, but then Mom escaped, and they got a priest to marry them in Jersey. Grandma sent the uncles after them, but it was too late, so they stayed in Brooklyn, and my dad runs the fruit market now."

"What a romantic story," I said, smiling at him. "And you have brothers and sisters?"

"Sure. Three brothers older than me in the import business with the uncles, and two sisters younger, who hide every time my grandma comes to the house. They don't want to get roped into doing the cooking over there like Rosaria."

"Salvatore! My child! What have they done to you?" A chunky, middle-aged woman with a nose much like Salvatore's, but smaller, burst into the room with Detective Benitez in pursuit. "First, you tell me you're going for a job interview; now I find you're in jail. What has happened?"

"He's not in jail, Mrs. Calogero," I assured the poor woman. "He's just being questioned about an . . . an incident in Lower Manhattan."

"Who are you? A policewoman? How could you think

my son would do anything bad? He's a good boy, an honor student." She clasped both hands to her bosom as if she were having a heart attack.

"Come on, Mama," said Salvatore, evidently embarrassed at his mother's theatrics. "She's just a nice lady. She got them to give me a sandwich and a Coke. Her name's Mrs. Blue."

"Blue?" Maria Calogero frowned. "Carolyn Blue? I've heard about her. She's an enemy of the family. A woman who created a big scandal so that her book would outsell your grandmother's." She turned on Detective Benitez. "And you left my son, my baby boy, alone in a room with an enemy of the family? I want to call our lawyer immediately. You can't talk to my son until Mr. Colleone is here to represent Salvatore."

"That's your right, ma'am," said Detective Worski, coming into the room behind his partner.

"Hey, I don't want Mr. Colleone here," Sal said. "He's Nonna's lawyer, and she got me into this mess. He'll look out for her, and I'll go to jail. Mom, promise me you won't call him. I want to go to college and become a famous computer scientist, not go to jail."

"What are you saying, Sal? You blame your grandmother for whatever—"

"You stay with me when they question me and just listen."

There were tears in his eyes, so I passed him another tissue, surprised that all mothers didn't routinely provide their children with a little travel pack. I'd always made sure Gwen and Chris had them before they left for school.

"Are you crying, Salvatore? Look what you make him do," she said to me.

"Mrs. Calogero, he's afraid of his grandmother, who forced him into doing something that got him in trouble."

"The cops even think she killed Grandpa, Mom, so she could take over the family. Grandpa loved us, but she never did, because of dad being just off the boat."

Mrs. Calogero looked shocked.

"Why would she send Dad out in a snowstorm to pick up fruit in New Jersey? She's got lots of people who could go, but she sends him? He's not even a good driver."

The poor woman had turned pale and blinked back tears. I handed *her* a tissue, in case she didn't have her own. "Salvatore is, as you said, a good boy, Mrs. Calogero. I really don't think he'd have done what he did if he hadn't been pushed into it. Why would he? He didn't know me. You need to listen to what he has to say. The poor child was so frightened he asked Detective Worski about the witness-protection program, but then he changed his mind because he'd never see you and his father again if he—"

"Never see his mama again?" She dabbed her eyes with my tissue. "I'll listen, and Salvatore, you better be telling the truth. You know I can always tell. If you're making up stories about your grandmother, you'll be grounded until you graduate from high school. I promise you that."

The poor boy sighed and said, "You may decide to ground me anyway, and not because I'm telling lies about Grandma." Then they went off to some other room where there were no doubt one-way-glass windows and cameras to record the proceedings.

35

Mrs. Calogero's Heart Breaks

Luz

While Carolyn was locked in with the kid, a uniform outside the door in case Sal attacked her, or his mother, who showed up later, attacked him, Abe and I discussed the case and said goodbye to DeShawn, who wanted to go home because tonight was rib night at his mother's house. I'd have joined him if I'd been invited. I was so hungry my stomach was starting to hurt more than my knees until Abe found us a snack machine and we treated ourselves to sodas, chips, and candy bars, all recorded in his Pettigrew expense book.

Then the two detectives, Sal, his mom, who'd been crying, and Carolyn edged out of the room. Worski pulled us aside with Carolyn and said we could watch and listen in a side room with one-way glass while he and Benitez questioned Sal with his mother present. I thought that was damned decent of him. In his place, I might not have been so nice. "We're doing this by the book," he added, staring at Abe.

"You wouldn't be doing anything at all, if I hadn't found him for you," said Abe, and then the kid and his mother went into another room with Benitez while Worski showed us into their viewing room.

"If you really need to let me know something about what the kid is saying, you can push this button and I'll come out, but I don't like an interrogation interrupted once it's going, so don't piss me off."

"You're a sweetheart, Worski," I said, forestalling Abe from being the first one to piss Worski off and get us sent away before the interview began. Our private detective had been getting short-tempered himself. Probably had indigestion from the junk food. And thinking of food reminded me that Carolyn and I were supposed to be meeting Roberto in Queens for dinner. I took out my cell phone and called him. Big surprise! He wasn't pleased to be ditched on such short notice until I explained that we'd discovered who'd sabotaged Carolyn's turkeys.

"You mean someone actually did?"

"What, Roberto? You thought she did it herself? I'd tell you about it, but the cops are about to question the suspect, and we get to listen in."

"Fascinating. You and your friend are two amazing ladies. Why don't we meet tomorrow at noon, same place."

"Sure, if the case ends tonight." Where did the NYPD get these chairs? I wondered, shifting uncomfortably. "Gotta go."

With the glass and the mike we could see and hear Worski going through the identification of people who were present for the interrogation. He didn't mention us.

"You're going to make another tape?" asked Sal, looking upset.

"You're treating my boy like a criminal," cried his mom. "I won't have it. He's a good boy."

"Ma'am, what he's admitted to doing *is* criminal. It's the extenuating circumstances, one being that he's a kid, that we figure to nail down in this interview," said Benitez. "You don't want to go over all this, we can just arrest him and—"

"No, no," cried his mother. "I've got to hear it, too. Salvatore, you answer these people truthfully."

The kid rolled his eyes and nodded. When Worski

pulled out some glasses and perched them on his nose to look at his notes, Carolyn said, "Poor Detective Worski. He didn't use to wear glasses. I suppose he's going far-sighted." Abe shushed her.

"So start by telling us how you got into this mess, Sal," said Worski, like he felt sorry for the kid. That settled the mother down some, and she said, "The whole story, Salvatore. Don't leave anything out to spare my feelings just because it's your grandmother you're talking about."

"Ma'am, don't prompt the suspect," Benitez snapped.

Before his mom could take offense at the word *suspect*, the kid said, "I was over at Grandma's, pulling up dead tomato plants and stuff like that, which I have to do every year since Grandpa died."

"I can't believe that people are saying my mother killed Papa," said Maria Calogero, patting her eyes with a soggy tissue.

"I should have given her the pack," Carolyn murmured to me.

"We can dig the old man up, ma'am, but that would come later." Worski made a note, and Mrs. Calogero burst into tears again.

"Do you think I should tap on the door and offer a pack of tissues?" Carolyn asked.

"Let them take care of it," I told her. "They can get Kleenex, food, sodas, whatever."

"I wish you would find out," said Sal. "I really loved Grandpa. If she killed him, I hope she goes to jail for life."

"Salvatore! How can you say that about your grand-mother?"

The kid sighed and hung his head. Benitez started drumming her nails on the table, and Worski said, "You were saying about the tomatoes—"

"Yeah. Every November after school. Sometimes October, but I been ducking her because I got a lot of home-work, and I wanted to get started on my projects for this year. Winning prizes doesn't hurt when you want to go to college. That's what my counselor says." Worski looked impatient, so Sal gulped and continued, "Anyway, she called me into the kitchen and offered me some of Rosaria's cake and a cup of espresso."

"What, so close to dinner?" gasped his mother.

"Yeah. That's when I knew something was up," agreed Sal. "She doesn't waste her espresso on the likes of me, son of just-off-the-boat, even when I painted the outside of her house."

His mother looked devastated to be reminded again of the family's contempt for her husband.

"That's when she said that, me being such a smart chemist, she had a job for me. She wanted me to make up a liquid the color of cognac. She even got out a bottle and poured some so I could see the right color, like I've never seen cognac, what with all the uncles making big money importing it and swilling it down at family dinners, that and grappa. The liquid had to burst into flames when it was lighted, she said, and keep burning until whatever it was poured on was burned all up.

"I told her I didn't know how to do that, and of course she got mad and snatched back the cake I hadn't finished eating yet and threw it in the garbage can. Mean old woman. I was hungry. I thought she was gonna hit me. Wouldn't be the first time."

He glanced at his mother like he thought she should have protected him, and maybe he had a point. It would make good testimony against the old woman. I could see Worski making a note—probably "child abuse." That would be my guess.

"So I said maybe I could ask my chemistry teacher how to do it, and she got madder and said this was between me and her if I knew what was good for me. I wasn't supposed to tell anyone, and I'd have to figure out how to make the stuff myself. I knew I probably could by checking out the Internet, but I didn't want to, so I said, where was I gonna make this stuff if I found out how? I couldn't use the chemistry lab at school since she didn't want anyone knowing about it. She told me to make it in the basement at home, and she'd pay for whatever I needed to do it, but I'd have to do it at night when the family was asleep."

"You made it in *my* basement?" gasped his mother. "We could have burned to death in our sleep—your papa, your brothers and sisters, all of us dead."

"Well, it wasn't *my* idea," he said defensively. "I was scared to death. Jesus, Mom, I'd have been the first one to go up in flames."

"Don't use the Lord's name in vain," Mrs. Calogero snapped.

I clapped my hand over my mouth to keep from laughing out loud because Carolyn was nodding with approval. Obviously she and Sal's mom saw eye to eye on some things.

"She said I should make at least six cups of the liquid and hide it in the basement till she was ready for it, then clean up after myself so no one would ask what I was doing down there. So that's what I did."

"No wonder it's been so hard to get you up in the morning lately." His mother looked pretty upset. "Salvatore, I can't believe you'd agree to such a thing without telling me."

"She said if I really wanted to go to college, I had to prove myself to the family. I said I didn't understand what she'd want with something like that, and she said it had to do with an enemy, and it wasn't any of my business, that maybe she'd tell me later if I turned out to be reliable."

"I suppose I'm the enemy Mrs. Randatto was talking about," said Carolyn. "What a horrible woman. She'd never even met me when she recruited that poor boy."

"I told you she was bad news," I replied.

"Will you two shut up?" Abe snapped. He was right. The interview was going on. Well, Mrs. Calogero was going on.

"Oh, dear. Holy Mother watch over us! My mother is from Sicily," she explained, turning to the detectives, "which is still a place of feuds and mistrust, even killings. Not that I believe Mama would kill anyone, but she's al-

ways thinking that someone is our enemy. I do remember
her saying that her publisher was giving a big party for another author, and Mama was convinced that they were trying to replace her as the bestselling cookbook author, and
she couldn't have that. I told her it would never happen,
Mama's cookbooks being so popular, with such wonderful
recipes. And I thought that was the end of it. Salvatore, you
should have told me!"

"Right, and then Dad would have lost his job at the fruit
store, and she wouldn't have even given him a recommendation. That's what she said. How's he gonna get another
job at his age? So I did what she said."

Maria Calogero exclaimed, "My heart is broken!" She
really started to cry then, so Benitez had to send for tissues
and water, and they took a break.

First, Carolyn said Annunziata Randatto was a terrible,
terrible woman. Then she said she was really hungry, so
Abe had to show her where the snack machines were and
provide change. I figured that this investigation was going
to cost Pettigrew's a bunch if we didn't get it settled
tonight. Not that their costs were any skin off my nose, but
I did want to meet Roberto for lunch tomorrow. I didn't
plan on sleeping with him—Carolyn was probably worrying about that—but at my age it was fun to have someone
sexy to flirt with.

36

Salvatore Continues

Carolyn

I felt better after the first chocolate bar. Maria Calogero was still sobbing into the police department's tissue, and I couldn't blame her. She and her mother and all the rest of them had to be the most dysfunctional family I'd ever run into. I'd had my differences with my father after my mother died, but he'd never asked me to do anything illegal or dangerous. I'd have to give him a call when I got back to El Paso.

"Mom, could you stop crying, so I can get this over with?" said Salvatore, his voice coming over the microphone into our room.

"Of course, my son," she agreed after a few more hiccupping sobs. "You must be so hungry. It's past dinnertime." She reached into her capacious handbag and fished something out, which she handed to Salvatore. He forgot about his testimony and began to eat.

"You brought me cannoli," he mumbled happily around a mouthful, the cream catching in the bristles of his sprouting beard.

Detective Worski snapped the recorder back on and told the boy to start talking. Everyone wanted to get home to dinner. "Okay, but I'll have to talk with my mouth full," said Salvatore. I was surprised that his mother didn't protest, but she beamed at him, as if the treat made up for the fact that she'd evidently never defended him from his grandmother. "So I searched on Google, looking for a liquid the color of cognac that would burn a turkey to ashes when it was set on fire and make Grandma happy."

"Hold up," said Benitez. "You said she wouldn't tell you what the stuff was for."

"That was before I actually figured out something that might work and synthesized it."

"What was it?" asked Benitez.

The boy asked for a piece of paper and drew a formula on it with a pencil. "I forget the name, but that's it. I learned how to make it on the Internet, too—there and from some books I borrowed from my chemistry teacher. I can write down the experiment if you want. Took me forever to get six cups, and I was scared to death the whole time. Like Mom said, I could have burned down the house and all of us with it. So then I hid it in canning jars and went over to Grandma's to tell her. She'd been paying for the chemicals and the equipment, and she gave me more money. She was real happy and called me a good boy. Not often she's said that to me."

"Where's the money? Did she give you a check?" asked Worski.

"Cash. I hid it in a shoebox and stuck it under a sheet of plywood in the attic, as far away from that liquid as I could get it. I was going to buy a subscription to *CPU* and a secondhand exterior hard drive for my computer."

"Oh, Salvatore, we'd have helped you with that," said his mother.

"I know you'd have wanted to, Mama, but we never have any extra money."

"That's her fault, too," muttered the mother. "She doesn't pay your father what he's worth, and now your sister Agata needs her tonsils out, and Mama wants her own doctor to do it in the kitchen."

Salvatore looked terrified. "Don't do that, Mama. I'll

give you the money in my shoebox." He turned to Worski. "Will you let me do that? Grandma's doctor will probably kill Aggie. He's a hundred years old, and nobody does operations on kitchen tables anymore."

"So how did you get the stuff you made into Pettigrew's?" Worski asked.

I thought he could have at least reassured Salvatore about his sister's operation.

The boy's shoulders sagged. "She got this uniform from our cousin in Queens. He works for the gas company."

"He owes her money," said Mrs. Calogero.

"Figures. Then she made Rosaria take the uniform in. Rosaria's not so good at that kind of stuff, and I looked like a dork. I figured no way were they gonna let me in the back door when Grandma told me I had to pretend to be a gas man and order everyone out of the kitchen because of a gas leak so I could pour my stuff into the cognac bottles or whatever."

"How were you supposed to find the cognac?" Benitez asked.

"Grandma sent Rosaria over with crostini first so she could look around for the pitchers with the stuff. Rosaria had to skip a whole day of school, and Grandma slapped her when she complained. She wouldn't even write an excuse for her, or me either. You remember when they called you, Mama, to ask where I was, and you chewed me out for ditching school? Sorry I lied to you, but I was scared to tell you about Grandma and the stuff I'd made."

"I'm the one who's sorry, Sal," said his mother.

"Anyway, they let me in with no problem. I'd have been twice as scared if I'd known there were cameras taking my picture. And then no one complained about leaving when I told them about the gas leak. I think they all wanted to have a cigarette or something. The hall was full of smoke when I left. And I found the pitchers right away, but one of them had this long spout. That was a bitch." His mother frowned, and he murmured an apology.

"I had to pour the cognac out in a sink and run water to

take the smell away while I poured in my stuff, which was in my tool chest, and man, my hands were shaking so bad, I spilled some and had to mop it up and stick the dish towel in the tool chest.

"I got the liquid on my clothes, too, and kept thinking all the way down to the street that I was going to catch on fire if I ran into someone with a cigarette. I had to take the stairs, because I smelled like the stuff, and then I threw up in the alley from being so scared."

"Where in the alley?" asked Worski.

"Other side of the Dumpster from the back door."

"Okay, anything else, Sal?" asked Worski.

"No, sir. I went back and told Grandma I'd done what she told me, and she gave me some more money and ordered me to keep my mouth shut. Then I went home and got balled out by Mama, and that was it."

Detective Worski leaned so far back in his chair I was sure he'd fall over. Then he thumped the front legs down on the floor and said, "Here's what we're gonna do. Benitez, I want you to call out an evidence team to check for vomit behind the Dumpster."

"In the snow? There's not going to be anything left."

"Don't argue. Call the D.A.'s office, and tell them to get an arrest warrant and a warrant to search the Calogeros' basement and attic."

"What are *you* going to be doing?" she asked angrily.

"Taking a piss." He glared at her.

"You're arresting my son?" cried Maria Calogero. "I knew I should have called a lawyer."

"I'm not arresting your son. But I'm getting a warrant for your mother's arrest, ma'am. I hope you got no problem with that."

"Of course not. I can't believe my mother betrayed us the way she did. You can search my house without a warrant. Should I write out my permission?"

"That would be good," said Detective Worski. "Makes our job easier. Benitez, just get the vomit taken care of, round up a couple of uniforms, and we'll head for Mrs. Randatto's house."

Benitez groaned. "Four people to arrest one old lady? You don't need me."

"Depends on the old lady," said Detective Worski.

Salvatore asked what he and his mother were supposed to do, and they were told they had to stay at the station house until the grandmother had been interviewed.

"But you can't let her see us," said the boy, looking terrified.

"You can wait in the lounge with a female cop until it's all over." Detective Worski called for a woman in uniform to escort the Calogeros out. I suppose he was afraid they'd leave without a guard posted. Then he and Detective Benitez left, without even giving a thought to us in the next room.

"What are we supposed to do?" I asked.

"Go back to the hotel?" Luz suggested.

"No, I want to see this through. In fact, I want to sit right here while they interview Mrs. Randatto. Remember, we can buzz Detective Worski if we have anything to ask. We need to stay. We know more about what happened than he does. But maybe we could follow the Calogeros to the lounge for the time being. These are terrible chairs."

"Right," Luz agreed. "If you ass aches as much as mine does—"

I rolled my eyes and hissed, "Language," at her.

"Come on, Caro. The kid can't hear me. Anyway, he's in high school. He probably knows more dirty words than you do. Lighten up, will you?"

"How did you two ever get to be friends?" Abraham asked, standing up to find, I assume, more comfortable chairs.

"It's one of the miracles of the twenty-first century," I replied, and collected my gloves and handbag, my coat, and my earflap hat, which I hoped never to wear again after that trip.

37

The Rescue of Rosaria

Luz

When we got to the lounge, it had sofas and chairs with cushions. They weren't great cushions, lopsided and lumpy, actually, but I'll tell you, my butt didn't complain. It was happy to find a soft place to rest.

Maria Calogero was on her cell phone talking to her husband. "So where are you, Angelo? . . . Lost in New Jersey? I knew it as soon as Salvatore told me Mama had sent you out, and on a night like this. Do you even know what town you're in? . . . Well, can you see a motel? . . . Then pull in, Angelo . . . I don't care what she thinks. She may not even be part of our lives anymore, so don't worry about it. Just get some sleep. We got enough credit left on the card for a night at a motel . . . Tomorrow maybe the snow will stop, and you can find the fruit. Maybe we ought to move to California like we talked about before we got married . . . I know we got six kids . . . Well, then my brothers are gonna cut us a break, or they'll be really sorry. I know stuff, Angelo . . . Yeah, honey, things are gonna be better, so get some sleep. Promise me . . . I love you, too, sweetheart. Night." She hung up, looking about as tired as a woman could.

"Mama?" said Sal, his eyes young and worried.

"It's okay, honey," she said. Then she turned to me. "What are you doing in here?"

"Looking for a soft seat, same as you," I replied.

"I got something else to tell you," said Sal. "Something I forgot in there when I was thinking about the stuff I made for Grandma. Maybe you could call Detective Worski." Sal looked from Carolyn to me, but not at Abe. "See, Grandma, she caught Rosaria with this Chinese guy. They been meeting, talking about Wall Street and stuff like that, going to movies. They really like each other, but Grandma, like, had a shit fit. Sorry." He bit his lip and glanced at Carolyn. "She locked Rosaria in the attic. When they arrest Grandma, unless Rosaria manages to get out, what's gonna happen to her? There's no heat and no electricity up there. No bathroom. Grandma left a pot, and told her to shit in that. Sorry, ma'am." He looked back at Carolyn.

"How'd she meet this boy?" I asked. The whole thing was making me real nervous. "What's his name?"

"I don't know. He and some others were hanging around the neighborhood. His name's Charlie. Charlie Li, I think."

"Shit," I said and looked at Carolyn myself, but not because of my language. "The Wise Dragon guys. The youngest one dropped out the last couple of days."

"Well, I'm sure he means her no harm," said Carolyn.

"Oh right. If they know what we know, they think Rosaria's cousin Sal put their cousin in a coma."

"What are you talking about?" cried Sal. "I never hurt anyone. I just fixed some turkeys to—"

"No one told you those turkeys got heaved into the street and blew up a car, caused a bunch of accidents, and hurt a bunch of kids in a VW? What was the Chinese girl's name, Carolyn?"

"Birdie Li," said Carolyn.

Sal looked panic-stricken. "Did you know that, Mama?"

"I saw it in the paper," she confessed, "but I didn't know

you or my mother had anything to do with it. What are you saying, Lieutenant? You think the Chinese have Rosaria? Rumors are circulating they're moving in on our neighborhood. What can we do?"

"Can you get hold of Worski?" I asked the female cop, who'd been leaning against the wall looking like she couldn't follow the conversation.

"Don't know. I think he took his own car because he's got chains. Maybe he has a radio; maybe he doesn't."

"Well, try to get him. Try to radio the uniforms he took with him."

"I'm not supposed to leave here."

"Christ. Call downstairs. You can use my cell phone." I tossed it, and she caught it, but she couldn't get a dial tone.

"Abe, we better go. Rosaria's a good kid. She doesn't need to get caught in all this."

"How are we going to find her?" Abe wanted to know. "And I don't have chains, in case you didn't notice."

"We'll stop downstairs and put the desk sergeant on it. Then we'll head for Annunziata's house. If the girl's still in the attic, we'll get her out."

"Go next door to my brother's," said Maria. "She's his daughter. He'll help."

"If she's not in the attic," said Carolyn. "I mean if she's left with Mr. Li's grandson, call Mr. Li. I know where the Wise Dragon Benevolent Society is. I can show you." She wrote down phone numbers and passed them over.

Sal was shivering, his mother's arm around him. "I should go. She's my cousin, and this is my fault."

"You and your mother can't leave," snapped the policewoman, putting her hand on her holster and scaring both Calogeros half to death.

"Carolyn, how are you going to show us how to get anywhere, and in a snow storm, for God's sake? You stay here. One of us has to stay and listen to what Annunziata has to say when they bring her in."

Carolyn nodded. "This is terrible. I should have listened to you about *Signora* Randatto, but I really think the Wise Dragons won't hurt Rosaria. They were guarding me, not—well, as far as Annunziata's concerned, I thought because she was teaching her granddaughter to cook—"

"Rosaria's mother taught her to cook," said Maria Calogero angrily.

"Less guilt and more help," I ordered. "Come on, Abe. We need to get on the road."

"Salvatore and I will want to listen to what my mother says, too," Mrs. Calogero told the policewoman, as if she wouldn't take no for an answer.

"That's up to Detective Worski," said the cop, and leaned back against the wall.

After we talked to the desk sergeant, we made the long hike to Abe's car and slipped and slid our way to Bensonhurst. Thank God there weren't many people dumb enough to be driving that night. No cars were parked in front of Annunziata's house, and we didn't know if Worski had already picked her up, or if she was still inside. Neither one of us had a gun, but I didn't trust Annunziata; she probably had one stashed someplace. We talked it over and decided to knock.

"Between the two of us we ought to be able to overpower her if she answers," said Abe.

"The woman's built like a Humvee," I muttered, "but at least I've got plastic cuffs in my purse." So we knocked. And knocked. "Guess they picked her up," I grumbled. I was freezing to death, with snow piling up on my head and shoulders and trying to squeeze in around my collar. What a crap place to live!

Muttering curses that would have turned Carolyn gray, I took a whistle out of my purse. I carry that for protection if I can't carry my gun. It's not like I'm up to running away if I get in trouble that I can't take care of myself. I gave it two good, loud blasts and yelled, "Hey, Rosaria. It's Luz Vallejo. You up there?" Nothing. I yelled again. "We've come to get you out of the attic, Rosaria. If you're up there, break out a window and yell down to us. Your cousin Sal sent us."

Lights started coming on up and down the street, just smears in the falling snow, but I figured people were sticking their heads out their doors, probably all Randattos. I should have thought of that. If I told them what we were doing here, they'd probably take Annunziata's side and beat us up. From next door a guy came stamping toward us, Rosaria's father maybe, so I took the Mace out of my purse. I'd picked that up while Carolyn was shopping for fuzzy gloves to replace her leather ones.

"What's going on here?" the guy demanded in that Brooklyn accent that makes me grit my teeth. "Why you yelling at my mother's house?" His wife was right behind him, hugging herself and shivering. She got right up in my face, me with my can of Mace clutched in one freezing hand. "You're too old to be a friend of Rosaria's. You, too." She was peering at Abe. "You look Jewish to me."

"Yes, ma'am. Half anyway. Abe Cratchett." He held out his hand to the male Randatto. "I live a couple of blocks over."

"Barney Cratchett's boy?" asked the father. "Your dad's a cop, right? I think you went to junior high school way back when with my oldest boy, Carmine."

"Right," said Abe. "My mom buys her fruit from your brother-in-law's store."

Old home week, I thought. *Like Segundo Barrio in El Paso. Every one knows everyone.* I wished I were back home instead of exhaling ice crystals out here on the street.

"Look, sir," I said politely. "Your nephew Salvatore sent us. He says Mrs. Randatto locked your daughter Rosaria in the attic."

"You from the neighborhood?" asked Mr. Randatto.

"No sir, but I did meet your daughter while I was having lunch at your mother's." Shit. Maybe I shouldn't have mentioned that. "Nice girl. Great cook."

"Thank you," said Mrs. Randatto. "I taught her myself. So you know my mother-in-law? If that's so, you'd know she wouldn't lock Rosaria in the attic. There's no heat up there. And Rosaria's scared of spiders."

Smashing sounds crackled above our heads, and we all got showered with falling glass. "Help. Help me!"

Once I was sure no more glass was going to fall on me, I looked up, but shielded my eyes to be on the safe side. "Someone's up there waving her arms and crying for help," I said to the mother, thinking she was the best bet to rescue the daughter since she wasn't a blood Randatto.

The woman leaned over to shake the glass bits out of her hair, which was braided in a long plait that hung over the shoulder of her robe. Then she looked up and shouted, "Rosaria, is that you? What are you doing up there?"

"Freezing, Mama," the kid called down. "She locked me up here and then drove away with some people."

"I'll get the key," called her mother, and she stamped off to her own house.

"I thought Rosaria was just spending a couple of nights at her grandmother's," said the father. "I'm Luigi Randatto, by the way. How do you two know my nephew Salvatore?"

"Because he's such a sharp kid, I was offering him an after-school job doing computer work for me," said Abe, "and . . . well . . . it's a long story, Mr. Randatto. Maybe we'd better get your daughter to safety first. Frostbite, hypothermia—they're no joke. She may need medical attention."

Once Mrs. Randatto opened the door, with all the neighbors gawking, crowding around, and shivering, we closed it in their faces. The Randattos and Abe stampeded up the stairs. I limped up. But when I got there, poor Rosaria, covered with dust and cobwebs, crying hysterically, threw herself into *my* arms. "I knew you were my friend, Luz."

"Right, kid. Now we need to get you somewhere warm. You're shivering worse than I am." Wrapped up in ancient tablecloths and rugs with mothholes, she was shaking like a mule caught carrying smack over the border.

"I'm never coming into this house again," she whispered into my ear. "Grandpa's ghost is up here. Do you hear that, Mama? Grandpa's up there. She must have locked him in the attic, too."

33

Annunziata's Interrogation

Carolyn

While we were waiting, Salvatore fell asleep on one of the lumpy couches. His mother brushed his hair away from his face tenderly and whispered to me that her boy should have a blanket.

"Mrs. Calogero, it must be nearly eighty degrees in here. With a blanket he'll start sweating and wake up, and he's so tired. Look at the poor boy. He has circles under his eyes."

She looked, nodded, and said, "You have a boy of your own. I can tell."

"Yes, Chris. He's finishing his final undergraduate year in chemistry." Should I have said that? Would she try to save Salvatore by suggesting that my Chris made up the flaming liquid? "It's wonderful to be proud of one's children, isn't it? I know you are of Salvatore. Such a smart boy."

"He is. Salvatore wins prizes in chemistry, and in computers. He wants to go to college, too, but now my mother may have ruined all that. When he gets out of jail, she'll put him to work in the fruit store like my husband."

The policewoman had given up her manly stance against the wall and taken a seat on another couch. Now she, too, was sprawled out asleep, so I put my arm around Maria and led her out of the lounge. "We won't let that happen. Let's go to the little room where we can watch your mother being questioned. There's even a button to push if we know something the detectives should know." We walked quietly down the hall and slipped into the observation room.

"Umph," said my new friend. "Hard seats."

Then we waited silently, and uncomfortably, until Annunziata Randatto was led into the interrogation room, demanding that she be told why she was here and allowed to call her lawyer.

"If you haven't done anything, ma'am, why do you need a lawyer?" asked Detective Benitez, brushing snow off her coat, shaking it from her hat, and looking innocently at Mrs. Randatto while Detective Worski held out a chair for the grandmother.

"You take me for fool just off the boat?" snapped Annunziata before she sat.

Beside me the daughter stiffened.

"I want my lawyer. Guido Colleone. You've heard of him, no?" She shrugged off her heavy coat and narrowed her eyes at them. "Is a very good lawyer, Colleone."

"Benitez, have him called," Worski ordered. Then he sat down across from Annunziata. "Ma'am, you asked why you're here. Being as you're a famous author, I know you'll have heard about the turkeys that caught fire at the Pettigrew book party. Likely, you were there yourself." She nodded, rather regally, I thought, as if Worski were some peasant and she a Sicilian noblewoman deigning to acknowledge his question. "Well, ma'am, we think you had something to do with that traffic accident down on the street."

"Nothing. I no cook turkeys. Must be mistake by the cook, a woman from Texas, a place of many fires last summer. You read about them? Probably set by women cooking turkeys."

"You didn't get your grandson to make up a liquid that would burn those turkeys to a crisp?"

"Of course, no. What grandson? I have many. No grandsons cook. No grandsons at party. Where is my lawyer?"

"He's coming," said Detective Benitez as she entered the room. "You want a Coke? Some coffee?"

"Only coffee I drink, I make," said Annunziata with great disdain. "What grandson you think is cook? Randatto men no cook. Is woman's work."

"Salvatore," said Worski. "He confessed and said you put him up to it."

"He lie, or you lie. Probably you."

Annunziata's daughter shifted beside me and muttered something in Italian. It sounded to me like a curse. If she knew more about her mother's plots, hearing her son called a liar might bring the information out.

"Well, your grandson didn't even know the woman from Texas. Why would he want to mess up her party? He says you threatened him, so he had to do what you said."

"All lies. I know *Signora* Blue. She comes to my house for lunch after her party. Maybe she tell you these lies."

"Nope. It was your grandson, ma'am. Maybe he did it for you without you asking, because he loves you, but why would he think ruining the party would please you, ma'am?"

She sat silent for a minute. "I think I tell someone in family that giving party for new author and none for other authors causes resentments, but I don't resent. I am famous writer of cookbooks, bestselling author *Signor* Pettigrew have. I don't know. Maybe his mother tell Salvatore what I say, but the boy is stupid if he thinks I mean me. Look how it turns out, what he did. Bad, no?"

"The who-will-rid-me-of-this-pesky-priest defense," I murmured.

"What priest?" asked Sal's mother. "And now she's blaming me. My own mother blames me, and my son."

"It's a quotation," I replied. "Probably not exact, but

Henry II said that to some courtiers, and they killed St. Thomas a Beckett to please the king," I explained. "Of course Henry said he hadn't wanted his archbishop killed."

"Right, they killed an archbishop in a cathedral. I remember. An English king," said Maria, as if that explained such a horrible crime.

"But I never tell Salvatore to do such a bad thing," said his grandmother.

"So he did it on his own?"

"Is hard to believe, but then he is like his father, stupid."

I had to keep Sal's mother from pushing the button to get Detective Worski's attention, probably to defend the intelligence of both husband and son.

"And what about the gas-company uniform he says you got from a cousin in Queens so Sal could get into the kitchen at Pettigrew's? Incidentally, we've got security photos of him wearing the uniform into the building that day."

"Maybe Salvatore call Antonio. I no call Antonio. Ask him."

"Okay," said Benitez, and wrote down a name and address for cousin Antonio, "but you got your granddaughter Rosaria to tailor it for Salvatore."

"Rosaria don't sew so good. Not likely Salvatore ask her, but you ask Rosaria, if you can find her. She run off with a Chinese boy. No respect for her grandmother."

"A Chinese boy?" Worski looked worried and excused himself. I rushed out into the hall to meet him.

"We know about it," I said. "Salvatore told us Rosaria was dating Charlie Li and Annunziata had locked her up in the attic to keep her away from the boy. Since you were already gone, Luz and Abe went over to get Rosaria out of the attic or to find her in case the Lis kidnapped her in revenge for Birdie Li, who's still in a coma."

Detective Worski grabbed his head as if he had a terrible headache. "Italian families. I hate cases with Italian families. Unless it's families of chemists; they're worse than Italians. Either way, you're the one who gets me mixed up in this crap."

He stayed away from the interrogation room to track down the cousin by phone and have him brought in. Twenty minutes later the cousin was announced.

"Detective, a guy named Antonio Borreo from Queens just arrived," a uniformed officer informed Worski. "He says he was told to come in and ask for you, but he wants to see his cousin Annunziata first if she's here."

"Right. Like that's going to happen." Detective Worski told me to go back to the viewing room, which sounded as if he was sending me to a funeral parlor. Then he popped his head into the interrogation room and told his partner to stay with Mrs. Randatto until he got back. "Parlotti, go downstairs and run a check on a Charlie Li—Chinese, maybe related to that guy who's head of the Wise Dragon Benevolent Society. Possible kidnapping of Rosaria Randatto there. I got that name right?" he asked me. I nodded. "And Parlotti, where'd you put the cousin from Queens?"

Having been told, Detective Worski rushed off before I could complain about the way he'd spoken to me, and after all the help I'd given him on both cases. I was about to return to Maria when she rushed out of the room and threw open the door to the next, shouting at her mother, "You liar! Telling them you liked Mrs. Blue and invited her to lunch. You told me you hated her, that she was a stupid Texan, and why would people want books with recipes from every silly place she went?

"And I didn't tell Salvatore anything. I've never betrayed you, but you never even warned my poor son that your treachery had hurt that Chinese girl. Now Rosaria may have been kidnapped by one of their relatives. This is all your fault, Mama. All your fault. How could you do it?"

"Maria, be quiet," ordered an elderly, swarthy man who had just reached the top of the stairs, panting. "Don't talk to your mother that way." He pushed past me into the room and snarled at Detective Benitez, "Have you been questioning my client?"

"Who are you?" she snarled back.

"He's my mother's lawyer. He'll probably try to put my son in jail, but don't believe a word he says." Maria Calogero's voice had risen to a scream.

I grabbed her arm and pulled her out of the room without being spotted by Annunziata. Maria did try to resist me, but I kept whispering, "Hush, hush. It's coming to a head. If you have to, you can testify when they get through with your mother."

After that we watched while Detective Benitez left the room and Annunziata and her lawyer whispered together. In about ten minutes Detective Worski returned, looking smug. "So Mrs. Randatto, I just talked to your cousin Antonio from Queens. He says he owes you money and you threatened to call the loan if he didn't provide you with a gas-company uniform and hat."

"You lie. Antonio never say that."

"Maybe he doesn't want to be arrested as a coconspirator in the turkey bombing of Lower Manhattan. By the way, he's still got the uniform with the stains on it, where Salvatore spilled stuff because his hands were shaking. We can test the stains."

"My client knows nothing about any uniform or any stains and refuses to answer any more questions," said the lawyer.

"Sal was probably too scared to tell her he spilled the accelerant on the uniform, so your client gave it back to her cousin. The kid is seriously scared of grandma here. Oh, and Cousin Antonio is pissed about the fact that his uniform doesn't fit him anymore and his wife has to hand-wash the ones he has every other night because they can't afford a washing machine because of the vig Mrs. Randatto here is charging them on the loan. That's loan sharking, along with arson, assault, contributing to the delinquency of a minor—"

"If you're planning to arrest my client, she will post bail," said Colleone.

"Not until Monday she won't," said Worski. "No judges who do felony charges until then."

Maria and I looked at each other and breathed sighs of relief.

"So you're arresting my traitor grandson, I hope," said Annunziata fiercely.

"I'll release him to the custody of his mom. I think he's been through enough already, don't you, Benitez?"

"Whatever you say." She stood up and, looking at Mrs. Randatto, added, "You're a piece of work. Anybody ever told you grandmothers are supposed to be sweet old ladies?" Then she turned back to her partner. "Can I go home now?"

"No," said Worski.

Maria Calogero jumped up and hugged me. "I'm going to wake up my Salvatore and take him home." I nodded and went with her, wondering where Luz and Abe were. They'd missed all the fun.

39

The Sins of the Grandmother

Luz

Mrs. Randatto, who was married to Luigi and whose name was Magdalena and later insisted that we call her Magda, wrested her daughter away from me and wrapped her up in comforting arms while she murmured assurances that Grandpa wasn't really in the attic, and that they needed to get home.

"Mama, you're cutting me," complained Rosaria, who was calming down. Her mother jumped away and brushed at some glass shards that had stuck to her big boobs.

Then we all shuffled downstairs and out the door of Annunziata's house, which Luigi carefully locked behind him. "Where did your grandmother go?" he asked his daughter.

"How would I know? I was locked in the attic," came the resentful reply. "And you're never sending me over there again. I could have died up there from . . . from cold, or a spider bite."

"Do you have bites?" asked her mother anxiously.

"How would I know? There's no light up there."

"Might be a good idea, ma'am, to put her into a warm bath," said Abe politely. "Maybe give her something hot to drink."

"I haven't even had dinner," said Rosaria. "I'm hungry."

I was, too. It had been a while since my last candy bar, but evidently if you tell an Italian mother her child is hungry, she forgets about spiders and hypothermia and serves food. We all ended up in another big Randatto kitchen eating warmed-up pasta, garlic bread, and great little sausages and drinking red wine, Rosaria included. I told Magda it was the best pasta I'd ever eaten, and she gave me a recipe. Carolyn would be really pleased with this one. "I'm not like my mother-in-law," said Magda, shooting her husband a dirty look. "I like to share recipes and good food."

Luigi rolled his eyes and said, "Okay, *carissima*, but for the love of San Gennaro, Mama's in the recipe business."

"San Gennaro is my saint, not yours, Luigi. I'm the one from Naples, as your mother is always telling everyone, as if it's a sin or something. And what kind of woman locks her granddaughter into a disgusting attic? I've been up there. You have, too. This is the end of your mother picking on *my* children and bossing them around."

The kid crossed herself and murmured a prayer of thanks. Then she went back to her food. I had to wonder how long she'd been up there.

"Maybe you should tell us *why* you were locked in the attic, Rosaria," suggested her father.

"Don't try to blame it on me. I didn't do anything wrong. I just fell in love."

"Oh my sweet Rosaria, who did you fall in love with?" Her mother was looking all soppy.

The dad said, "She's only sixteen, Magda. She's a smart girl who wants to go to college. You want her to give that up and—"

"I wasn't giving anything up. I'm in love with a smart boy who wants to go to college, too. It was so romantic. We took walks, and we went to a gelato shop in Manhattan—"

"In Manhattan?" asked her mother. "Why in Manhattan? We don't have good gelato here? Who is this boy?"

"—and we went to the movies, and we sat on a bench

in Washington Square Park and talked about how we were both going to be big successes on Wall Street."

"Doesn't sound like any boy I know," said Luigi suspiciously.

"And then she ruined it. She caught us on the street together, getting off the subway, and said I couldn't ever see him again, and she was going to call his father and tell him what was going on, and then she locked me in the attic after she dragged me home, yelling at me all the way and embarrassing me."

"Why wouldn't his father approve of a fine girl like my Rosaria?" wondered Magda. "Maybe your mother has been telling lies about our Rosaria, Luigi. Anyone would be happy to have Rosaria for a daughter-in-law."

"What was it your grandmother didn't like about him?" asked Luigi. "What's wrong with him? You're not sneaking around with some gangster are you, Rosaria?"

"No. There's nothing wrong with him. He's wonderful, and I'll never see him again because of Grandma. I hate her. I—"

"Rosaria?" Her father looked stern.

"He's Chinese," she said defiantly. "And so what? He's handsome, and we'll have beautiful children, and—"

Both parents looked at each other like she'd said her true love was a Klingon who was going to take their daughter away in a starship.

"The bath was a good idea," said Magda and rushed her daughter toward the stairs that ran down into the hall.

"The thing about Charlie Li," said Abe soberly, "that's the boy's name—is that we think he's related to Li Cheng Bao, who's the head of the Wise Dragon Benevolent Society."

"I don't know the man, but I don't want my daughter dating an Asian. Bad enough they're opening stores here in Bensonhurst."

"Well, I hope you don't approve of your mother locking your poor kid in an attic full of spiders," I said. "Not that I think Rosaria should be dating the Li kid."

"At least someone has a sensible point of view. So Salvatore sent you over here to rescue my daughter from the attic and from the Li boy, Luz? Is that what my daughter called you?"

"Right, Luz Vallejo. And Sal doesn't know that the Li kid might be dangerous to Rosaria. The name Li doesn't mean anything to you, Mr. Randatto?"

"Call me Luigi. Never heard of any Lis. Maybe they're from Manhattan."

"They are, and the thing is the granddaughter in that family is in a coma because of that flaming turkey business. Maybe your mom told you about it."

"I read about it," he said, "but I don't remember Mama mentioning it, although she was at Pettigrew's that night for a party."

"I'm afraid she did more than attend the party," said Abe. "Your mother's not here because the police picked her up. She talked your nephew Salvatore into substituting a strong accelerant for the cognac that was supposed to be used to flambé the turkeys. Then when the turkeys set fire to the party room, they were thrown into the street, causing accidents, one of which almost killed the Li girl, who's expected to die. So you can see that the Li family might have a quarrel with your family. We were afraid Charlie Li might kidnap your daughter if she managed to get out of the attic."

"Charlie wouldn't have kidnapped me!" Rosaria cried. She was standing in the doorway with wet hair straggling down onto the NYU sweatshirt she was wearing over her jeans. Her mother stood behind her, rubbing her head with a towel. "You're saying Grandma made Salvatore attack one of Charlie's relatives? That really, really sucks." And she burst into tears again.

"Look, my mother wouldn't hurt anyone," Luigi protested.

"She does it all the time," snapped Magda. "She's a mean woman, and I remember her sneering the next day about how badly that party had gone for the woman from

Texas. Lock my daughter in an attic, will she? I'm going to tell the police what she did."

"Me, too," said Rosaria. "If anyone kidnapped me, it was her, and I heard her telling poor Sal his dad would be out of a job if Sal didn't do what she told him. That must have been about the turkeys. No wonder she didn't like Charlie. She tried to kill his cousin. Besides that, I saw the article in the newspaper about the accidents and asked her about it, and she got mad and said I wasn't to tell Sal, and if I did, I'd be sorry. I'll bet she's down there blaming him for the whole thing. Come on, Mama. Let's go to the police station."

"You can't testify against my mother," said Luigi. "Anyway, it's snowing. We might be able to get you to the hospital to see about spider bites, but—"

"She doesn't have any spider bites, thanks be to the Blessed Virgin," said his wife. "And it's about time you and your brothers took over the business, so let's go to the police station."

"Randattos do not turn one another in to the police," said Luigi. "It doesn't happen."

"I don't think you need to feel responsible for your mother's problems," I said. "I'm sure she's already under arrest. When Sal found out about the injuries, he told the whole story. Anyway, we need to get back to the station ourselves. The woman whose turkeys Mrs. Randatto sabotaged is waiting for us there."

"I'll go with you," said Rosaria. "I want to file charges."

"I'm going, too, " agreed her mother.

"I'm not driving you," said Luigi, "and I'm not letting you go off with two strangers."

"If they were good enough to help us rescue our daughter from Annunziata's attic, they're good enough to give us a ride to the station. Where is it?" Magda asked Abe.

"Lower Manhattan," he replied.

"Manhattan?" Luigi groaned.

"Don't worry, sir," said Abe politely, "since I live here in Bensonhurst, too, I'll see them safely home."

Randatto mother and daughter were already pulling on their coats, so the dad caved and came with us. It was a tight squeeze for the three of them in Abe's backseat, but even without chains, Abe got us there safely.

I had my first taste of Penne all'Arrabbiata in Sorrento, but a friend from El Paso had it at the home of a lady whose family was from Naples, and my friend loved it because the Italian peperoncini, chili peppers to Americans, make it so spicy. She got the recipe from her hostess and passed it on to me. *Arrabbiata* means *angry*, as in "an angry pasta sauce just attacked my mouth."

Penne All'Arrabbiata

- Cook *1½ pounds penne pasta* in a large pot of lightly salted boiling water for 8 to 10 minutes or until al dente. Drain.

- Heat *1 tablespoon extra virgin olive oil* in a large skillet and sauté *1 chopped onion* until translucent. Add *5 cloves sliced garlic* and sauté until soft, and then *6½ ounces finely chopped pancetta bacon* and cook until bubbling and transparent.

- Add *4 tablespoons capers, 1 cup fresh sliced mushrooms, ½ cup pitted, halved green olives, 1½ teaspoons crushed red pepper (dried peperoncini if available), 1 teaspoon salt, ground black pepper,* and *⅔ cup red wine*. Simmer until wine is reduced by half.

- Add *4 cups canned whole tomatoes crushed by hand*. Cook 10 minutes longer, add *6 fresh basil leaves*, and toss after pouring on cooked pasta.

- On top sprinkle with *one bunch chopped flat-leaf parsley* and ½ *cup grated Pecorino or Romano cheese.*

- Serve immediately. Around 5 servings.

Carolyn Blue,
"Have Fork, Will Travel,"
St. Louis Bugle

40
"Crazy Soap-Opera Italians"

Carolyn

We were all on the first floor, Worski explaining to a young man who had identified himself as ADA Prolick from the District Attorney's office, that Salvatore should be sent home in the custody of his mother since both of them had given statements against the accused, Annunziata Randatto. She stood scowling, hands cuffed behind her back, in the custody of Detective Benitez, who looked as furious as her prisoner. I was wondering how I'd get home; Luz and Abraham hadn't returned. I certainly didn't want to try to find the subway in a snowstorm and ride it uptown by myself at night. Maybe it wasn't even running. Detective Worski was growling, "You wanna make this case, you gotta send the kid home with his mom. In fact, they'll need a ride in a squad car."

"Haven't got one loose right now, Worski," shouted the desk sergeant. "We got accidents, some involving our own cars, and emergencies all over the place."

"Oh, thank you, Detective," cried Maria Calogero. "We can wait a bit. I never come to Manhattan. Goodness knows how I'd get back in Brooklyn on public transportation, and I don't—"

"We'll call you a taxi, ma'am," said the ADA, "but I think the boy should stay here. Social Services will—"

"No," wailed Maria, and her ready tears began to fall. "I won't be separated from my poor son, who has been led astray by my mother. I couldn't leave him here in the same building with her, and I can't afford a taxi because my mother won't pay my husband a decent wage."

"Basta," snarled her mother. "Keep your silly mouth shut if you know what's good for you."

"She's threatening me," sobbed Maria. "Just like she threatened my Salvatore."

"Okay." The ADA sighed. "Send the kid home with his mother."

"I protest," shouted Mr. Colleone, whose protests hadn't gotten a thing for his client so far.

The ADA worried me. He was a spindly, lank-haired fellow who looked too young to try serious cases. I hoped the District Attorney's office could find someone more experienced to take Annunziata to trial. I'd been about to ask if I could have a ride home as well, but if no car was available, I'd wait to see if Luz and Abraham returned. I wouldn't want to leave her stranded, although it occurred to me that they might have been in an accident. After all, Abraham had no chains, and the snow was still falling. New York was evidently looking at a white Thanksgiving.

Just then Rosaria Randatto burst through the door with a middle-aged couple, the woman held up by the man and Abraham, and Luz cursing and limping behind, saying the *f* word in its adjectival form accompanied by *snow*.

After casting one malicious glance at her grandmother, Rosaria headed straight for the desk sergeant and cried out, "I want to report a kidnapping."

I immediately assumed that the Lis had kidnapped her and Luz had taken part in her rescue. It must have been very exciting. "Good for you," I said, hugging Luz and patting Abraham's arm.

"Good for me, *what*?" my friend asked through gritted teeth. "Good that I fell down in the frigging snow? Good that my damned left knee is swelling up like a soccer ball?"

"I'll get some ice for it," I offered.

"Stop right there," Luz ordered. "What are you going to do with the frigging ice? I'm frozen as it is. We had to walk forever to get here. Every bastard in New York parked his car on this street, half of them cops. Magda fell down and can hardly walk at all. I fell down. Even Luigi fell down."

"It's about time one of my sons arrives to save me from these Mafioso *polizia* and my worthless lawyer," said Annunziata furiously. She tried to pull away from Detective Benitez and got yanked back for her trouble.

"Please treat my mother with respect," said the man named Luigi—Randatto I assumed—and then I wondered, not for the first time, if *frigging* was a more polite term for the *f* word.

"Is that all you can say?" his mother demanded. "Where were you when I was arrested and dragged from my home by these *banditti*?"

"Well, Mama, I was rescuing my daughter from the attic, where you locked her up and left her."

"Without dinner," said the middle-aged woman, who had been deposited in a chair and was inspecting her swollen ankle sadly. "My mother-in-law, who is an evil woman, involved my daughter and my nephew Salvatore, innocents both, in her crime, may the good Lord condemn her black soul."

"I do nothing," said Annunziata. "If the children are involved in crime, they do it themselves, maybe to please me, but I am not pleased. I do not approve. That Rosaria, she is a slut who chases Chinese boys and even her own cousin Salvatore, luring him to my house. Looking at him in his underwear. Disgusting girl. She has lust for her own cousin."

"I do not," protested Rosaria. "You said I had to fix that uniform. Like I wanted to see Sal in his underwear. Gross."

"Hey," said Salvatore, "I was more embarrassed than you. I don't even let my sisters see me in my underwear."

"He's a very modest boy," said his mother.

"And I'm the one who was kidnapped," Rosaria repeated, pouting because her first announcement had been ignored. "By my grandmother. Right there." She pointed at Annunziata. "I could have frozen to death in that attic. Or died of a poisonous spider bite. And my grandpa was up there. He told me she put him there, too."

I noticed that Detective Worski had straightened up, suddenly alert. "Your grandfather's in the attic, kid? You saw him there?"

"Of course no in attic. He die years ago," Annunziata said impatiently. "The child's a hysterical liar, not to mention a slut. Her and her Chinese boy."

Jumping up from her chair, Rosario's mother screamed, "I'll kill you, you evil old witch!"

However, she then screamed with pain and fell down when her weight hit the swollen ankle. Luigi Randatto ran to his wife while his mother shouted, "You choose her over me, Luigi? The useless woman from Napoli? Take care, or I bring you down!"

"Annunziata," cautioned her lawyer, but seemingly hopeless at the prospect of trying to advise his client.

"You! Shut your mouth. Another useless man," Annunziata snapped.

"So, young lady," said Detective Worski. Before he had been muttering things about *crazy soap-opera Italians*. "You saw your grandfather in the attic?" He nodded to Detective Benitez. "If we dig him up, what are we gonna find? An empty coffin? Some poor schmuck they killed to bury in his place? Maybe we can close a cold case."

"My Ettore no in attic," said Annunziata. "Everyone see him in his beautiful coffin."

"He spoke to me," Rosaria insisted. "While I was locked in up there. I couldn't see him because it was dark."

"Lies," snarled the Italian grandmother. "I am surrounded by liars and Mafioso *polizia*. Me, a famous cookbook writer."

"Most of your recipes are mine," claimed Rosaria's mother, who had been resettled, sobbing, in the chair by her husband. "I'll sue you for taking my recipes, like you poisoned Mrs. Barbaro for using our recipes in her *ristorante*."

"You know she poisoned the Barbaro woman?" asked Worski.

"Everyone thinks so," said Magda Randatto.

"Everyone thinks she killed the old man, but we can't take gossip to court," said Worski, disheartened. "Benitez, take Mrs. Annunziata Randatto to be printed and photographed. That all right with you, ADA Prolick?"

"Sure," said the young man and followed after Detective Benitez, his eyes glued to the detective's shapely, if overgenerous, bottom. I'd thought only women wearing high heels had that seductive sway to their hips. Evidently not. Detective Benitez was wearing what looked like black-laced shoes constructed for men, probably police issue. She hadn't worn such practical footwear when I saw her the first time. But of course she'd met my mother-in-law since then. Vera had probably told her about the male-chauvinist footwear conspiracy.

It seemed to me at that point that the evening would never end. A fellow with a red nose sticking out beneath his woolly hat sidled up beside me and asked, "Anything interesting going on? Lots of people in here for a night with a shitload of snow coming down."

"You have a nasty mouth, young man," I said, "and as far as I know, you have nothing to do with this case. I suppose you're just some passerby trying to get in out of the storm."

He looked rather surprised to be reprimanded for his language, but he rallied and said, "Sorry to offend you, lady, but every police case is my business. I'm a reporter just checking in to see what's happening."

"Really? Well, I'm the Incendiary Gourmet, whom you people have been writing false stories about all week. I hope you print a retraction, because my colleagues and I have discovered the person who arranged for my turkeys to flame out of control."

"Yeah?" He fished a notebook and pen from the deep pockets of his heavy overcoat. "Your colleagues, you say? So you're Carolyn Blue, right? Who are they?"

"I *am* Carolyn Blue. That's Luz Vallejo, retired vice lieutenant from the El Paso Police Department." I pointed to Luz, who was sitting on a bench massaging her knee. "And over there is private detective Abraham Cratchett. His office is in Bensonhurst, but he's under retainer by my publishing house, Pettigrew and Sons. We were the people who ferreted out those responsible for sabotaging my turkeys and how it was done." I gave him a detailed explanation of our investigation, all of which he took down, which assuaged my anger to some extent.

"Detectives Worski and Benitez are, I'm sure, good investigators, but like most police persons, they have more cases than they can handle. In my case, they simply settled for the simplest explanation of what happened that night, so we had to do the legwork, I believe it's called, ourselves. They have, however, been very cooperative about interviewing the suspect and witnesses and arresting the guilty. Is there anything else I can tell you, Mr. . . . I don't believe you mentioned your name."

"Downey, Bart Downey. Wow! What a story. And who are all these other people?"

"Aside from Lieutenant Vallejo and Mr. Cratchett, they are mostly relatives of the accused."

"And the grandmother did all this to—"

"Protect her place as the bestselling food writer at Pettigrew's, it would seem."

"Well, thanks, Mrs. Blue. Do you have a phone number I could call if I need to check my facts?"

"Actually, I have a cell phone," I replied, feeling quite proud to be able to say that. People in France had been

rather judgmental about my failure to own a cell phone. I
gave him the number and went off to confront Detective
Worski, who was still being harassed by excitable Randattos and Calogeros. Mr. Downey ambled over to Luz to ask
questions.

"Detective Worski, am I free to go home to El Paso
now?" I asked, after stopping to hug, shake hands with, or
be introduced to various members of Annunziata's family,
all of whom seemed to be nice people.

The detective scratched his head. "I guess I owe you
one, Mrs. Blue."

"Two," I replied. "Don't forget our other case. I was
very helpful in that one, too."

"Yeah. You're a regular Carolyn Spillane. So go on
home. You may have to come back to testify when she
goes to trial, but maybe I can get you out of that. I don't
know if I'm up to another round of your help."

Luz had limped up and agreed with him. "Working with
Carolyn is hard on the nerves. Stay out of her way,
Worski." Then she held my hand up and slapped it with
hers.

"What was that for?" I asked.

"That, my friend, was a high-five. We're a frigging success, you and me."

"About the word *frigging*, Luz."

"Forget it. Let's get back to the hotel. Why don't you
call Mr. Ming? I do *not* want to fall down again. I'll kick
in half for cab fare."

"Excellent. I'll use my new cell phone." Shortly there-
after, we waved to Abe, who was still being interviewed,
and stepped out into the street, where Mr. Ming's unheated
cab and smiling face awaited us. I tipped him 15 percent
for venturing out in the snow, regardless of Jason's belief
that 10 percent is quite enough.

41
A Message from Mr. Li

Carolyn

Vera was asleep in my bed when Luz and I returned to the hotel room, feeling both relieved and proud of ourselves. Luz even admitted that traveling with me was more fun than anyone would have believed. I decided to take that as a token of her friendship and went to my lumpy cot, smiling.

However, the next morning my mother-in-law awakened us at 5:00 A.M. with complaints: Where had we been the night before? She'd been worried about us. Even worse, where had Detective Benitez, who was to have attended an organizing meeting of the Hispanic League of New York Policewomen, been? We explained and were forgiven for worrying her, although she thought Benitez should have called her a second time to clarify the situation.

Then we got a lecture on matriarchal societies, the gist of which was that just because Annunziata Randatto had ruled her clan and misused her power over them, we weren't to think that matriarchal societies weren't better than patriarchal societies. "True," I agreed. "Look at the world today. Just because two flaming turkeys landed in the streets of New York, everyone jumped to the conclusion that it was a terrorist incident."

My mother-in-law nodded but still had that let's-irritate-Carolyn look on her face, so I forestalled her by mentioning the matriarchal society of ancient Crete, which had been very peaceful and successful. That well-chosen example placated Vera, who then pulled on fuzzy lined boots, put on her winter coat and hat, grasped the handles of her suitcases, and departed to catch her plane home, mentioning as she left a few of the terms of her contract with Pettigrew, terms which were much more generous than mine had been. Obviously Loretta would have to do some sharp negotiating on the *Eating Ethnic in the Big Apple* contract, for which I hoped to have another sellout book signing at Cooks and Books when the time came. I planned to swallow antiinflammatories *before* the event this time.

"Okay," said Luz, "why don't you see if you can get us tickets home for tomorrow, and I'll go to that museum that has the whale and dinosaur. I wouldn't put it past my nieces and nephews to meet me at the airport, demanding pictures and stories. We'll meet in Queens at Inti Rami on Eighty-seventh Street at twelve-thirty for Peruvian food with Roberto. And why don't you call Abe? Maybe he and DeShawn would like to come, too. We could make it a celebration."

"But I thought we might be able to book a plane today," I said as she disappeared into the bathroom. The answer was *no*, so I went back to sleep in the real bed, more worried about catching up on my sleep than catching feminism, as Luz had suggested the first morning I did that.

She woke me up at nine, ready to leave after having had breakfast, and insisted that I read the instructions she'd written out for getting to the right station in Queens and then to the restaurant. "The snow quit sometime last night, and big machines are tossing it up into piles in the gutters. Wear your boots." And she was gone.

I made plane reservations for the next morning—horrid seats at the back in a three-chair row—and was just dozing off again, having set my alarm clock for eleven, when the first phone call came, an invitation to be interviewed on TV that night about my exciting experiences as the Incendiary Gourmet and my adventures in clearing myself of turkey-tossing charges. Remembering Loretta's insistence that all publicity is good publicity, I agreed, although it meant that I'd get to bed late and be exhausted on the airplane, where I'd have to try to sleep in the miserable middle seat. Luz, with her puffy, fall-damaged knees, would need the aisle.

Within an hour I'd received more invitations for magazine, TV, and newspaper interviews, one from Bart Downey, who was in a state of high delight because his story had made the front page of his newspaper with his name on the byline. "You've changed my life forever, Mrs. Blue. Can we do an interview with photos for the Sunday section?" I arranged to be interviewed by telephone when I got home and, in return, allowed a photographer to come to the hotel room at 11:15, providing he arrived on time. Otherwise, I'd be gone.

I had to refuse one invitation because they wanted me to be the star of a Thanksgiving cooking show, making my famous flambéed turkey. As if I'd ever flambé another turkey. As if I'd be anywhere but with my family on Thanksgiving Day. In fact, I thought as I hung up, if Jason agreed, I'd much rather go out for Thanksgiving dinner. The prospect of cooking another turkey so close to the terrorist turkey incident really didn't appeal to me.

I gave up on more sleep, bathed, and dressed in a fashionable black pantsuit with teal insets in the flared legs. I'd bought it from Uncle Bernie several years ago. The photo shoot was conducted downstairs, and I then headed for the subway and a very long, very stressful trip to Queens, much of it made in tunnels through which the train rattled so badly that I was sure it would fall apart, leaving me injured, dead, or stranded in the dark under the earth or river or whatever the tunnel tunneled under.

When I finally arrived, we'd climbed onto tracks high above a busy street, and I had to pick my way down icy stairs bedecked with WATCH FOR ICE signs, as if I couldn't see and feel it under my feet. Salt had been flung everywhere, so I trudged for blocks, or so it seemed, taking tiny steps and asking frequent directions from people who spoke mostly Spanish.

With the trains thundering above and the structure holding the subway casting a dark shadow over the traffic, I was convinced that at least one car would slip off the track and plummet down onto me and the crowds around me. One man I asked for directions to Inti Rami kissed his fingers and waved them in my face when I mentioned the restaurant for which I was searching. Then he took my arm and escorted me there, a block and a half, kept me for falling several times, opened the door for me, and shouted something in Spanish that brought a waiter rushing over to greet me.

I was early, and the only person there was Janet Fong. That was a surprise. She explained that Roberto had invited her and several others from Pettigrew to join the celebration. After telling the waiter that two more people than however many he'd already been instructed to prepare for would be joining us, Janet and I sat down with menus, and she whispered to me, "I have a message for you from Mr. Li, which I've been trying to deliver since yesterday."

"Oh, my goodness. I forgot to call him, and I promised."

Janet frowned and said delicately, "I don't think that's necessary, or even wise, Carolyn."

"But I have to tell him that I found the person culpable, at least indirectly, for his poor granddaughter's precarious situation."

"It was in all the papers this morning," she pointed out, "and as his granddaughter has come out her coma—"

"She has? That's wonderful!" Then it occurred to me that she might be brain damaged. "Will she be all right?" I asked nervously.

"They think so, but the family is also upset about other matters, particularly a grandson named Charlie—"

"Rosaria's Charlie?" I asked.

"Perhaps." She looked confused. "The grandson has been caught falling in love with a girl from Bensonhurst and is being shipped off to Hong Kong to an elder brother for training before he goes to university here."

"That's so sad," I murmured. "A sort of Romeo and Juliet story."

"Yes," Janet agreed, "but Mr. Li doesn't see it that way. Still, I must give you his message. He tells you that you will no longer be followed by his grandson and the other two."

"Well, of course. I don't need bodyguards any longer. Perhaps I should write him a note."

"Carolyn, Mr. Li was not happy to hear that instead of being frightened by the men following you, you kept talking to them. They were not bodyguards. He told my grandfather that you are a very naive woman whose husband should keep her at home."

"That's insulting!"

"You must understand that Li Cheng Bao is a powerful but old-fashioned man. He did not want his granddaughter associating with Occidentals any more than he wanted his grandson falling in love with one, especially one associated with a family who—"

"I understand, Janet, but he shouldn't blame the rest of the Randattos and Calogeros for Annunziata's sins. I'll just write Mr. Li a nice note. Have you noticed this Peruvian drink on the menu? It's made of purple Peruvian corn, pineapple, and other things. Shall we try it while we're waiting for the others?"

We did and found it very tasty with a rich, winy color and pineapple bits floating on top, not to mention cinnamon and, I think, lemon or lime. I later learned that one of the chemicals in purple corn is supposed to prevent weight gain and improve eyesight. The drink wasn't hot, which would have been nice after the frigid wind outside; nor was it cold—more or less room temperature, and served in a pitcher with goblets. Festive but nonalcoholic. I proposed a toast to Birdie Li's complete recovery. Wonderful news! I'd send her flowers. Surely her grandfather wouldn't object to that.

42

A Serendipitous Cilantro Incident

Luz

Boy, that Natural History museum is something. I had stuffed animals, books, and dinosaur assembly kits for my nieces and nephews that were going to blow them away, and maybe me, too, since I'd been carrying the gifts in bags on subways and now out on slippery sidewalks looking for this Peruvian restaurant Roberto was so crazy about. It better be good since I was risking my mobility to get there, not to mention traveling on subways that should have been retired a hundred years ago. Thank God I'd got a seat. All that shaking, if I'd been standing, would have been the end of me.

Ha, there it was. Nice to know Inti Rami was so discreet I'd already passed by once. I shifted two bags into one hand, which no longer had any feeling so it didn't mind the extra load, and opened the door. A waiter came over, but I just nodded my head toward Carolyn and Janet Fong, sitting at a long table with no one else. How many people were coming to this party who were already late? I could see it now: We'd end up paying another bill for a meal that we were supposed to be guests at. I plopped my bags on an empty chair, said hello, and looked at the menu. The prices weren't bad, or wouldn't have seemed bad if I hadn't just maxed out my credit card at the museum shop.

Carolyn ordered me a purple corn drink, which didn't sound all that great but was evidently the real Peruvian thing. At least there wasn't any ice in it. I didn't think my hands were up to any more frigging exposure to below-freezing temperatures. "So where's everyone?" I asked.

"Probably stuck in traffic," said Janet. "I would be, too, if I hadn't been staying in Queens with my mother. I walked over."

"Your mom live in one of those tall brick apartment houses off Roosevelt?" I asked. "They look pretty grim— like the one with the bright red fire escapes all over the front. But the one with the gatehouse sticking out front was pretty funky." Evidently Janet's mom didn't live in either one of those.

About then Abe and DeShawn piled out of Abe's old car and blew in on an arctic blast of cold air. DeShawn announced that he needed food, which was no big surprise, but Carolyn ordered him the Chica Morada. He didn't get too excited about purple corn juice.

Abe got one, too, but paid it no attention. "You're not going to believe this," he said, "but I got seven calls this morning, new customers wanting the detective who solved the terrorist turkey case—some of them called it the turkey toss case. I've signed on to find their missing husbands, investigate insurance scams, clear clients of false charges, chase down an accountant who ran off with a truckload of money. Luz, if you want to come on board, I could use the help."

"You got me," said DeShawn.

"I told you you're on full time if you want it, and you said you weren't giving up your bicycle business until you saw whether this was a onetime rush of clients. Sal can't start until he's been to court. Worski thinks it would look like I bribed him with a job to get him to rat out his grandmother, so I—"

"Count me out," I said. "I'm going home, where it only

turns cold at night, and I can stay in the house until it warms up. If I wanted to be a private eye, I'd set up on my own."

"What a wonderful idea," said Carolyn. "I could help you."

"Uh-huh." I drank some more corn juice. The stuff kind of grew on you. "Anyway, good for you, Abe. Now maybe you can get an office that isn't in your mom's basement." Abe didn't know about that. He wasn't paying rent, and the basement was cool in the summer.

"But not all that impressive clientwise," said Carolyn. "You don't actually interview prospective clients there, do you?"

"I go to see them. I don't invite them—"

"I've never seen that done in the movies. And Robert B. Parker's Spencer has his own office in Boston."

We all rolled our eyes and then turned to the door, where several more people were arriving. Roberto was embracing the waiter, Jack Armstrong was saying he was a vegan, which the waiter obviously didn't understand, and Allison, the deadbeat—why the hell had Roberto invited her?—was turning up her nose at the décor. I thought it was pretty nice. They had cute hanging lamps and tables with tops made of wood bits pieced together. The swinging door to the kitchen squealed, but there were great paintings on the walls, guys with donkeys following narrow trails up steep mountains and the like. And the place smelled good.

Then a big limousine pulled up outside, delivering Mr. Pettigrew, Mrs. Christopher, and Petey. They filled up the last of the seats.

With Roberto there, we switched from corn juice to Pisco Sours and ordered food, a good thing, since a Pisco Sour has a lot of alcohol in it. Not that I complained. When the drinks came—Janet stuck with the corn juice—Roberto said that Pisco was made with some grape introduced by the Spanish for wine but produced in mud jars by the Incas. We all toasted Carolyn with the stuff, for being

cleared in the terrorist-turkey case, although both Allison
Peabody and Jack Armstrong bitched about the fact that
Carolyn and I had accused them of the crime. I gave Jack
a mean look and he shut up, probably afraid I'd show up at
his door again.

Then I decided to teach Allison a lesson, since Carolyn
didn't seem about to do it. "You're complaining about us,
Allison? After you invited us to dinner at Daniel, ran up a
big bill, and then ducked out and stuck us with it?"

Mr. Pettigrew's eyebrows went up, a weird sight since
the flaming turkey seemed to have singed off part of one.
"Allison?" he asked. "You invited guests to dinner and—"

"It was a mistake, sir," she said, turning pink. "I received a distressing phone call, and I'm sorry to say, I had
to leave immediately and didn't even think about the bill.
Of course, I'll reimburse you," she said to Carolyn. "I
imagine you, rather than Ms. Vallejo, paid it. Feel free to
send me a statement care of Pettigrew."

Carolyn smiled brightly and said, "No need. I have the
receipt in my expenses notebook," and she produced it.
"Cash or check will be fine."

"I'm afraid I have neither that amount of cash nor my
checkbook with me," Allison replied, cool as an iced bottle of Negro Modelo, which I'd rather have been drinking
than the Pisco Sour.

Mrs. Christopher offered to write the check for Carolyn
and deduct it from Allison's royalties. "Here our new star
food writer was falsely charged for something another of
our writers did. We wouldn't want her to think we're all
people of dubious ethics, would we?" As she said this, she
pulled a big checkbook out of her purse, wrote a check,
and passed it over to Carolyn. "There, my dear. You've
been very brave during this entire distressing incident, and
we appreciate not only your spirit, but the fact that you
pitched in yourself—both you and Ms. Vallejo—to help
Abraham get to the bottom of things."

Jack glared at us, evidently still mad about the way we
pitched into him.

"Isn't it hard to believe that Annunziata Randatto would do such a terrible thing," Mrs. Christopher continued, "and evidently because she thought she was being superceded in our affections? We're very loyal to our authors, as Mr. Pettigrew can tell you."

"Indeed," he responded, still staring at Allison with a big frown. "I haven't been so disappointed since Abraham found out that our comptroller was stealing from authors. It's a sad world when one can't trust one's associates." He looked down at the stew, which he'd just sampled. "This dish is quite tasty. Haven't had such a nice stew since the days when my mother did a bit of cooking herself. Has some unusual flavoring. What is it, Roberto?"

"The dish is Seco Combinado," Roberto replied, beaming at his publisher. "The herb is cilantro."

"Lovely, thick gravy," said Mr. Pettigrew. "Don't recall that I've had gravy with light beans and rice before. Allison, is something the matter with you?"

Allison said, "This dish smells terrible."

"You can't be serious!" Carolyn exclaimed, folding her check and thanking Mrs. Christopher, then digging back into her Seco Combinado with gusto.

"Oh, do call me Terri, dear," Mrs. Christopher replied. "Allison, perhaps you'd better excuse yourself. You don't look well." Allison leapt up and dashed toward the swinging door that led to the kitchen and the johns. Evidently she didn't make it, because first she screamed and then we heard loud retching and moaning.

The waiter returned to our table to announce that the lady had been frightened when he came up from the basement through the trap door and that now she was throwing up in the hall. He wanted to know what he should do with her.

Mrs. Christopher rose immediately, wavered once—maybe she hadn't drunk Pisco Sours before—and went back to tend to Allison while the rest of us ate heartily. I tried Carolyn's beef stew and thought it was great. I'd ordered Chorosa la Marinera, which turned out to be mussels in shells covered with a great salsa. Reminded me of ceviche at home—lime, onion, tomato, and stuff. I even liked the mussels, which I'd never had before.

DeShawn had almost finished his dish when Allison came staggering out, held up by Mrs. Christopher, who was scolding her for having had too much to drink, which Allison denied. She sat back down, looked at her plate, and said, "I can still smell it. It has something rotten in it."

DeShawn said, "Say, you don't want it, I'm still hungry." She clapped her hand over her mouth and headed back to the ladies' room. DeShawn reached across the table to take her plate and began to eat immediately. "Tastes good to me," he declared.

"Don't you have a hearty appetite!" said Mrs. Christopher. "I'm reminded of when my boys were still at home. Always hungry, those boys."

"Allison must be one of the 10 percent of the population who have an unfortunate reaction to cilantro," said Carolyn, "something to do with an enzyme that makes the herb smell and taste bad to them. Some people who have the enzyme even become violently ill. A reader of mine from Michigan emailed me about it. Very interesting."

"Divine retribution," I muttered.

"I wouldn't be surprised," Mr. Pettigrew said to me. His eyes were twinkling.

Our entrees were taken away, and Roberto advised that we try Peruvian ice cream, which was like nothing we'd ever had before. Carolyn ordered a light tan variety, and I had orange-colored ice cream that didn't taste like oranges. They were both pretty good, made of fruits as fibrous as jicama, one nutty and one sort of like licorice. Of course Carolyn wrote everything down.

Allison staggered back and fell into her seat. "Thank God that awful smell is gone." She refused dessert and didn't seem to appreciate Carolyn's diagnosis of her cilantro problem.

"You should check out the website, ihatecilantro.com," Carolyn told her. "I'm sure you'd identify with the readers who've written in about their trying experiences with cilantro."

"Very funny, Carolyn. There was something rotten in that stew, and it wasn't an herb. Probably I've been food poisoned."

"In that case," said Janet, "there's a good doctor at a clinic just a few blocks from here. I'm sure he'll be happy to see you immediately if I ask him."

"What's his name?" asked Allison suspiciously.

"Dr. Urdinola. He's from Peru."

"Waiter, would you call me a cab?" Allison called, rising and clutching the back of her vacated chair. "Cab, taxi. *Comprendo?*"

"*Sí,*" said the waiter and pulled out a cell phone while Allison fumbled in her purse, pulled money out, and threw it on the table.

"I wouldn't want anyone to think I'm trying to avoid paying my share," she said and rushed out into the street.

"I must apologize for Allison," said Petey. "She's a bit of a snob. You should have told me about the Daniel bill, Carolyn."

"Oh, we're having too much fun to worry about that," Carolyn replied and tried mixing her *helado* with her drink, which evidently didn't work out too well. She passed the little dish holding her latest culinary experiment to the waiter.

I had to pour a lot of coffee down her throat when we got back to the hotel in order to get her ready for her TV interview, and to stop her from crying over a pretty ivory carving Mr. Li sent her. She kept saying, "Wasn't that thoughtful? I don't believe for a minute that his young men weren't protecting me."

She was wrong about that, but she was right when she told Petey that we were having too much fun to worry about his snobbish author Allison. We did have a good time in New York. As Carolyn put it when we boarded the plane, still hung-over but game, "All's well that ends well, especially Allison turning out to be sensitive to cilantro."

If you never get to visit Peru, at least you can eat and drink Peruvian with these two recipes. The Pisco Sour started with Quebranta grapes brought to Peru by the Spanish, but they just made wine with the grapes. Then a Spanish king a hundred years later outlawed wine, so the Indians in Peru made their own *aguadiente* with the grapes, Pisco (45 percent alcohol), an indigenous brandy.

The sour part of it was reputedly a cocktail fashioned in a Lima bar in the 1920s and picked up by hotels popular with tourists. After 2003, an ad campaign boosted exports of Pisco more than 300 percent, and Americans buy 30 percent of those exports.

As for the beef and cilantro stew, both ingredients came to the Americas from Europe, brought by the Spanish to Peru. Cilantro, or Chinese parsley, is a name for the leaves of the coriander plant. It grew wild in Southeastern Europe and was cultivated in China, India, and Egypt for thousands of years. Interestingly, it smells terrible to some Europeans and was named for the smell of the bedbug. The beef stew recipe is as close as I can come to one I ate in Queens at a Peruvian restaurant.

Pisco Sour

- In a pint glass pour two *2 ounce shots of Pisco* and one of freshly squeezed *lime juice*.

- Make simple syrup ahead of time by adding *1 part boiling water* to *2 parts sugar*. Pour in a half shot, 1 ounce, of simple syrup, and the *white of one egg*.

- Cover the glass and shake until the egg white is creamy and frothy.

- Pour the drink over ice and add *two dashes of Angostura bitters*.

Seco Combinado (Beef and Cilantro Stew)

- Mix *4 cloves crushed garlic, 2 teaspoons ground cumin, salt*, and *black pepper*.

- Cube *2¼ pounds braising or stewing steak*, place in large dish, add garlic mixture, and mix thoroughly with hands. Cover and marinate 30 minutes or more.

- Heat *1 teaspoon vegetable oil* in large saucepan, add meat, and brown on all sides.

- Add *1 large chopped onion*, and stir until soft and transparent.

- Add 8 ounces from a *16 ounce can of beef stock* and bring to a boil; then reduce heat a little and cook 45 minutes, stirring occasionally and adding more stock when needed.

- Chop *2 tablespoons cilantro* and *12 ounces spinach*, put in blender or food processor with *6 ounces water* and process until smooth. Set aside.

- Peel *1 large potato*, cut into small cubes, and add to cooked meat with spinach-cilantro mixture. Mix thoroughly and cook for another 15 minutes or until potatoes are tender.

- Add *5 ounces frozen green peas* and cook another 5 minutes.

- Stir in *zest of one lime* immediately before serving hot with white rice or beans or both.

Carolyn Blue,
"Have Fork, Will Travel,"
Phoenix Sun

Recipe Index